Praise for *Prison Stories*

*"Seth's **Prison Stories** is a full course meal for a gangsta novel reader's appetite!"*
Joe Black, Author of Street Team

*"Seth Ferranti knows the darkness of prison. **Prison Stories** grabs the reader in a chokehold and shows how American prisons make bad people worse. To know Ferranti's work is to know prison."*
Michael G. Santos, Author of About Prison

*"**Prison Stories** is vicious. Everybody should read it. It will give you an inside look at the FEDS. Prison is no joke!!!"*
Robert Booker, Sr., Author of PUSH

*"The language in **Prison Stories** is a dense pastiche of slangs that is very effective, beautiful, and intense."*
Richard Eoin Nash, Soft Skull Press

*"**Prison Stories** sheds light on many aspects of the criminal justice system and is fascinating to read."*
Mary Bosworth, Ph.D., Author of Prison Encyclopedia

*"**Prison Stories** is engaging, readable and thought provoking."*
Dr. Stephen Richards, Author of Convict Criminology

*"**Prison Stories** brings 'the netherworld' to life and creates a distinct portrait."*
Helen Breitwieser, Cornerstone Library

"Seth's a talented writer and one with a unique perspective."
Karen Rothmyer, The Nation

"Seth's style is light, involved and at times lyrical."
Robert Gannon, Author/Journalist

PRISON STORIES

By
Seth "Soul Man" Ferranti

Copyright © 2004

Library of Congress Control Number: 2004114918
ISBN 0-615-12685-5
Printed in the United States of America
First Printing: February 2005

Edited by Ben Osborne
Book Design by E-Moxie Data Solutions, Inc.
www.e-moxie.com

SECOND PRINTING

Gorilla Convict Publications

URL: www.GorillaConvict.com

ii

PRISON STORIES

To order additional copies of
PRISON STORIES

Visit www.GorillaConvict.com

ISBN 0-615-12685-5

LCCN: 2004114918

. . .

ACKNOWLEDGEMENTS

I would like to thank all the convict authors that came before me—Jack Henry Abbott, George Jackson, Edward Bunker, Mumia Abu-Jamal, Dannie Martin, Jean Genet and Leonard Peltier.

I would like to thank my beautiful mother, Anne S. Ferranti, and my gorgeous wife, Diane. None of this would have been possible without their efforts. Their love and support has sustained me throughout my bid and both of them mean the world to me. Also much thanks to my natural father, Robert Feeney, for his contributions to this project, my education, and my work ethic. I just wish it hadn't taken me so long to find it.

I would like to thank my publisher, Gorilla Convict Publications, for putting me on and my editor/writing mentor/friend, Ben Osborne, from *SLAM/XXL/KING* magazines for being there from the jump. Good looking out bro. Also big props to GCP's in-house artist, Charles "Chuck" Waldo for the awesome cover art and vicious logo design.

I would like to thank all the magazines, editors, and websites that have given me a forum for my work and provided me with the inspiration I needed to tackle this project—Kevin and Tiffany Chiles from *Don Diva*, Jesse Pearson from *Vice*, Anselm Samuel from *The Ave*, Meghan Conaton from *FHM*, Susan Price from *Slam*, Jorge Sierra from hoopshype.com, Jason Lomberg from prisonerlife.com, and Susan Hampstead from *Don Diva*/Hamstead Publishing.

I gotta thank my two main dudes who preceded me in this game, showed me how to put it down and helped me get my shit together—Michael Santos (see MichaelSantos.net) and Joe "Black" Reddick (Check out Illstreetz.com). Without their examples I might still be adrift. Also, I got to shout out the following—my main man and #1 BOP baller Ronald Paul, aka Ron Jordan aka The Abuser, Robert Booker, Sr., (author of *PUSH*), Chris Mullin (writer of *On X*), Terry Trice, Kenneth "Supreme" McGriff, Ronald Tucker and David Robinson.

I would like to thank Dr. Stephen Richards from the University of Wisconsin-Oshkosh, all the Convict Criminologists and Professor Mary Bosworth for providing support, opportunities, and guidance. Plus I'd like to thank Monica Pratt and FAMM, Nora Callahan and November Coalition, and Karen Bond and Federal CURE for fighting the good fight and trying to stop this madness.

I'd like to thank the old and new friends and family members that have given me a lifeline to the real world—Sue Mecca, Andy Maloney (Go Arsenal), Marcy Cortese, Alison Litton, Carey Smith, Kathleen Murphy, Daniel Dean, Tricia Maloney, Daniel Desindes, Calvin Coohey, Carolyn Rogers, Daniel Ferranti, Lela Ferranti, John Ferranti, Banks Tarver, Elizabeth

Lavelle and Dreamhaven Books, Mickela Gay, John Gay, Jerry Capeci, Christine Gowen and Valery Gailiard.

And finally I'd like to thank all the dudes I've done time with who provided me with stories to tell, checked out, read and critiqued my writing and taught me how to be a man and a convict in this netherworld of corruption and violence. From FCI Manchester—Mike Magnum, Robert Salazar, Vincent Martinez, Dave Miranda, Ceasar Delanoy, Larry Galloway, Marc Duncan, Mike Simmons, Roy Payne, Geoff Webb, Bob "Breeze" Kaplansky and John Bierle. From FCI Beckley–Paul "Stump" Arhens, Daniel Perkins, Denny Gullett, Antonie "Monkee" Rogers, Clay Warren, Rupert Pitters, Barry Thompson, Randell "Skripcha" Williams, Dean Valley, D. Parker, and Glen "Ill" Wiltshire. From FCI Fort Dix—Tidy Yates, Joe Maldanado, Pete Hockford, "Foundation" Wiggans, Saul Salazar, "Noodles" Drummond, Ernie Fhleur, Jonathon McDonald, Juan Cintron, "Pup" Collier, Mustafa Jefferson, Ali Hall, Paulie Harris, Matty Ward, Ron "Catch-me-if-you-can" Hammond and Jeff Reynolds. From FCI Fairton—Efrain "Pelu" Rosa, Carlos "Cheeky" Lopez, Jimmy Curcio, Jesse Carter, Mike Malloy, Kenny W., Princewell "Dread", Paul Green, Cliff Mitchell, Tim Dunn, "Pop" Alteiri, Mikey Perna, Mike Ryan, "T-Y" Whittaker, Jade "Polo" Best, Naim Gore, Big Troy, Angelo Perry and Juan Martinez. From FCI Gilmer—Darryl "DJ" Hairston, Lamar Bell, Randy Gustave, "Wild Bill" Jenkins, "Judge" Broman, Harlemworld, Sharn "LeBron James", Stan, Smoke "The Gangsta Poet", "Tennessee" Cannon, "Mike" Petaway, "Chris" Chu, Tone, Big Sid, Laruan Queen, Turtle, Chris Fannon, Tank, Dirty Red, Mike Clemons, Mondo, Choke, Jab, Stef, John L., Chris "Gutter" Collins, Dog, Escalade, Big Jack McConnell (author of *Twisted*), Eyone, Rich and Ty from Cali, and Quincy "Trini God" Joseph. Anyone I missed, my bad. I got you in the next *Prison Stories* because you know this shit is gonna be a series.

Take care and later.

Seth "Soul Man" Ferranti
December, 2004

I dedicate this book to all the prisoners doing football numbers in the feds due to the War on Drugs. For real when they can't even keep the drugs out of the prisons you know the Drug War isn't working.

Also I would like to dedicate this book to all prisoners everywhere. When your friends and family members ask you what it's like living in the belly of the beast, tell them to read this book and then they'll know.

Seth "Soul Man" Ferranti

"The degree of civilization in a society can be judged by entering the prisons."

—Fyodor Dostoyevsky

"Some guys have it real fucked up in prison, real hard. Some guys will be doing somebody's laundry. Some guys will be on their stomach with the pillow in their mouth, some guys will be getting stabbed. If you're a man on the streets and you eat well, you'll eat well in prison. It just might be different food."

—Suge Knight

"Teachers are heroes—Not drug smugglers."

—George Jung

...

PRISON STORIES

Table of Contents

DRUG DEALER
BOOK ONE

"Another chapter in the tragicomedy called the Drug War."

—Mumia Abu-Jamal

PART 1: BEGINNINGS

I hit the compound in '93. Never been in prison before. Fresh from my sentencing and angry as fuck. I had to face facts though; I was a skinny white kid from the suburbs. I had to get my swoll on. Because you can't be selling no wolf tickets in the pen, unless you want six inches of steel in your gut.

I was looking to become fierce, lean, and muscular. I scoped the dudes in my unit to see who went hard. The unit was multi-tiered with three different rows of cells formed in a triangle. In the middle of the unit was the common area with phones and the C/O's station. While I was calling my peeps one night I noticed these two Detroit cats holding court. They looked thorough and cut up so I stepped to them and asked if I could ride. Steve, the black con who was driving the car told me, "You can ride, but if you jack rec, you out." That was how he pumped.

Steve was ripped up and strong. He claimed to have run track at Michigan State before he caught his charge. He was a pretty smooth character. Straight Motown and way serious, just finishing up a 10-year bid. The other cat was Dave. A loud, boisterous Puerto Rican with a 17-year conspiracy sentence. He had black, slick-backed hair and sported a matching goatee. He told me, "I used to be a fat fuck. Everybody called me gordo. But since I've been working out with Steve, I'm a beast." Dave was a funny dude. Always up for a laugh. I started pushing iron with these cats everyday to start my bid. It was a mean workout.

The weight pile in the yard wasn't fancy. Just the basics. Barbells and plates, benches and racks, and some dumbbells. Cracked, black rubber mats lined the floor and a fiberglass awning stretched overhead to at least deter the weather. We worked out rain or shine. In freezing temperatures or blazing heat. The iron was rusted, cracked, and chipped. The bars were bent and the benches wobbly. But it served our purpose and anyway, I was in the pen. I was going hard.

Before long the whole compound started associating me with these dudes. I worked out with them, went to meals with them, and lived in the same unit with them. They were solid convicts and they played it straight so I just rode.

After a couple of months, though, all the white dudes started stepping to me asking what was up. I didn't know what the fuck they were talking about so I told them nothing was up. Then my homeboy Mike from VA stepped to me. Mike was a ink-slinging, go-hard white boy who had come down from USP Atlanta. He was like, "When you gonna start kicking down, dog?"

I was like, "What the fuck are you talking about, dude?" He looked at me like I was stupid and said, "The tar, dog. Can you hook me up?"

This shit really blew my mind. I didn't know why the fuck Mike and the other white cons thought I could hook them up. I mean, who the fuck was I? I hadn't even been down a year. I had blazed some weed with my homeboys, but fucking heroin? They were crazy. Where the fuck was I supposed to get that? I didn't even know that shit was on the pound.

Then Mike explained, "Those dudes you work out with, the Puerto Rican and the Black, they're holding. They're running the show, dog. I would step to them, but I don't fuck with them like that."

Damn, I thought. Mother... fucking...hell. All this time and I didn't even know. But I told my homeboy, "Naw dude, I don't fuck with them like that either."

The months rolled by and I got tighter with Dave and Steve. I never asked them to kick down and they never offered. This loco, tattooed vato, Travieso, a straight gangbanger out of South-Central LA, got busted with three grams of heroin in his cell. They locked him and his cellie, Frenchy, a fat junkie from Canada, in the hole. The thought that Travieso was down with Dave crossed my mind but I never heard Dave or Steve mention the bust.

Dave liked buying hobbycraft stuff for his peoples. Leather purses, cases, or wallets, and ceramic vases, figurines, or china. Dave was always spending money. This white dude in our unit, Larry, who worked in rec, used to hook him up. Larry was a country boy from North Carolina. I mean redneck. A big cocaine dealer with a 20-year bid was how he told it. Larry was a little older and kinda frazzled from the coke, but he was alright. Talked like a hick, though. Larry hooked me up with a job in recreation working in hobbycraft. Dave told me it was the thing to do because I could get my hustle on selling ceramics. I figured it was all good.

When Larry's cellie went to the hole I moved into his cell. It was like all the others—sink and toilet apparatus by the door, with two wall lockers opposite. A long desk mounted to the wall and a metal bunk bed, all crammed into the 6-foot by 10-foot living space the two of us called home. It was a corner cell, so it was quiet and dark.

In the unit I would kick it with Larry, Dave, and Steve. Dave's cell was like a common area. Mucho trafico. We would kick it there, sometimes eight or 10 dudes hanging out at the same time. Dave's bunkie was a Cuban from Florida, Carlitos, who didn't speak any Ingles. Him and Dave were always back and forth in Español. Dave also had crazy Mexicans around him. Mostly Chicanos from Cali and Texas. La Raza, you know? They rattled away in rapid fire Spanglish. I didn't understand much, but it was cool. I felt like I was a part of a little crew, almost like a family.

I didn't really know about all the shit that was going down but I started catching on. The Detroit cats, Dave and Steve, were making moves. Big moves. Power moves. They were bringing in heroin and letting La Raza put the work out on the pound. It didn't seem like something I wanted to be involved with, especially since the whole scene was hot because of the Travieso bust. But like I said, I was riding and Dave was straight. He wasn't no petty cat. He looked out. There was always food, bullshitting, and weed burning. So a lot of times I was just trying to hang out.

After a while Dave grew to trust me. He would ask me if I knew this white dude or that one and then send me to pick up some commissary or stamps from them. I didn't mind running the errands. It wasn't like I was fucking with the heroin or anything.

One time I was on a visit with my parentals who had journeyed down from Virginia. The visiting room was kind of non-descript. Like a bus station waiting area. Vending machines and all. Except there were prison guards walking around monitoring you. After a couple of hours I saw Dave come out, all decked out in his visiting khakis, lined out, his black hair slicked back, fronting with a thick gold chain. A Spanish couple was visiting him. They jabbered away in Español and I remember being surprised when Dave cut out after about 20 minutes. When I thought about it in my cell that night, I figured he must've been copping.

Larry, my bunkie, told me in his country drawl, "You know Dave's into that bullshit." I guess he was scared I might hold some drugs in our cell or something. I told him, "Don't worry dude. I just fuck with him for a little weed. I ain't for all that other shit."

But to be honest, I was kind of fascinated by the whole scene. I mean, I was a drug dealer on the streets. That's why I was in prison. To imagine that the exact same thing, if on a smaller scale, was happening inside, was un-fucking-believable. It seemed Dave was getting crazy chedder too. Not on a street level but he was living large. He always had mad commissary. Bags were all up under his bed and shit. I'd be up at canteen everyday collecting for him. All the shit wouldn't even fit in his room. The dude had like 10 pairs of brand new sneaks and Timberland boots, which weren't even prison issue. The boriqua was styling.

It seemed like everything that was hard to get, Dave had. I'm talking about stuff you take for granted on the streets.

Champion sweatsuits, cassette players with the latest mixed tapes from the streets, gold chains and watches, Air Jordans, and crazy porno mags. Most people in prison have nothing; Dave had everything. He was the man. I liked being down with him because there was like this trickle-down effect. I guess he liked having me around because I wasn't really in the know and I didn't have my hand out like most of La Raza, who circled him like vultures.

The different aspects of the prison hierarchy were sinking into my stoned mind. Dave controlled the drugs, so he had the power. And with that power came respect. Big respect and bigger props. And in prison it was all about what you can do for me, and Dave was showing mad love. To La Raza, to motherfuckers in the unit, and convicts on the pound. He had it all. But with the drugs came the money. And when money is involved, problems will always arise.

PART 2: BLOWING UP

I liked being associated with Dave. I came in a scared white kid from the suburbs, but hanging with Dave gave me props. I learned how to carry myself by watching him and his people. I guess the other prisoners figured I had to be thorough because I was down with Dave and La Raza. I got a rep by association and with that reputation came acceptance and, grudgingly, respect.

All the white boys still wanted me to hook them up. They thought I was playing them. But I really wasn't. I'd never brought the subject up with Dave and he never talked about it. Steve was getting ready to hit the streets so he started laying low in the unit while Dave gradually took control of the whole show.

I could tell Larry started to get involved because one time he asked me if I wanted to make some moves but I told him, "Heroin ain't my thing." And it wasn't. Finally they let Travieso out of the hole. He told Dave that Frenchy was about to be deported so he took the rap for the 3 grams of tar. It was just hole time for him because he was Canada bound. When Travieso found out that I was born in Cali, he and this other vato Vince, who had a reputation for knocking motherfuckers out, took me under their wing. All these Chicanos liked to do was get fucked up on hooch, weed, and heroin, or whatever. I was way into the weed they were smoking so I was there. I had barely been in prison a year and already I was getting involved in the stuff that got me locked up in the first place. I gotta keep it real, though, I was a marijuana fiend.

Eventually I started getting a little more involved. Compound-wise, Dave was bringing in mucho dinero, and he needed to turn it into street money, because you can only have so much commissary. And not a lot of junkies can do sendouts. They're living month to month on that UNICOR check.

The common currency on the pound was stamps. A book cost $5.80 in the store but was only good for five dollars on the pound. With the drug trade in full swing in the prison a lot of stamps were changing hands and most of the books were making thier way into Dave's possession and our unit. The problem was stashing them.

Me and Larry were trusted with stashing the stamps and turning them into real money. For the stash spot we used the thermal coolers they sold in the store. By ripping the inner cylinder out and disposing of the styrofoam that insulated the cooler we found we could hide 90 books of stamps around the cylinder. Then we would slide the outer cover back on. A perfect stash. As the stamps started multiplying we found we had to stash the coolers in other prisoner's cells because having 10 thermal coolers in one cell is kind of unexplainable to the C/O's and definitely suspicious looking. And Dave didn't want that as he was trying to keep everything on the low. But it was hard because he was blowing up. The drugs, the money, the power, the respect. He was on Big Willie status.

At one point we had over 1000 books of stamps in the unit. I would just put the jugs in other convict's cells and ask them to hold them for me. Larry was selling stamps to the inmates in hobbycraft, who regularly mailed hobbycraft items they made out to the street, but it wasn't enough. We had too many fucking stamps and Dave wanted real money from them.

I knew some of the bookies on the compound so I started asking them what was up, if they could do send outs or not. Football season was about to start so I was in luck—all the bookies were gearing up for the season. Getting their bank ready. I would sell 125 books of stamps to the bookies for a $500 send out or street to street transaction. The bookies were jumping on this deal and Dave liked it even though he was losing 75 cents on every book.

But there were only so many bookies on the compound. Larry and I would literally be waiting every weekend for the bookies to get hit. And when they did they would run to us to re-up their exhausted supply of compound money that was paid out to the parlay ticket winners. It was a vicious cycle but it was one of the only ways to turn compound money into real money.

Another way was to offer dudes who had crazy bank mad deals on commissary. Me and Larry would find a high roller and offer him a commissary delivery service. Like $350 worth of canteen for a $300 send out. We had a string of regulars who did this. They had the money to make the transactions, but most importantly they liked the prestige of having other prisoners see us bringing them commissary. Like they were in the loop or something. It made them feel important and we didn't care because we were getting paid anyway. Dave used to say, "Canto de cabrones, I'm getting robbed." But that was just a front because he was making $1200 a gram and there was room for the losses since that same gram cost $75 on the street.

Larry was my partner but he didn't like to smoke out. He was styling because he skimmed money off all the deals, but I'd take my profits directly in weed. This made it easy for Dave as other cons were always trading him weed for heroin.

I was still at the beginning of my bid and escaping my sentence through marijuana was my thing. When I was stoned I didn't have to face the reality of my sentence, so I stayed stoned 24/7. Travieso and Vince were my stoner buddies. My carnalitos. We would sleep late, smoke out, get the munchies, work out, smoke some more and chill. I liked to hang with these vatos because they got mad respect. Travieso was considered one of the bad asses on the pound and Vince was also highly regarded. My association with them and La Raza changed the other prisoners' perspective of me. It was weird. I went from being accepted and respected, at least begrudgingly, to someone who you did not want to fuck with.

Motherfuckers would be real cautious of what they said around Travieso, so when I was with him I held the same notoriety. It wasn't like anyone was dissing me before, but you could definitely tell the difference. Fear breeds mad respect. All this perception shit really blew my mind, but then I found out why Travieso and Vince were held in such high regard.

I had heard that they were Dave's collectors but I never thought nothing of it because I used to collect commissary too. But these vatos were different kind of collectors. They handled the troublesome accounts. I knew Vince had a reputation for knocking motherfuckers out but I had never seen him in action before. Neither him nor Travieso were big dudes. Both were stocky and cut-up, with that classic Chicano gang-banger look, vato firme, you know. I thought they were real laid-back, mellow cats but like I said I had never seen them putting in work.

One morning when they called chow, Vince came and woke me up. "Levantate, buey, we got business," he told me. I was like what the fuck, but then again this was Vince, so I got up. Him and Travieso were decked out in their khakis and looked serious. When I walked up Travieso handed me two locks and a belt. "Dale, carnal," He said as I took the makeshift weapon that functioned as a medieval flail. As we walked out the unit Vince turned to look at me and said, "Listo Guero. We got to check this buey." I was like damn, what the fuck have I gotten myself into? But I couldn't turn my back on these two vatos—it wouldn't be healthy. So I just rode.

When we got up to the other unit a couple of Chicanos came up and told Travieso something. He nodded and motioned for me and Vince to follow him. We entered the unit and walked quickly down the tier and went into a cell. The morning light was sneaking inside the bars on the window, casting a dreary light over the cell with its off white walls and metal bunkbed.

An older white dude was sleeping on the bottom bunk and popped up surprised as he noticed us. I had seen him on the pound. They called him the captain. Supposedly he had a yacht down in Florida or something. He was a hardcore junkie. He looked startled, even annoyed. Like, what the fuck are these motherfuckers doing in my goddamn cell at 6:30 in the morning? But he didn't say shit. Just looked stupid. Then, as the captain was about to open his mouth, Travieso motioned for him to shut up as we all crowded into the cell. Vince shut the door and put the shit sign up. It was a piece of cardboard that covered the window slotted into the door, which allowed the C/O's to look into the cell when they counted.

"Mira capitan," Travieso said, "the money didn't hit. So what the fuck is up?"

The captain, looking all nervous and shit with his eyeballs sticking out, looked at Travieso and then at us as he tried to talk, stammering, "it should of hit. It was sent last Saturday. Overnight. Are you sure it's not there? Please check again."

Vince grabbed the locks and belt from me and stepped toward the captain menacingly. "Let me smash this Viejo." But Travieso put his arm out, stopping Vince and playing it cool as the captain tried to sink further under his covers and into the bunk. Like that would save him from Vince.

"Look captain," Travieso drawled all slow like in his South-Central, Cali accent, "Either that money hits or we come back to see you. Entiende?"

"Yeah I understand," said the captain. "It will be there. You know me. We've been doing this a long time. Just check again, OK? And let me know."

Travieso nodded his head as I took the shit sign down. Vince gave me the locks and belt which I disassembled and we cruised the cell making our way quickly out of the unit.

That was my first experience checking someone and I wasn't sure if I liked it. I didn't think I was cut out for that type of shit but when I passed the captain and his boys in the yard I could feel their eyes on me and as they nodded to me I could feel the fear they had of me and in a strange kind of way, that feeling was intoxicating.

I started going with Vince and Travieso regularly when they collected. A lot of prisoners owed Dave money. There were major heroin debts on the compound. I never realized how much credit Dave had extended people. The stamps were just the tip of the iceberg. I lost count of how many people like the captain owed literally thousands of dollars. There were mucho junkies on the pound. Most of them paid up with a little persuasion from Travieso and Vince—some didn't, though.

I remember convicts getting on the phone, begging their peoples to send the money. Travieso would be right there putting down his press game. And he had a mean press game. Sometimes the con would hand Travieso the phone to talk to their peoples. The person on the phone would assure Travieso that the money would be sent. And Travieso would imply what would happen if the money didn't hit. Still, sometimes it never came and then it was beatdown time.

I never applied a beatdown but I was in the cell a lot of times watching out for the man. I saw Vince break this motherfucker's leg once. For $300 dollars. Just broke the motherfucker's leg. It was brutal. The dude was just sitting on the bunk, all casual like, explaining how his girl would put the money on the wire when she got her paycheck that week. Vince told the skinny, tattooed, white junkie, "You are full of shit." And when the dude tried to jump out of the bed—to smack Vince I guess—this vato slammed his steel-toe, prison-issue boot into the convict's leg as it swung off the bunk toward the floor.

The junkie screamed as his leg splintered. The bone from his shin was jutting out beneath his skin and quickly turning blue. Vince then smashed the guy in the face with his fist and told him, "Make sure that money's on the wire or I'll break your other pinche leg, buey."

The beat down dudes would usually end up in the hole never to be seen again. Branded as a chump and a no good motherfucker. Other cats would escape the beatdown by checking in and snitching someone out. But never Vince, Dave, Travieso, or La Raza. They were too scared. And smart to be scared because these Chicanos were vicious and La Raza was all over the system. They would get you sooner or later. Especially if you were a pinche chota. I'm glad I was down with them.

Travieso had problems, though. He was bad on the heroin, too. He was always getting strung out. It wasn't pretty. The vato would OD and turn blue. Me and Vince would have to pack ice on his balls to revive him. A couple of times I swore he was dead but he always came around. The thing was, Travieso had a history of drug abuse so the cops were always pissing him, giving him urine tests, and he was always failing so he was in and out of the hole as the dirties showed up.

With so many convicts getting dirty urines for heroin, the compound got hot. Dave chilled out and started getting weed instead. It was more tolerated then heroin. Nobody was dropping dead because the dope was only tar, not china-white. But still, the SIS cops, who investigated prison events and were FBI wanna-bes, were looking for a bust. They had a unit town hall meeting where the prison administrators acknowledged a heroin problem in the prison. It was crazy. They wanted to know where the fuck the dope was coming from.

Dave told me, "Fuck that heroin shit. I'm only moving weed now." This was definitely more my style. I was a big weed dealer from the streets. I figured weed should be legal anyway and I knew a lot of white cons who would buy the weed. Especially if they couldn't get the tar. An addict was an addict no matter what the drug. The addiction feeds itself. Even in prison.

PART THREE: THE RUN

I was a stoner at heart, so in a way, the weed angle had me in heaven. And that is a hard feeling to get here. The marijuana I smoked helped me to transcend the drama of my environment. I was escaping reality.

I didn't know where Dave was getting the pot from and when you are a big pot dealer from the streets, the amounts were ridiculously small. But still to me it was perfect. We were breaking up ounces almost every day. And this wasn't no kiestered pot either. This shit was straight from the street. Whatever the situation was, Dave had a sweet connect.

A lot of drugs in prison are brought in through the visiting room. Prisoners swallow balloons full of drugs that their visitors smuggle in. It is a dangerous business, hustling right under the cops' noses, but this is how Dave was getting the heroin in. Another way drugs enter the prison is by being kiestered or stuffed. This is when a convict hides the drugs in their anal cavity. Stated more crudely, they shove the contraband up their ass. They stuff it. Usually the drugs are wrapped in some kind of plastic or duct tape for obvious reasons.

Dave's inner circle was steadily shrinking. Going home to Motown like Steve, the hole like Travieso, or transferring to another institution like some of the other vatos. As people left, I slowly became more involved. I went from being a fringe player to a main dude. It wasn't something I planned. It wasn't even something I wanted. It was just something that happened. I mean, I was down with the smoke and all. But the other stuff—putting in work—was just a means to an end. I was down with the clicka. I was riding, you know.

When I think about it all now, smoking weed was the real reason why I was in prison. That was the reason why I sold drugs, to support my habit. But with the easy money I just got a little carried away. Now I realize that not only are the drugs addictive but the lifestyle was too. Maybe even more so. You get accustomed to living a certain way. You also get accustomed to being high all the time and the drugs cost money. So if you want to do drugs all the time, you have to be rich. And if you aren't rich, you have to do something to support your habit. Be it robbing, stealing, or whatever. Selling drugs was just the logical conclusion for me. I was not the robbing or stealing type. But when you're dealing with drugs and money, there are always consequences.

In prison, drugs are dealt just like they are on the street. Everything is just done on a miniature scale. What they sell for $25 in here, weed-wise, is just the leftover shake from rolling a joint on the street. In prison an ounce goes for about $800. That same ounce might cost $100 on the street. And we're talking commercial bud. Mexican brick pot. Wasn't any kind bud making its way into the penitentiary. And if it was, nobody's selling it. They're keeping it and firing it up themselves.

I remember one time Dave and Larry came back to the unit with a laundry bag full of popcorn packets from rec. They picked one of the packets of popcorn out and ripped it open. What the fuck, I thought, as the popcorn scattered on the floor. I saw a salt-shaker sized black electric taped cylinder fall out of the bag.

They both looked at me as Dave said, "Yo kid, unwrap that."

Without thinking I did. Ripping layers of black electric tape that was wound tightly off and uncovering a compressed ounce of weed. Only then did I smell my hands. Looking disgustingly at the unwound electric tape I realized my hands reeked like ass. I gave Dave and Larry a look like, "You motherfuckers," as I ran to the sink to wash my hands.

They laughed their asses off as Dave smirked, "Smells like shit, right cabrone?"

The norm on the inside is smoking tiny toothpick joints. You can get maybe four hits off of one. A straight New York joint, you know? These go for like ten bucks each. And don't be wasting no smoke either. You better inhale all that shit. No

Bill Clintoning it. It's brutal, but if you are a stoner, you learn to live with it. This same scale is representative for all the drugs making their rounds in the prison also. And they got everything in here too. Life in prison, drug-wise, mirrors life on the streets. Again, just on a miniature scale.

When Dave broke out a new ounce he would always bring it to the cell Larry and I lived in. Our room was the official stash house. "Time to work," he would say. There was this flat, platter-like tupperware bowl that Dave used to put the ounce in when it was time to break it up. Every time I saw that white, platter-like bowl I knew what was up. I was a conditioned stoner. It was working time.

There were no scales in the prison so we used chapstick caps as a measuring device. A cap full of weed cost $25. And if you stuffed the cap you could get three or four pin joints out of it. Dave liked to look out so we were always stuffing the caps full of weed. "Make it nice," he would say. "I ain't trying to rape nobody."

Dave had a different attitude then most drug dealers in prison. I guess that was because he had a sweet connect. He wasn't hustling balloons in the visiting room. Most dudes moving drugs in prison try to kill you and maximize their profit. Dave was different. He had an abundant source, so he showed love.

My cell was used so much because it was a corner cell. We always broke the marijuana up there. We had an assembly line-like system. We could break up a whole ounce pretty rapidly. It had to be quick because the cops were always making rounds. Looking in your cell and shit.

I always liked to see the ounce in the plastic sandwich baggie. It reminded me of la calle. I reminisced back to my younger days in Cali, buying quarter bags and shit. For a second, at least. I remembered my first days of taking drugs— the excitement, curiosity, and experimentation. It was nice to go back but the weed wasn't all that good. Most times it was garbage, but it was better then nothing. I was like an alcoholic and if you can't drink the whiskey, drink the wine. Mad Dog 20/20.

The assembly line-like system worked like this. One person, usually me, would cut off the corners of the institution issued envelopes to place the caps of weed in. The triangle corner of the envelopes opened up into a little pouch baggie—perfect for the tiny amount of weed going into it.

At the front of the line was usually Carlitos, Dave's Cuban cellie. He was entrusted with breaking up weed in the tray and stuffing it into the measuring cap. Larry was next, using a seam ripper, obtained from UNICOR. He would pull the stuffed marijuana out of the chapstick cap and put it into one of the envelope corners I had prepared. Vince would be last, taping the envelope corners shut and taping them together in groups of five.

Dave would always be out on the tier looking out. As the big man, he didn't like to handle the weed unless absolutely necessary. We would repeat this procedure every time Dave broke out an ounce. And he was breaking out a new one three or four times a week. So there was a lot of working time. And a lot of weed burning. We tried to be careful and sometimes we would hold off because every now and then, a supercop was on.

Supercops are usually stupid but in general, they are nosy motherfuckers. All up in your business. They are always walking around, going into your cell, and shit like that. They either take their job too seriously or are some untested rookie who is scared to death from all the movies he grew up watching. Some C/O's are just petrified of their own Lieutenants. It doesn't pay to try and get over on a supercop because their work is their life. They have nothing better to do.

Most other cops were chill, though. The veterans didn't sweat you. They know the system is fucked up and they don't give a fuck about the Lieutenant's bullshit. Plus, they have seniority and job security. They're not on probation like the rookies, who are always getting their balls busted by the LT's.

An ounce would make between 60 and 65 caps. As long as we got 60 Dave was happy. He was always like, "Necisito sesenta, cabrones." As part of the assembly-line crew, we would always get a cap or nice little bud for ourselves. Just for the head, you know. Putting in work was what we called it, and I enjoyed the fringe benefits. Kind of like a prison corporation. Dave was the CEO and we all held various titles. And as CEO, Dave was always sure to bust out a big finger-sized joint too. This brought the streets right back. I lived for these moments. The smoke slowly slipping out of my lungs. In my drug-addicted mind, this was heaven. Paradise in the penitentiary. "Guero," Dave would say, "tienes fosfero? Damme cabrone. Light it."

We would smoke the fattie between the two of us. Dave was showing love. I enjoyed watching the smoke trail my fingers and seep out of my mouth. Dave would revel in the moment telling me as he took a hit, "I'm running this shit, kid. I'm the man." I would nod my head in agreement as he passed the joint back to me. He could've told me he was god. I didn't give a fuck. I was mad stoned and happy like a cartoon. It was motherfucking Bugs Bunny time, you heard.

For selling purposes, five or six caps made up a hundred dollar piece. This was usually a street-to-street transaction. Other prisoners would have their peeps put the money on the wire or send a money order to the address Dave provided. If the feria didn't hit there would be problems, and Vince took care of that, but most times the money was straight. The weed was a different scene then the heroin. Not so much fiending and jonesing. Dudes weren't getting out of line with the weed. It is a much more laid back business. Ain't nobody getting strung out or dropping dead on pot. Marijuana provides a more relaxed and controlled atmosphere. In the prison everybody was just chill. The weed kept the whole compound on stoned status. No beefs, no drama, just love.

Convicts would buy caps for commissary or stamps. Sometimes they would trade other contraband items like some smuggled in coke, shit from the chow hall, or hooch from their wine hustle. In prison, dudes got all kinds of hustles.

Dave was making about $1200 an ounce. And he wasn't paying no eight bills either. He had himself a sweet connect. As far as I could figure a cop was bringing in the weed. The ounces were fat so the shit wasn't being kiestered. Sometimes Dave would have a quarter pound at a time. I didn't know what the setup was. I mean, I heard rumors, but for a long while I just wasn't sure. Eventually, I scoped the situation out.

Before long, Dave started to get sloppy, overconfident, and brash. Everything was going to his head. He would tell me, "This is my compound, Guero. I run this." He thought he was the John Gotti of the pound. Talk about vanity. The money, the drugs, the power, and the respect were inflating his ego. He was bragging big time. Talking crazy shit. Like he was Scarface, Jr. or something. He had a hustle, sure, but in perspective it was just some small-time prison shit. No big operation. He had the compound on lock and all, but you know, dudes revel in their own glory and that usually leads to their inevitable downfall. I just hoped I wouldn't be caught up in it. I liked the smoke and all but I wasn't trying to catch another case. The sentence I had was enough.

Dave was all blown up and having a nice little run but I soon found out through careful observation that he wasn't even the man. He had the whole compound fooled. He was just the front man. The real man, the one who pulled the cops strings, was a behind the scenes type of dude. He let Dave have the limelight. It took me a while to catch on but when I did I saw that Dave was just the man on the street so to speak. He was nothing without this other boriqua. The other Puerto Rican was Leonardo and this dude was el magnate. Better yet, he was the man behind the man. The puppet master, manipulating events from behind a curtain. Pulling the strings of his homeboy and the cop bringing in the drugs.

Leonardo was a smooth operator. Quiet, controlled, and violent. I would hear hushed whispers about him. Like dudes were scared to talk about him and shit. He was a Latin King from the street. Supposedly el rey. Straight outta New York. He had it all figured out too. With hardly any Latin Kings on the pound he went with the Mexican strength, La Raza, to control the flow of drugs on the compound. And he did this through Dave, who was already established and working with the vatos. Leonardo's ace was the young Puerto Rican cop he had working for him. The cop, Flores, would bring in the weed. Quarter pounds at a time in his lunch cooler and shit. Then he would make the transfer to Leonardo who would front it out to Dave, who in turn let the Mexicans put it out on the pound. Everybody was getting a piece of the action but Leonardo was cleaning up. Almost all the send outs for weed were being sent to the same Puerto Rico address. Every time I made a move Dave would give me the same Puerto Rico address to send the money too.

I don't know exactly how much money made its way to that address, but it was a lot. It was like a running joke on the compound. "Puerto Rico?" dudes would ask when they bought a hundred dollar piece. "You know it," I would answer nonchalantly. Every time Larry and I sold stamps or whatever the money was always going to Puerto Rico. Before Dave would have the money sent here or there or wherever, but now everything was being funneled to Puerto Rico.

Leonardo had the shit on lock. The whole compound. And in secret too. Nobody knew for real. Only a select few. I remember the young PR cop working our unit. And when he did Dave would be real relaxed. Like he was on teflon don status and shit. We would break up ounces, get drunk, or whatever. When that cop was on the unit it was like party time. He wasn't sweating us; we were his feria. I don't know the deal between him and Leonardo, but by the way he acted, it had to be his money. It was so sweet that if the LT or another C/O were making rounds the PR cop would give Dave the heads up. It was all very coordinated. Under wraps and the like. Through Leonardo, Dave had a cop at his disposal. His head got even bigger then. Dave thought he was king shit. Running the compound and all. I would hear Dave tell new dudes that came in, "You know I'm that man around here."

He was really proud of it, too. I guess that is what he based his self worth on. Dave wasn't the smartest of guys. He couldn't read or write. I was always writing his letters for him. To his kids, old lady, or his madre. I didn't mind, though, because Dave was cool. He was real. He was street. A nice guy, funny and all. He just got caught up in some serious powertripping. Leonardo was different though. I didn't know him at all. But all the whispers spoke of menace, violence, and ruthlessness. I hoped Dave knew what he was doing because to me it seemed Leonardo was playing him for a fool.

PART 4: THE CUBAN

"That's how you pump?" Dave demanded. "That's how you motherfucking pump, cabron? Me cago en dios, I can't believe this shit." Dave was fuming. The man was losing his cool. He had this little bamma hemmed up in the cell. Shorty was getting pressed. "Don't be selling no wolf tickets on this pound. You got it, cabron? Me entiendes? This is my compound. So take that country-ass bamma shit outta here. Me entiendes? And don't let me find out you're a snitch. Because if I find out you're a rata—muerta, oistes, cabrone? Now get the fuck outta here."

With that, the shorty scrammed. He made tracks, you know. Dave was hot. His face all red and shit. The man was out of control. He looked to me and Vince like he would justify himself but said nothing.

Not that he had to. Because like he informed us everyday, he was the boss. El jefe. A prison-styled scarface. Not that it mattered. If he wanted to be the boss, more power to him, he was the boss. I was happy smoking weed. And Dave was the man with the plan. But the heat was turning way up. Muy caliente, you know. This little venture seemed ready to implode just like the veins in Dave's temple.

Later on, as me and Vince were toking on a joint, Vince told me, "That vato's tripping, verdad esse?"

I answered in the definitive—the man was tripping lately. He was losing it. Irrational tendencies were taking hold. Like the way he treated shorty. All shorty did was cop some of his own weed. Trying to get his hustle on. Dave thought he had the compound on lock. But damn, everybody's gotta get theirs, right?

Dave was high profile. I wondered whatever happened to all that keep it on the down low shit. I guess that was out the window. Now Dave was going around running his mouth. Bragging and the like. Flaunting everything about his drug dealing. The man reveled in his popularity. But it was false popularity. The cons just wanted the drugs. They could care fuck else for Dave. But I was his friend; I liked the guy. Hung out with him. He was straight, looked out and the like. But shit definitely wasn't kosher. The whole prison was stoned and everyone thought Dave was the man. Even though he wasn't. He was set up to take the fall. It was getting brutal. The drama was about to happen. I could feel it.

The members of La Raza were infighting, trying to stay in Dave's good graces. A lot of backstabbing and hating was going on. I was surprised no violence broke out. Dave would flip on dudes and switch alliances like crazy. He was trying to play La Raza off of each other.

But these Mexicanos were vato locos. They weren't gonna let no boriqua twist them. So they stepped back from Dave. These esses were gangbangers and owed allegiance to La Raza. The money and drugs were powerful temptations but by stepping back from the situation, they killed the jealousy that might arise and divide them. For a minute, I thought they were gonna stab Dave. But they didn't. They just stopped fucking with him. All but Vince, that is.

Dave was in a fucked up situation. His ego was on one million and he was power tripping something fierce. There were some major mind games going on and in reality it was all unnecessary but you can't tell nobody that in the moment. Especially when feria is concerned. Everybody wants to get theirs, you know.

A lot of times when things heat up in the joint, dudes just back off, not wanting to take it to the next level. Because the next level is a mess—blood, shanks, and murder. Who needs all that? But the fact is, in prison some dudes do need it. So it happens all the time. I was just hoping this wasn't going to be one of those times. Everything settled down, though, and nobody lost face, so that meant no killings and that was cool by me.

Leonardo clocked what was going down on the pound. He heard the rumors like everyone else. He became invisible and started melting deeper into the shadows. Removing himself from dealing with Dave and La Raza. Leonardo wasn't very visible before except for those in the know, but now I hardly saw him on the pound or in the chow hall. I guess he was always on the unit—avoiding the yard. A silent partner so to speak. Because the drugs were still flowing; it was still marijuana time.

So for the moment, everything was about Dave. He made all the moves. He was the front man, the street dealer, and the big man all in one. Like he was fond of saying over and over, "I'm that man around here."

Dave and I used to chill a lot, in the unit or on the yard. He would always go on about this or that. The man loved to talk. "Sabes que, Guero. These esses—they don't know shit. A little dope. A little money. What is all that? Nothing—entiende? You gotta look at the bigger picture. That's what I'm about. The bigger picture. Me entiende, cabrone?"

I would listen and nod my head yes as I passed the fattie. I liked Dave. He was a cool dude. A little full of himself but he never tripped on me. And he looked out, big time. I guess that is because he saw me as something different. From the suburbs and all. I wasn't street like him and most of the other cons. I didn't know for real, though. Maybe I was just his yes man. It didn't bother me one way or the other. I was down with the weed.

But sometimes it seemed like Dave was grasping. For what, who knows? It seemed he wanted a higher calling. He was definitely up in it and I'm not sure if he could see what was going on around him. And I wasn't really sure it was my place to inform him. I was just riding, you know. I didn't really want to get more involved because the whole scene was frayed, and like the decaying end of an old rope it was ready to unravel.

In prison, transfers are common. Buses were always rolling in from other joints. Convicts would transfer prisons when their security levels dropped or they would hit the pound fresh from their sentencing or just back form court. You would always know who just came in because they would be wearing the elastic waistband khakis and the blue slip on shoes. Standard bus gear, or bus clothes, as we called them.

Diesel therapy is what transit was called and when dudes hit the pound they were usually happy. They could get hot food, commissary, cigarettes, and stretch their legs. The new arrivals just off the bus would chase down their homeboys to swap stories and the like. The newly convicted, fresh from sentencing, look out of place and unsure of themselves. Disoriented. Coming to prison ain't no homecoming, but the others—those who had done time—were just happy to be somewhere besides the buses, holdover, and bullpens of transit.

One week, a bus rolled in and they put this new Spanish cat on our unit. He had long black hair and a beard. He was still in his bus clothes when I saw Dave step to him and check him out. He wasn't a new prisoner, I could tell. He had a convict air about him. He was trouble, I thought.

Apparently the dude was Cuban. He had just come from Leavenworth and was 7 and 1/2 in on a 30-year bid. Him and Carlitos, Dave's Cuban cellie, hit it right off. Homeboys and all that. The Cuban's name was Roberto. There was something menacing about him. Something not quite right.

Maybe it was the USP time he had did. A lot of dudes come outta there fucked up. But for real, I didn't know. He carried himself like a convict, though. He was smooth and portrayed intelligence when he talked. He kind of whispered. He wasn't very big, but he was stocky. He definitely had been hitting the weights. For all outward appearances he seemed a solid dude. Plus he came from Leavenworth. A brutal penitentiary. All the Latinos gave him big props. He got mad respect on the pound. Dave welcomed him with open arms, like he was a long lost brother or something.

From day one Roberto was hanging tight with Dave. Walking the yard with him, going to the chow hall, all over the pound. You would have thought they were homies from the street. I guess Dave felt he needed some back. Since the beef with La Raza I guess he felt exposed, and maybe he figured the Cuban would watch his back. I don't know for sure but all of a sudden this Cuban, Roberto, was like Dave's best friend.

"What's up with este Cubano, Guero?" Vince asked me.

"I don't know, dude—I guess he's Dave's boy," I answered. But maybe I had it wrong. Maybe Dave was Roberto's boy. Because Roberto was all up in Dave's business real quick. Roberto was smart, too. He didn't step on any toes. He scoped out the scene real quick. He convinced Dave to give La Raza some action again, thus cementing an alliance with them. It seemed this Cuban was an ace poker player and Dave was his mark. And nobody would step to Roberto either because he seemed like the type to strap up if called out.

It was only a matter of weeks before Roberto was heavily involved in the whole affair. He was breaking up weed with us, selling it, and making moves for Dave. He became Dave's front man on the pound. Giving La Raza just enough weed to keep them happy and stoned. Suddenly the whole pound was kissing Roberto's ass. I didn't fuck with him on that level because I was already down. But I smoked out with him a couple of times. Me and Larry had our stamp thing anyhow—that was our hustle. We turned the stamps into street money. I was getting my smoke on and living large so I didn't give a fuck about Roberto. He was cool with me, but there was something about him—I just couldn't place it.

PART 5: THE STAMP BUST

The prison was chilling. Stoned to death, you know. All the convicts were high. No beefs, no drama, no static. The Cuban, Roberto, was making moves, establishing his rep on the pound and the like. Do as thou will and all that. In no time at all it seemed Roberto was running the whole operation. Dave was even telling me and Vince to cop from Roberto, and we were his road dogs. I couldn't believe it. Things can change fast, can't they?

Anyway, this one day Dave, Vince, and I were getting stoned something fierce. Bien arrebalado, you know. Smoke drifting out of the cell and shit. Through this smoky haze appeared Leonardo, all agitated and the like. He was hollering at Dave in rapid fire español. Talk about a buzz kill. His words shot out like they'd been burst from a Spanish-language machine gun. Rat-a-tat-tat. In my stoned state I was struggling to understand what the fuck Leonardo was telling Dave. I couldn't translate the words quick enough but I caught the gist of the conversation.

Basically, Leonardo was telling Dave that he had heard about the Cuban and he didn't like what he had heard. More importantly, he didn't trust the Cuban and couldn't believe Dave was working through him. Supposedly some of Roberto's stories didn't match up. Leonardo was a Latin King so he had mad connections in other prisons. Including Leavenworth. Leonardo was essentially calling Roberto's character into question. As Dave stood there stoned and gaping, Leonardo told Dave, in heavy accented ingles, "Keep my fucking name out of your motherfucking mouth in front of the Cuban." Dave, still stoned and trying to deal with this barrage of complexities, nodded in agreement. Not wanting to burn bridges with Leonardo, who could always cut off the flow of drugs. I guess Leonardo still had a hand in such things. The man behind the man, you know. Like a bad dream Leonardo was out of the cell and the unit with the end of the move. The whirlwind of threats and insinuations seemed surreal in our stoned minds. I looked at Vince like, what the fuck and he said, "Politics, esse."

Dave seemed to blow Leonardo's warning off, though. Leonardo was Latin King but Dave wasn't. He was from Motown and he was used to calling his own shots. He wasn't taking orders from a gangbanger. El Rey or not. Leonardo was boriqua also and he was Dave's homey, but Dave was his own man. He started this whole shit with his Detroit homey Black Steve anyhow. Who the fuck was Leonardo to tell him what the fuck to do and who to do business with?

Dave kicked all this to us as he sat there, clearly angry at the tongue lashing he had just received from Leonardo. Me and Vince just looked at each other as the marijuana smoke was sucked into the vent of the modern-day prison cell's ventilation system.

So things kept rolling, big money and all that. Business as usual, you know. The quarter pounds of weed did not stop. We were breaking up an ounce a day. It was a stoner's paradise. Football season was coming up again and me and Larry were moving a lot of stamps. The bookies were gearing up, setting up their banks and the like. Getting their tickets ready—Black Gold, Hit or Miss, All the way to the Bank—these were the names of their parlay tickets. Every bookie's wet dream. Pick 5, 10-point teasers, a sucker's bet, you know?

Gambling was illegal in prison but that didn't stop anybody. Anyway, the administrators couldn't even stop the drugs so good luck with the gambling, right? Like the drugs, the betting action was heavy. Prison is a maze of gamblers, cut throats, and drug addicts. It's just the nature of the beast.

Everything was tranquilo. Then one day when I was coming in from the yard this asshole cop stopped me to shake me down. It was no biggie—the normal routine—but for some reason on that day I wasn't feeling it. So I bucked. The C/O was rude and disrespectful to me, or so I felt, so I let him have it. I cussed his sorry hack ass out.

This motherfucking cop trying to front me out on the pound and shit. I told him he was a sorry motherfucking excuse for a man who was making money off my misery. I asked him why he didn't get a real job instead of being some lame ass rent-a-cop. Needless to say, he was not pleased. He took me to the hole and wrote me a series of petty shots—insolence, disobeying a direct order, refusing a shakedown and the like. I didn't think nothing of it—a couple of days in the hole or whatever—but my bucking the shakedown set the asshole C/O off. He took it on a personal level and after he took me to the hole he was off to rip my cell apart. I'm talking major shakedown. As he put me through the security doors at SHU he smirked and said, "I hope you don't have any contraband in your cell."

I didn't sweat it because me and Larry were pretty careful. We had stash spots, yeah, but no motherfucking pea-brained cop was finding them. I knew my shit was together. I just hoped Larry's was. Because I knew that FBI wannabe hack was gonna rip the cell apart.

A couple hours later, my worst fears were realized as they brought Larry into SHU (Special Housing Unit—otherwise referred to as the hole). I found out from the orderly that the cops found 125 books of stamps in one of Larry's sneakers. I guess he was about to make a move because that shit should have been stashed. Now we were gonna both be under SIS investigation. Fucking great, I thought.

The hole sucks. 24-hour lockdown. No TV, no phone calls, very little rec and human contact. And no motherfucking weed, either. I was dying. Luckily Larry was locked in the cell beneath me so I hollered down at him through the vent.

"Whats up, dog?" I hollered.

"Fucking hell Guero," he yelled back in his redneck, North Carolina accent. "What you on about?"

"This is some bullshit, man," I hollered through the vent, "That pig is an asshole."

"They got the stamps, hoss. What you think they gonna do?"

"I don't know, Larry. Just chill. It will all shake out. Tell them you bought the stamps from the store. Fuck 'em, you know," I told him.

"Alright, Guero. Let me know what's up. I got this one. Tell Dave the deal."

With that straight, I was ready to hit the pound. No SIS investigation for me. Larry would handle that. He would take the fall for the stamps. He was a solid dude. It was his motherfucking fault anyhow. He would keep his mouth shut and I would get back on the pound and let Dave know the 411. I was just in on some bullshit shots. As soon as Larry took the heat for the stamps I would be scot free. No investigation. And Larry? Well, he might do a little hole time.

After a week in the hole I hit the pound. I let Dave know the facts about the stamp bust and Larry. "Five hundred dollars, Guero—I guess I gotta take the loss, verdad?" He didn't seem too put out about it, though. I guess $500 isn't such a big hit when you're making $1200 an ounce. But when I told him about the SIS investigation, he was tripping.

"He won't snitch, will he?" Dave asked.

"Fuck no, dude. Larry's solid," I told him. Dave seemed relieved. He also seemed to be under a tremendous amount of stress. I asked him what was up.

"You know, a lot of shit, Guero. The stamps, the investigation, and the fucking Cuban. Roberto keeps asking me for mas drogas—coca, chiva, whatever. The cabron is loco. Pero I can't get nada. Only mota and they gonna shut that down soon."

And I knew by "they" he meant Leonardo, because Leonardo was calling the shots for real. If Leonardo wanted to shut it down, shut down it would be. It was a nice run though, I thought. A year and a half of free drugs, big willie status and all that. Maybe it would be good to chill out for awhile. No more smoke, you know. Clean the system out. So much for marijuana dreams.

About a week later we got word from the hole. Apparently the SIS was onto something. Larry sent a kite out with homeboy. Prisoners call notes or letters to each other kites. Usually they only come from the hole so the people under investigation or in trouble can inform the convicts on the compound what the deal is, who owes money, or who the snitch is. Larry's kite said that the SIS was pressing him to connect the 125 books of stamps to Dave. They were implying that the stamps were from drugs. Supposedly quite a few notes had been dropped on Dave.

I wasn't surprised, snitches and all that. Always dropping notes on somebody. For what, who knew. Jealousy, trying to get Dave out of the way, it didn't matter. Everybody on the pound knew about Dave. He was high profile. Who knew how many notes were dropped on him? But I knew Larry wouldn't break—he was a good old country boy. Been in trouble with the law since the day he was born. Dukes of Hazzard and all that shit. Anyway, all SIS had were notes. No proof. They could pressure Larry all they wanted but he wasn't no rat motherfucker and Dave knew it. So he didn't sweat it. But the Cuban, Roberto, was sweating Dave. He wanted to make some moves. He wanted some coca. He kept pressing Dave to death. Telling him he needed money to send to his familia in Florida. For his niños, he stressed.

And the thing about Dave was that he had a big heart. You could work him if he liked you. And the Cuban worked him, sweating him like crazy. Dave went to Leonardo, asking him to make a move and get the ounce of coke. But Leonardo wasn't having it. He said, "Fuck that shit, cabron, no mas ahora."

So that shit was dead. Dave tried to make the Cuban understand but Roberto wouldn't listen. He kept pressing Dave to make a move. He told Dave to go right to the cop. "Fuck Leonardo," Roberto said. "Habla con el policia." But Dave seemed unsure. It wasn't like Dave didn't have the balls to do it, because he did. But he seemed tired, worn out, and used up. The whole run seemed to grind on him. All the pressures, the vultures, the demands. He seemed relieved it was over. Dave looked like a junkie who slammed one too many times. And you never knew if that next shot would be his last. Because whatever he did—Dave was hit.

PART 6: THE SNITCH

Without the drugs Dave's popularity took a nosedive. I mean, he was still the man but it just was not the same. A lot of prisoners kicked him to the curb. Dave's claims of "I'm that man around here" were ringing hollow with no drugs flowing. Most dudes were like, holler back when you hook up. And later. I still liked him, though.

Dave went from being the man to just another convict. I could tell he didn't like it. When he had the drugs he was always in demand but without them, he was just another number, just like the rest of us. Dave had this over-inflated ego and without the drugs he was just fronting like all the other wannabes talking about that Lexus they supposedly had. When you're rolling, you're rolling, big Willie status and all that, but when you're not you are just another number. This new nobody status was eating away at Dave. He craved the action, the moves, the limelight. He wanted to be Scarface but now he just seemed like a wannabe.

As the weeks rolled by, there was a dramatic affect. Only a couple of dudes on the unit still kicked it with Dave. Besides myself, there were Vince, Roberto and Fox, who was a hustler from NY. Travieso would have been down also but he was still in the hole with Larry. So our little crew, once on top of the compound, was now about little or nothing. That's the knocks of the drug game, I guess. Fast and furious, even on the inside. But Dave wasn't having it. Over the weeks of idleness the urge to act had been building. The urge plus the voice of the Cuban in his ear. Dave kept thinking, "I run this shit." He had made his own moves before with the chiva and the like. He didn't have the same set up now but fuck it. He decided he would shake things up. Fuck Leonardo, he thought.

With Roberto's constant badgering and Dave's own conscious playing him, he convinced himself to step to the cop himself. Dave was about action. He wasn't no fake-ass motherfucker. Fuck taking orders. Dave made arrangements with the Puerto Rican cop. We were back in business.

There were a lot of implications from this move, and I don't know if Dave really considered them all. First and foremost he was going behind Leonardo's back and against his will. The Puerto Rican cop just wanted money so Dave convinced him that Leonardo was just laying low trying to get a transfer and the like.

Dave was boriqua so he figured it was all good. But for real he got it fucked up. He was boricua, no doubt, but he was from Detroit, while Leonardo and the cop were from the island. They spoke ingles but with an accent. Dave talked like any joker from the inner city. Plus Leonardo was a Latin King—a gangbanger. Dave was making a dangerous enemy by crossing Leonardo. That took balls. Balls and the Cuban pressing him to death.

But really, I think Dave just wanted to be the man again. It wasn't about the money or drugs. For Dave, it was about the status. Dave was jonesing to be the man. He was like an addict for the power and respect. Plus he wanted to please people. Especially the Cuban, it seemed. For some reason Dave felt that he had something to prove to the Cuban. I don't know why. Maybe because Roberto came from the USP. Who knows? Maybe Dave had promised him something or more likely, Dave just wanted to prove that he was the man. He had made his own moves before when his homey Black Steve was around. I guess Dave figured he didn't need Leonardo telling him what the deal was anymore. But that was his worst mistake. Not listening to Leonardo.

Dave made his move and the Puerto Rican cop brought him an ounce of coke. Roberto was the front man on the pound, putting out feelers and taste testers, getting the cokeheads lined up. They tried to keep it on the down low but you have to realize a prison is like a fishbowl. Word gets around.

When Leonardo found out, it was on. But still, he played it cool. I was chilling with Dave when Leonardo stormed into

Dave's cell. If it was a rough off I was definitely in the wrong place at the wrong time but luckily at this stage Leonardo just wanted to holler at Dave.

"What's up?" he demanded in his rough, Spanish-tinged ingles.

Dave was like, "Nothing's up, Yo," not sure what Leonardo meant and trying to play it off. But it was clear Leonardo knew what was up. He was just playing this out.

"You got the coke, cabron? You got the coca? Word on the pound is that you got the coca. Tell me, cabron. You got the coca?"

"I got nada, cabrone," Dave answered defensively. "You know motherfuckers on the pound—talking shit and all that."

"Oh well, sabes que, I heard you got the coca. Just checking, cabrone," Leonardo concluded, playing it off.

But I saw in his eyes that he knew. That boriqua was angry. Before the move ended, Leonardo slipped out of our unit leaving Dave and me in silence. Dave looked at me and shrugged his shoulders, but I could tell he was concerned. I would be. Who the fuck would want a beef with Leonardo? That dude was scary.

"What's up with the moreno?" Roberto asked as he strolled into the cell, obviously amped up from the coke.

Don't get high on your own supply, I thought, as I imagined Roberto as a geeking crackhead. Dave shook his head. Roberto continued, "Dame mas coca—I'm ready to make some moves."

But Dave wasn't having it. "Mira, Roberto, we gotta play it cool. We got an ounce of coke, right? You just can't put it all out there. We gotta stash it first. Leonardo is onto us. He knows something is up. I got serious fucking problems right now." Dave didn't want to face Leonardo's wrath. He was shook. I didn't blame him but Roberto was persistent. He wanted to sell some coke. He had people waiting. He had given his word. And in prison if your word is no good then you are some shit.

Right then Vince walked in the cell and smiled, "What's up with the coke?"

Dave was at a loss. He told me to go get the ounce from the stash spot. I brought it back and Dave broke it open and started cutting lines. The NY kid, Fox, came over too. They were all doing lines. I wasn't down with the coke so I bounced. I told Dave I would catch him later.

They ended up doing about three grams. Carlitos joined the party and all five of them were geeking. I was tripping off their paranoid asses. Always thinking the cop was coming and shit. "Did you hear the keys?" I would say and Dave and Vince would be peeking out the tiny cell door window slit while Roberto would be looking around for somewhere to hide in the 12' by 7' prison cell. Dudes in prison are funny but some serious bad shit was about to go down.

All geeking and paranoid, Dave told Roberto to hold the coke and stash it. I would have done it but I was like, whatever. Dave's the man, right? So now the Cuban had the coke, which was exactly what he wanted. But for reasons none of us could guess.

Roberto was a smooth one. He had something planned that would stun us. He was about to pull out all the stops.

The next day was frozen into my mind. Dave and his cellie, Carlitos, got locked up. The LT's just went right to their job assignments and cuffed them up. Then a SORT team came down to our unit and locked the whole unit down. I saw the SIS dudes prancing in all important like with dogs and video cameras. A DEA-style drug bust, right in prison. Who would have thought? They went right to Dave's cell and proceeded to rip it apart. But boom, I thought, Roberto's got the coke. SIS won't find anything.

A few hours later SIS, the video cameras, the SORT team, and the dogs left. During the four o'clock stand-up count. I was wondering what the fuck was up. After the count when the doors cracked Roberto came down to my cell asking me what was up. I told him, "I'm not sure, but where's the coke?"

He said, "Dave took that shit back this morning." So I'm standing there thinking, What the fuck? Then we started walking toward Dave's cell and we ran into Vince on the tier.

"Go check Dave's cell," I told Vince. "Roberto says the coke is in there. Maybe they missed it." Vince knew the stash spot and luckily the room was open. The PM shift cop wasn't informed that both cellies were locked up. The cop would find out sooner or later. But now was our chance, I thought. We went into the cell which was all torn apart. Everything thrown all over the place. Vents unscrewed and all. Vince checked the spot. Nada.

Roberto said, "We gotta hold Dave's stuff. He's got too much property."

We started to pick out the choice items, including sneaks, sweats, boots, and commissary. I felt like we were vulturing Dave's stuff but Roberto and Vince assured me we were just holding it for him. Eventually the cop got a clue, locked Dave's cell, and started packing him out. But only after we pilfered his property in the name of holding it for him. I felt guilty for some strange reason.

Right after that we convened in my cell with Fox, the NY kid.

"Look," Fox said, "something is up with Dave. I'm not pointing any fingers but if they got the coke it was someone close to him who set him up. Dave ain't stupid, you heard. He wouldn't keep no ounce of coke in his cell. And the way Jake came in, all DEA like. I'm telling you son, it was a set up."

I was thinking, the only people close to Dave were the people in this room. I looked around at Vince, Fox, and Roberto suspiciously, not wanting to believe what Fox was implying.

Fox continued, "I'm not calling anyone here a snitch, but think, who knew?"

The question lingered in the cell as I looked around again, still not believing. Prison is a harsh reality where you have to take a man at his word until he proves otherwise. And I had a sinking feeling, one that sunk right into my gut, that I didn't want to believe. One person in that room set up Dave. Who was the snitch, I thought?

INTERLUDES 1

"The criminal's number one rule; thou shall not snitch, not even on a snitch."

—Edward Bunker

INTERLUDES I: SNITCH CULTURE

Ronny was an East Coast guy. Not made or connected, but he was a guido nonetheless. He was from Rhode Island or something. You know, a real mafia hotbed, and he was kind of dark-skinned to boot. At least for a white guy. It must have been that Sicilian blood, I figured.

He wasn't a bad dude. He was decent, fairly intelligent, and in good shape. Not a slob or loudmouth or nothing like that. He stuck close to the Italians and to the Boston guys in particular. He rooted for the Patriots and Red Sox. A regular New England kind of guy. Forget about it, you heard.

I don't know what his case was or even what he was really about. I just saw him around the unit. Figured he was OK because most of the Boston dudes went hard exposing snitches and the like. And the Italians had a pecking order and detested rats. Wouldn't be caught dead talking to one, you know. Not like Ronny was with the in crowd or anything. He was just a guy from Rhode Island. But he was one of the guys. On the block at least. I guess on the compound he was kinda on the fringes.

But it wasn't like he was a wannabe or nothing. He carried himself well, or so I thought. But that just goes to show you because Ronny was a snitch and he probably didn't even recognize it. A lot of dudes in the feds are like that now. They think they are Joe Citizen or something. Like they're on the streets, reporting something to the police. Like an accident or burglary, I don't know.

What I do know is that Ronny went to rec one day and when he came back he found that his radio was missing from his cell. So the first thing he did was come over to the table where some of the white guys sit and told them that someone stole his radio. And the second thing he did was run to the cop's office to tell the cop. Like they're gonna put out an APB or something.

Me and a couple of dudes were sitting there and we felt bad because Ronny got his radio stolen. But we then looked on with disbelief as Ronny went over to the cop's office. I looked at my homeboy and said, "He didn't just…" But my homeboy was already up and moving, walking by the cop's office and getting a drink of water from the fountain. He locked back over at me and nodded his head. Confirmation. Ronny was snitching to the cop. Unfucking believable, I thought.

As it turned out, Ronny's bunkie had had his radio the whole time. So Ronny jumped the gun and his true colors came out. He ran to the man and snitched for nothing. Did he think it's like when you're on the street and someone breaks into your house or your car and you call the cops? I guess he did but for real, he got it fucked up. I mean, this is prison. Dudes ain't going for that. Ain't no Joe Citizen shit flying in here. For the better good or not. You just don't go to the man for nothing.

Ever since then I stepped back from dude. But still I saw dudes fucking with him even after they heard the goods. That is just the state of the feds now. It's a sad, sad world.

Vinny was a straight thief. He would steal whatever wasn't bolted down. And if he had a screwdriver he would steal that too. He didn't give a fuck. He had a reputation in the prison as a thief also but he didn't steal from solid prisoners, only from snitches and the man. Onions and green peppers from the kitchen, C/O's pens and sunglasses, their lunches, whatever he could get his hands on.

One day Vinny made a score in Education. He got a little computer pocket dictionary that they let the students use in class. He got it clean, too, or so he thought. The teacher didn't even know. But Vinny didn't count on his fellow prisoners playing cop.

On his way through the metal detectors this black kid stepped to Vinny. "Yo, you gonna put that computer dictionary back or what, my man? You know we be using dem joints in education."

Vinny looked at the dude sideways and told him, "I don't know what you're taking about, man." The kid just shook his head and Vinny forgot about it. He was already trying to figure out who to sell the computer jammy to. He figured he could get 15 or 20 macks.

The next day Vinny got called to Education in the afternoon. They called his brother and his man in too. Vinny didn't know what the fuck was up until he walked into his teacher's classroom and saw the kid from yesterday standing with the teacher.

"That's him, Mr. Dennis. That's him," the kid said, pointing at Vinny like he was on the witness stand.

Damn, Vinny thought, this snitch-ass motherfucker. Vinny wanted to pop the dude in the face but he couldn't do it right in front of the man.

The teacher told Vinny that he had two choices—bring the pocket computer back or go to the hole. Vinny chose the former and counted himself lucky for not getting a shot. But still he wanted to bust that snitch motherfucker's ass. But Vinny didn't do it. He was too busy working on his next scheme. And he thought, just wait motherfucker, what comes around goes around.

There were these two Mexicans. They were bunkies. Homeboys, you know. Vatos locos. I used to eat nachos and burritos with them. You know, kick it in español.

One day I saw them arguing and the next thing you know they were fighting. They both got lumped up and went to the hole. I didn't think nothing of it.

A couple of weeks later one Mexican comes out the hole but the other one doesn't. I ask the vato what's up with his homie and he gives me this big story how his homie was using his phone because his was on restriction and how the other vato had used like $70 of his money.

This is what they had been arguing about and why they got into the fight. I told him he was smart to handle his business and get his respect and asked him if he gave the other vato a $70 dollar ass whipping? The Mexican smiled and nodded but then he got all quiet, looked around and asked me if he should tell the counselor that money was missing off his phone account and he didn't know where it went.

I looked at the vato and told him if he said that there would be an investigation most likely and the cops would put two and two together. He got angry and told me he just wanted his money back. I told him he would have to wait 'til the other vato came out the hole and get it straight then. But according to this Mexican the other vato wouldn't be coming back out to the pound. A lot of other Mexicans had found out how he got over on his homie and they looked down on him for the sneak thief move.

But I thought, ain't this some shit. Here is this Mexican who got his props for handling his business asking me if it was OK to snitch. Indirectly of course, but he was asking me to make the call nonetheless. I told him straight out—if you do that, esse, then you're a snitch. He got mad at me again. I guess because I wouldn't ride with him and condone his snitching. Like I was gonna tell him what he wanted to hear. But fuck that, I gotta keep it real. I told him, Do what you think you gotta do. He looked at me, smiled, and put his finger to his lips. Telling me to keep it quiet. Damn, I thought. These snitches are crazy. And for real, to this day I don't know what the Mexican did and for real, I don't care either.

Back to Ronny. So a couple of months roll by and I really forgot about the whole radio thing. I said what's up to Ronny. Treated him like a person. I mean there are so many snitches in here. But I didn't really fuck with him. I told my homeboy Chris from D-block about the whole thing but that was when it was fresh in my mind. Now it was a couple of months later.

I walk into the chow hall and see Ronny sitting with my homeboy Chris, who is a little dude. They call me over and I'm thinking, what the fuck is this about. Chris is looking like he doesn't want to be there and this guy Ronny tells me like he's some mafia guy or something, "What did you tell Chris about me? Did you tell him I'm a snitch?"

I looked at him, and then at Chris, not really prepared for a confrontation but fuck it, I dove in anyway. "Look Ronny, didn't you go to the cop about your radio?" I said.

He looked at me kind of stupid like."What are you talking about?"

"Didn't you go to the cop and tell him someone stole your radio? And then you found out later your bunkie had it," I continued.

"No, man. You got it fucked up. I think you owe me an apology. I went to the cop and asked him if he shook my room down," he said.

"I ain't apologizing for shit, man. If you went to the cop and told him your radio was missing, what does that make you?" I asked.

"Are you calling me a snitch? Did you tell this guy that I'm a snitch?" he repeated.

"I'm just saying, if you went to the cop about your radio what does that make you? I'm not playing all this he said, she said shit," I told him.

"Did you hear me tell the cop that my radio was stolen?" he asked.

"No, but someone told me that they heard you tell the cop that," I said.

"Well you better tell that person that they're wrong because I didn't say no shit like that," Ronny said.

"Whatever, dude," I told him. "I can only go by what I hear."

"Well, from now on you better keep my name out of your mouth or I'll bust you in your mouth," he retorted.

"Oh yeah, well, get to busting, kid. Go 'head," I dared him, but he didn't do shit. He got up and left the table.

Chris shook my hand and left also. I found out later that Ronny was trying to work out with Chris and them and that they told him he couldn't because they heard he was a snitch. Ronny got all mad and acted like he wanted to fight Chris. So when pressed, Chris said that I had told him.

But for real, Ronny was not only a snitch, he was a punk, too. Don't say you're gonna knock a man's teeth out and then when your bluff is called, do nothing. I wasn't trying to label dude but he should learn when to keep his head down and just ride. Most dudes had forgot about that shit anyhow and he had to bring it up again. He came to me later on the block and told me that shit was dead. And lately it seems like he's been walking around by himself a lot. That's just the way shit goes when you get exposed as a punk and a snitch.

Vinny was mad as fuck. He just got some bullshit shot for something he didn't even do. He wouldn't mind if he actually got caught at something but this shot was bogus. It wasn't a second later that he walked into the bathroom in the education building and who did he see but the black dude that had snitched on him the week before. The lord works in mysterious ways, Vinny thought as he sucker punched the black dude in the back of the head while he was taking a piss. The dude crumpled into the urinal and piss started going all on the floor and all over his pants. Vinny wasn't through. He kicked the dude in the back and the side, punishing him with his steel-toe boots.

It didn't last but a minute but dude was wasted. Punched, pummeled, and kicked from behind. He was out. Vinny put it on him and he figured that the dude didn't even know who did it. Vinny left him there lying in a pool of blood and piss. That's what you get you fucking snitch-ass punk, Vinny thought as he exited the bathroom and made his way back to the unit.

About four months later I thought back to the conversation I had with the Mexican. I still wasn't sure what he did but I knew that the other vato never came on the pound again. Maybe he signed a separatee or something. I noticed that all the other Mexicans still fucked with the dude so I figured he must be OK. But for real, you never know.

Then the Mexican went to the hole again for refusing to stand for count. Actually he didn't "refuse to stand," he was just sleeping but in here that is no excuse and they hit you with the refusal shot anyhow. All the dudes on the block were like, he'll probably be in there for a while because he got time on the shelf from the fight before. Usually when you see the disciplinary committee they give you time served in the hole and put some on the shelf so if you get in trouble again within six months they can hit you with the new infraction and make you do the time from the old one.

Dudes on the block figured the Mexican would be in the hole at least 15 days and maybe more. But to everyone's surprise he came out a couple of days later. When dudes asked him if he beat the shot he said no that the counselor took care of it and he didn't have to go to the disciplinary committee. It sounded funny but dudes didn't have nothing to go on. I did.

I know you only get preferential treatment from the counselors when you're a snitch so I drew my own conclusions. I didn't put it out there or nothing but I keep that Mexican at an arms length now.

INTERLUDES II: THE TRUTH COMES OUT

Dave Ellis seemed like an OK dude. Maybe a little pretentious. But he was the type of dude that would go that extra mile to make people think he was solid. He wanted to come off as a tough guy, a man's man, someone not to fuck with. He liked to brag about what he had on the street. Showing dudes pictures of houses and cars and girls. Like he was big money or something. The kid thought he was a major player in the drug game.

He was tight with the Boston dudes. The roughnecks from Charlestown and Dorchester. You know—the bank robbers, the hijackers, the Irish mob. But Dave wasn't like them. He was a marijuana dealer from the suburbs. Supposedly into tons and the like. He was always saying how some well-known millionaire's daughter snitched him out. Dave didn't come across as a bad guy, though. He just wanted people to like him. It was like he was in high school or something. Trying to be Mr. Popular. He was always trying to talk business or shop with dudes. Trying to make connections. He wanted to be down with the tough guy crew and the mob—both Italian and Irish.

Dave had like a little iddy-biddy sentence though. Something like five years or so. The dude was in his early 20's and he let everybody he talked to know that he wasn't through with a life of crime. He was always trying to network and hook-up—make connections, you know. He wanted to be seen as a solid dude so people in the so-called life would want to fuck with him when he got back on the street.

But the dude was a little much. He lived the Big Willie lifestyle in prison. Doing sendouts here and there, putting money on dudes commissary accounts, and taking care of his homies. He was always trying to impress like he was Mr. Moneybags or something.

There was this infamous reputed Italian mobster on the block and Dave was all up under him. Trying to position himself as one of the mobster's boys. Dave was all up in there with the pasta meals every Sunday and all. "All mobbed up," as the white dudes on the block put it. Dave even had his own personal bodyguard, Big Henry, a 20-year penitentiary veteran and Dave's homeboy from Boston. Whenever you saw Dave, Big Henry was not far behind.

Dave had been on the compound about a year. Transferred in from Fort Devens, a low in upper Mass. He was getting a rep on the pound due to association and dudes were giving him respect. Everybody, that is, except for the dudes on the block who saw him as a clown. Dave was trying to hang and be cool but he got into a few scrapes. Like the time he got into it with Big Hoss, a NJ kid and straight speed freak. Dave and Big Hoss had some words when they were drinking some hooch and Big Hoss didn't like the way Dave came out of his mouth so he jumped on him. He was punishing Dave but then Big Henry, Dave's homeboy, stepped in and hemmed Big Hoss up in a full nelson. That's when Dave got his, punching Big Hoss flush in the face. Just a little bust up but Dave got his respect, even though it seemed like a chump move. But that's how the notions of respect and honor get perverted in prison.

Dave fought, though, and this counts for something in prison. At least he wasn't a pussy like some dudes previously thought. His homeboys were psyched that he held his own and represented for Boston. That is how dudes carry it in here. Every little thing gets blown up. A lot of distorted reality, you know.

So now Dave was carrying it like a Boston hardman but it was kind of farfetched because for real, the dude looked like a Backstreet Boy. And like all Boston dudes he claimed to know the dudes from New Kids on the Block. Those go-hard popstars from Beantown. Supposedly Dave grew up with the Wahlbergs. But it's all relative, you know. It's all about your reputation and your crew, New Kids on the Block or not.

Dave was getting on with everybody. Kissing up to the Italians and trying to get in with the Colombians. He was real interested in dudes who were getting out soon. Always saying that he could have his boy pick them up. Dave was always pressing dudes for contacts on the street. Wanting to hook them up with his boy and shit. It seemed he saw his whole prison term as a way to make future contacts for possible criminal enterprises when he hit the street. But that ain't nothing new. Dudes are always trying to get the hook-up so they can make moves when they get out.

But with Dave it was different. The dude was pressing. Always trying to make a move. Get an address, a hook-up or anything. The dude was a connect fiend. Like he wanted to catalog them or something. He was always saying he could make things happen. Like drug deals and the like. And his boy, another Backstreet-looking dude, was always visiting Dave with an assortment of nice-looking chicks who Dave would promise to hook dudes up with. Of course Dave claimed they were all his girlfriends. Dave would be trying to introduce his boy to other prisoners in the visiting room and shit.

The funny thing was that Dave wasn't into the prison drug scene. Not like most dudes who are trying to make moves. Dave acted like he had big money and was all about conducting business on the street. Fuck all those little prison hustles, you know. He portrayed himself as a stand-up guy so dudes took him under their wings. The mobsters, his homeboys, and the white dudes on the unit. They called him Hollywood because he would always say how he wanted to break into movies and be an actor like his boys Matt Damon and Ben Affleck, who of course he claimed to know from Boston. Dave even made the big power move jumping into a two-man cell with an Italian guy from Philly who was the grade one plumber and got a lot of respect on the pound. So Dave was styling now. He thought he had his shit on lock.

A little situation happened, though. A white dude in the unit started talking shit about Dave. This dude was supposedly a white supremacist, Nazi motherfucker. He lived with another Boston dude, a druggie named Kevin.

This is how the scene went down: supposedly Dave heard the Nazi dude talking shit about him in the yard so his homeboys geeked him up and he confronted the Nazi dude in the chow hall. Not the best place for a confrontation but Dave apparently wanted to make a show of it for his homies. Dave stepped to the Nazi dude and basically punked him out in the middle of the chow hall with the cops all around and everything but this Nazi dude didn't do shit. His bunkie Kevin, who was from Boston, convinced him he didn't want no drama with the Boston crew. So the Nazi dude tried to let it die. But

Dave wasn't having it. He made a big scene and brought a bunch of his homeboys down to the unit to see if the Nazi dude wanted to go to rec and handle his business in the bathroom. But Kevin, the Nazi dude's bunkie, came out and talked to his homeboys and Dave, telling them that shit was dead. The Nazi dude didn't want no problems.

It was weird how it all went down because it seemed like the Nazi dude could have whipped Dave, but that didn't happen. Dave got big props and moved up in status in the eyes of his homeboys because supposedly the Nazi dude wasn't no joke. But clearly he got punked out by Dave. So now everybody was fucking with Dave like he was a tough guy or something. He was so confident in his new-found hardman status that he kicked his homeboy, Big Henry, to the curb. Like he didn't need him anymore. He still fucked with him, but it wasn't the same and it was clear Dave thought he was destined for bigger and better things.

Dave began to act like a shotcaller for the Boston dudes. Checking in snitches and the like and mediating problems. The dude thought he was all that. But he had everybody fooled. He was just playing a role. Maybe he was an actor on par with Matt Damon and Ben Affleck, but eventually it all came to a head. Dave's bunkie the plumber stepped to Dave and told him he had to move out of the two-man room they shared. Dave was stunned. He didn't know what was up. He moved back into a 3-man with two white kids his age. Supposedly the plumber found something out about Dave but he wasn't letting on. He just told Dave to get the fuck out of the room.

A couple of days later Dave came back to the unit all fucked up, shaking and shit. During the lockdown he told his two bunkies that his homeboys got paperwork on him. But he said it was all a mistake because he wasn't no snitch. The Boston dudes told him to get the fuck off the compound though so Dave told his two bunkies that he was gonna check in until he could get it all figured out. The dude was scared shitless. His homeboys put a serious scare into him. Before the count cleared the cops came and got Dave. Dudes on the unit didn't know what was up but in the yard that night everybody heard.

This dude Dave had supposedly been working for the feds for years! His boy and the chicks who visited him were DEA or something. So Dave was a full-blown rat and now it was in the open. Recently a guy on the street had gone to trial and when he got his discovery, Dave Ellis' name was all over it as the informant. There was like 80 pages on all the snitching Dave had done. Dudes on the compound were passing around copies of it. And it seemed like Dave wasn't through with all his networking and the like; on the pound he was trying to make more busts and hang cases on dudes. Life in the feds is fucked up. Especially when dudes got DEA agents coming to see them in the visiting room during regular visits when all the prisoners are out there with their people. Dave fooled a lot of people and his homeboys from Boston were fucked up because they were tight with him. But they did the right thing—they got his snitching ass off the motherfucking compound. That is a rare thing in the feds these days. Usually the snitches are right out in the open and nobody does nothing.

It's like Dave's old cellie, the plumber, said, "I didn't want any problems. I just wanted the rat out of my cell. I let the Boston dudes handle it. He was their problem."

Prison is like a fishbowl. And dudes will always find out the deal. It doesn't matter if you are a good actor or not. When snitches front like solid dudes it's sad. Actually it's a real bad scene but the truth will come out in the end. Somebody will call that bluff. And Dave got lucky, he was just checked in. In another spot he might have got stabbed or beat down. You never know. Because that is prison life.

INTERLUDES III: PAPERWORK PARTY

"Yo, main man. What's up? Where you coming from?" Dusty asked the new jack holding a bus roll. Dude entered the unit sporting the blue slip-on skippys, the elastic- waistband khakis two sizes too big, and the soiled t-shirt that looked like it was his kid brother's, all of which marked him as in transit. Dusty knew he was straight off the bus, probably straight out the county, too. The dude looked up at Dusty and gritted on him before answering.

"I was in Mecklenburg County, nigga. What's up?"

"Damn, nigga," Dusty replied. "Chill the fuck out. I'm just checking you out. So you from Carolina, right?"

"Yeah, Charlotte, Newsome Projects," dude said.

Dusty's eyes lit up. "Oh yeah? That's around my way. I'm from Crutchfield Street. They call me Dusty. What's up, homeboy?" Dusty smiled and put out his hand. Dude paused, unsure for a minute, then shook hands with Dusty.

"Alright, cool, they call me Murder," the new dude said.

"Damn," Dusty said with surprise. "Murder, huh?"

"Yeah," the dude said. "Murder."

Dusty had been in the system a minute and he'd met a lot of brothers and seen a lot of shit but he was still surprised at what dudes called themselves these days. Maybe dude thought he was straight out of a rap video or something. Dusty didn't care. At least he was a homeboy. And he was a stocky little dude, too. Straight pitbull-looking muthafucka.

"So how much time you got, Murder?"

"What's it to you, nigga," Murder shot back.

"Damn, playa, don't take no offense. I'm just making conversation. I been in six years on a 15-year bid. I got busted back in '93 on the Toppy Smith case. You heard of that, right?" Dusty said.

"Yeah, I heard of that. I got a gun charge. 60 months," Murder said.

"Alright, it's all good then. I'll introduce you around to the homies on the block and on the pound. You probably know some of them. I think Popcorn and them from Newsome projects. Anyway, chill homey and if you need something, holla."

"Alright, bet," Murder said as he hit rocks with Dusty.

Dusty walked over to his man Johnny Blaze. "Who the fuck dat?" Johnny Blaze asked.

"Some young nigga outta Newsome Projects," Dusty explained.

"Oh yeah? He know Popcorn and them?"

"He didn't say," answered Dusty. "The young brotha seem kind of high strung."

"He probably just scared, man. You know, first time in the feds and shit," said Johnny.

"Yeah, you right," Dusty said. "These young niggas always trying to go gorilla on a muthafucka and shit." Johnny Blaze nodded his head in agreement.

Later, Dusty and Johnny Blaze were in the gym balling with some DC cats. Popcorn came in the gym with his boys. "Yo, Dusty my man," called out Popcorn.

"What's up kid?" Dusty said as he nodded to Popcorn's boys as they all nodded to Johnny Blaze. When Dusty and Johnny Blaze's team lost they joined Popcorn and them on the bleachers.

"Damn Dusty, you let them DC niggas rough the court off?" Popcorn joked. Dusty and them laughed.

"You win some and you lose some," Dusty said as he and Blaze hit rocks with their homeboys. "What's up though?"

"Did you see that nigga Antawn last night? The muthafucking Tar Heels were killing them cracker-ass Blue Devils," Popcorn said.

"Yeah," piped in his man Baby. "Ain't no true nigga like Duke. It's Carolina blue all the way. MJ and all that."

"You right," Blaze said and pounded rocks with Baby.

"Did you hit or what?" Popcorn asked. "I know you took the points."

"No, man," Dusty said dejectedly. "I took the over. I didn't hit shit."

"Damn, nigga," Popcorn said. "That shit was a lock. We tore the bookies' ass up."

"Straight up," added Shane, Popcorn's other homeboy.

"Yo," Dusty jumped in. "You see that new young nigga from Newsome Projects?"

"No, man," Popcorn said. "What's his name?"

"He said it's 'Murder.' He a little dark-skinned, pitbull-looking muthafucka."

"Maybe I know that nigga," Popcorn said. "I wonder if he's on my man Big G's case. You know that nigga got life. Fucking snitches, be making people's families cry. The feds is full of them hot-ass muthafuckas. Is that cat straight, Dusty?"

"Shit, I don't know," Dusty said. "He from your hood. Said he got 60 months for a gun charge."

"Word," Popcorn said. "You seen his paperwork?"

"I ain't seen shit and I ain't co-signing nothing either but dude seemed alright, you know?"

"Well, damn nigga, we still gotta check that shit out. Can't have no hot-ass Carolina niggas walking the pound giving us a bad rep," Popcorn said. "Introduce me to that nigga, alright?"

"Alright, I got you," replied Dusty.

"Yo," Blaze piped in. "There goes that nigga now."

Dusty looked over and saw the dude doing pullups.

"Yo, Murder, homeboy, what's up?" Murder heard Dusty and them and nodded. Dusty was waving him over. "Let me holla at you," Dusty continued.

Murder stopped his workout and walked over. "What's up?" Murder asked as he looked around. All eyes were on him.

"What up, man?" said Popcorn. "I'm Popcorn, this Baby, and this Shane. We from Newsome, too."

"What up," Murder said while hitting rocks with them all.

"And this Blaze," Dusty said. "He on the block with us." Murder hit rocks with Blaze, too.

"We on A-block. You need something, just holla," Popcorn said.

"Alright, bet," Murder said as he started to walk back to resume his workout.

"Yo Murder," Popcorn hollered. "You know Big G and them, right?"

Murder kind of looked down at the ground before he met Popcorn's eyes. "Yeah, I know Big G. The feds did him dirty," Murder said.

"Yeah," Popcorn said. "My peeps said the nigga got life."

"That's what I heard at the county. He was over on 4 South," Murder said.

"That shit's fucked up. Fucking hot-ass niggas," answered Popcorn. "You know who snitched on him?"

"I heard some shit and read the papers but I didn't know the niggas. They said some boys down Carson Street testified against him," Murder said.

"Damn," Popcorn said. "Hot-ass Carson Street niggas."

With that, Murder took off. "Alright, I'll holla at you all."

"Alright, later."

A couple of days later Popcorn saw Dusty on the yard in the afternoon.

"Yo, my nigga, what's up?" Popcorn said.

"What up, homeboy?" Dusty answered. Popcorn took him aside and told him he wanted to holla at him.

"Check it, Dusty, I was hollering at my sister on the phone, right? And she was telling me about Big G's case. She said some nigga called Anthony Simmons was the star muthafucking snitch at Big G's trial. And she said she heard that nigga Anthony Simmons go by Murder."

Dusty looked at Popcorn, taking in the implications of what he just said. "You think it's the same nigga?"

"What the fuck do you think?" answered Popcorn.

Dusty shook his head. "That shit is fucked up, dog."

"Fuck yeah, it is. Me, Baby, and Shane gonna check that nigga in. Unless he show some paperwork proving it ain't him," Popcorn said. "Damn, I thought that nigga was straight. We gonna find out one way or another. You down or what?"

"You gonna check that nigga's paperwork?" questioned Dusty.

"Yeah," Popcorn said. "He gonna have to show it or he gonna have to check in. We can't leave no hot-ass Carolina nigga running around the pound."

"Damn, Pop. I mean, I don't know if I'm down with some shit like that," Dusty said.

"What? You soft now nigga?"

"Don't go there, homie," said Dusty. "Cuz I'll bust a nigga's ass. But I ain't into all this paperwork shit. Why don't you just leave the nigga alone?"

"Fuck that, Dusty. You let one of them rat muthafuckas on the pound and then they'll start running shit," said Popcorn. "Snitching to the man and shit. I ain't going out like that. I represent for my hood. For Carolina, nigga. We can't be letting them other niggas think that Carolina dudes are soft. Know what I mean?"

"Yeah, I know what you mean," Dusty replied.

"So you down, right? Bring Blaze, too. On the yard tonight. We gonna have a paperwork party. I'ma tell that nigga Murder at recall."

"Alright, homeboy," Dusty said.

Dusty saw Murder on the block after count. He noticed Murder was eyeing him suspiciously. For real, Dusty wasn't down with that paperwork shit. He was just trying to do his time. He didn't care what another muthafucka did. As long as it didn't concern him and his. Those Newsome Project niggas be wilding anyhow, he thought.

"Yo, Dusty, what up?" Johnny Blaze said. "You trying to ball tonight or what?"

"No, fuck that. I ain't going anywhere near the yard. Popcorn talking about a paperwork party for Murder. I ain't fucking with that shit. He wanted you to go too. To represent for the homies." As Dusty spoke, Johnny Blaze looked at him, taking it all in.

"Well fuck that, I ain't going out there either then," Blaze said. They both looked up to see Murder gritting on them from up on the tier. When their eyes met, Murder turned and walked away.

"That nigga shady, Blaze," Dusty said. "I ain't fucking with him."

That night, Baby, Shane and Popcorn were in the yard with some other Carolina dudes. Not many, but enough. The 6:00 PM move ended and they started toward the gym. They saw Murder and cornered him.

"So what up, nigga," Popcorn began. "You brought your paperwork or what? My peeps from the street say a kid named Anthony Simmons snitched on my man Big G and gave that nigga life. My peeps told me Anthony Simmons went by Murder and was from Newsome Projects. So is that you, or do you got paperwork proving it ain't you?"

Murder glared around at the group that had surrounded him. They could tell he had some type of folder behind his back. "Yeah, I got some paperwork, nigga," Murder said.

"Well let's see it, homeboy," answered Popcorn. "Because we don't like no hot niggas around here representing Carolina. And if you Anthony Simmons you need to check the fuck in or else."

Murder brought the folder out from behind his back and as the Carolina dudes looked on he ripped two nine-inch shanks outta the folder, which promptly floated to the ground. "Or else what, nigga," said Murder with a snarl. "I'm Anthony Simmons and I snitched on Big G and his whole crew. So what the fuck is up?"

Everybody jumped back and Popcorn, Baby, and Shane were definitely startled for a minute. But Popcorn kept his nerve. "What you gonna do nigga? Stab all of us? We 10 deep," Popcorn said.

"I don't think so. I think I'm just gonna stab you three. I ain't got no beef with the others. They didn't say shit to me," explained Murder.

Popcorn looked around and saw his other homeboys backing up and then he realized that Dusty and Johnny Blaze weren't even there. Bamma-ass niggas, he thought. But Baby and Shane were still with him.

"So what's it gonna be, nigga. You think you some Big Willie shot caller. I ain't checking the fuck in. In fact, I think you the one that checking the fuck in," Murder said.

Popcorn looked at Murder's eyes and thought, this nigga crazy. He looked at Shane and Baby right beside him and realized they were thinking the same thing.

"So what up niggas," Murder said. "You got your cutcards or what? You ready to play? Cuz I'm strapped and I am all about murder."

He yelled the last word and lunged forward with both shanks. And with that, Popcorn, Shane, and Baby took the fuck off running for dear life. And they ran all the way to the lieutenant's office and checked the fuck into PC.

"Fake-ass hard niggas," Murder cackled after them as he watched them run.

After that, Murder was the talk of the pound. Wasn't nobody fucking with him. Dudes started calling him the killer snitch. Didn't nobody want no drama. Nobody really messed with him but they kept their distance. Because for real, wasn't nobody trying to fuck with a known snitch but wasn't nobody trying to beef with him either. He had earned his respect.

Popcorn and them became laughingstocks as did the Carolina dudes on the pound. But after awhile it all died down and was forgotten.

Back on the block, Murder stepped to Dusty and Johnny Blaze. "We straight, right?" he asked. They both nodded, telling him, "Yeah, we cool, Murder. We cool."

They didn't want no drama.

INTERLUDES IV: TV MAN

Dude was a straight TV monster. Thought he owned the television and shit. He had that joint on lock, too. Dudes on the block were like, that's L's TV. He was the head orderly on the unit and had gotten a remote control that he kept up in his cell.

He programmed the TV so that only his remote could change the channels. So when he wasn't on the block the TV would be locked onto whatever channel he left it on. Usually BET or MTV.

But that wasn't often. If you ever wanted to find L he would usually be up in front of the TV. He didn't watch no sports or movies, either. He was a straight video and sitcom man. Plus reality shows. He went hard on reality shows, and stories too. All afternoon it was all stories. General Hospital, Days of our Lives or whatever.

L worked as an orderly, so his day would start with buffing the main floor. Then he would set up his chair right in front of the TV. He would bring out his bowl, some snacks, his coffee mug and something to drink. He was marking his territory, so to speak. He was demonstrating and letting it be known that the TV and the area right in front of it was his domain. He had his newspaper, TV Guide, and everything right there. Dudes in prison are bad about that, laying claim to some government shit, you know. I guess it makes them feel like they own something because for real, they got nothing. And if they once had something, the government took it. Ain't no Lexus parked out front, you heard. But anyway, after L finished his work he wasn't leaving for nothing. He did his bid with the TV.

And for a brother from DC he watched some corny shows, too. I remember seeing a lot of sci-fi/ superhero stuff on the TV. But BET was the staple. And no one ever argued with him, either. I guess he had dudes up on the block shook. I don't know. He wasn't no super-imposing dude but he carried himself well, was in good shape and the like. Everybody on the block just knew that it was L's TV. Knew it and accepted it. The rest of the block contented themselves with the four other TVs on the unit. They didn't fuck with his.

But one time this dude came in from Lewisburg, and he was thorough. They called him J-Bo, and J-Bo was a mean dude. And for some reason he took a dislike to L. J-Bo liked to cause problems. Create some drama, you know. Stay in the mix. That was just how he did his time. J-Bo started fucking with L and the TV. He wanted to try the man. I don't know why. Maybe cuz he saw that L had the TV on lock. For whatever reason, J-Bo wasn't having it. He wasn't on the block a week when he started challenging L about what was on the TV.

"Damn, nigga," J-Bo said. "Put that shit back on BET. Fuck that sitcom shit. What you watching some Mutant X shit for? We ain't no crackers."

"No, brother," L said. "We watching this."

"What the fuck you mean, we watching this," J-Bo replied.

"This what we watching," L said. "This what we always watch."

"Only person I see is you, nigga," J-Bo said as he looked around. "What do you mean, we?"

L didn't say shit, just sat there and watched the TV.

"Fake-ass nigga," J-Bo said as he walked off.

L watched him go and then spoke to his man T, who was sitting right beside him. "Watch that nigga, T," L said. "Watch him."

Now, T was a bigger dude but not the brightest. He was loyal to L, though. L took care of him, cooked for him, and let him hold the remote on late night. So for real, T had a stake in the whole TV thing and he was smart enough to know that J-Bo was a threat to this.

J-Bo was mad that his manipulation technique didn't work. He figured L for a bamma-ass dude. Well, he thought, if the press move don't work I just got to rough it off. For some reason he was obsessed with that TV. Not for the fact that he was a TV monster but just because he considered that DC cat L soft. And J-Bo couldn't abide no soft dude running nothing. That nigga ain't built like that, he thought. In the pen he'd be hiding up in his cell. He ain't running shit.

At the same time, L was thinking, why this nigga hatin' on me? I don't know this nigga. But I got something good here. I ain't letting this new jack fuck up my bid. L thought about the steps he might have to take to preserve his TV.

T was thinking, too. He was like, damn, I gotta punish this dude J-Bo if he step to L again about the fucking TV. I can't let no nigga disrespect my man. Plus it's my TV, too. L be letting me hold the remote. Fuck that nigga J-Bo. If he fuck around I'll punish his ass.

The next day a bunch of dudes were watching Rap City on BET. L watched it everyday, T also. But when it was over L flipped the TV over to the news. Most of the dudes left not saying nothing, but J-Bo spoke up. "Yo, my man, put that shit back on BET. We ain't watching no corny-ass news."

L just ignored him like if he did he would just go away but T looked back. "Check it out, playa. You new here," said T. "You ain't running shit. We watch Rap City everyday and then we watch the news. That's how it goes. You don't like it, you don't gotta watch shit, but you ain't running shit around here." T turned back around to watch the news and that was his first mistake.

"What?!" J-Bo shouted as he jumped up and slapped T in the back of the head. L turned to look at J-Bo, who was all agitated. T got up and threw his chair at J-Bo. J-Bo's slap against T's head had attracted the attention of the whole unit.

"You gonna throw a chair at me like a bitch, nigga?" J-Bo said to T. T just stood there like he was gonna do something but he didn't do shit and that was his second mistake. J-Bo sensed T's hesitation and took it for weakness. J-Bo was surprised, as he had geeked himself to pound L instead of the bigger T. But whatever was whatever, he thought. And now this big dude T was hesitating after J-Bo had bitch-slapped him in the back of the head, so J-Bo figured the brother was shook.

J-Bo popped T in the nose and followed with a flurry of five more punches straight to T's face. L jumped back and held up his hands in surrender like he didn't want no problems as his man T went to the floor. Blood flowing and his face swelling up.

"Yeah, nigga, that's what I thought," J-Bo told L as he turned to face him.

"Fake-ass niggas," J-Bo said as he went to his cell to check his hands for marks. L helped T up and a couple of other prisoners got a mop and bucket to clean up the blood that was flowing onto the floor from T's face.

In T's cell L tried to patch up dude's face but it was fucked up and looked a mess. T didn't need no stitches but he would have two black eyes. L went and got some ice for him. As he did, he thought about how to get rid of J-Bo. L didn't watch no TV that night.

The next day J-Bo got locked up under SIS investigation. Supposedly someone had dropped a note. T got locked up too but was released a couple of days later. J-Bo never came back to the pound.

A lot of J-Bo's homeboys from Philly said L and T were snitches. But they never said nothing to L and T's faces—only behind their backs. And L and T never followed up on the rumors. They were content to let them lie and eventually blow over. That is how things happen in prison a lot of time. Dudes just don't want to deal with the drama so they let it lie until it becomes dead. L had taken care of the problem. He had his TV, watched his shows, and didn't pay attention to what people said behind his back.

DRUG DEALER
BOOK TWO

"Prison has two sets of laws, those of the administration and those of the convicts."
—Edward Bunker

PART SEVEN: THE AFTERMATH

"Esse, we gotta find out what's up?" Vince told me later. "Sabes que, mañana I'm gonna go to el hoyo and talk to Dave."

We decided that this was the best course of action for now. Because shit was off the hook. And for real Vince was the only vato I trusted with Travieso still hemmed up in the hole on the dirty urine trip. When the fuck is that vato getting out anyhow, I thought. He would know what the fuck to do. I was at a loss and didn't trust the Cuban, Roberto, one bit.

"What about the Cuban?" I asked Vince.

"Don't worry, Guero, he's cool. Maybe la policia didn't get the coca."

I knew this was wishful thinking but maybe everything wasn't all doom and gloom. Maybe some sucker-ass, clown-buster just dropped a note. That was how SIS and the LT's got most of their information—from notes slid under C/O's doors or placed in the institutional mailboxes for outgoing mail that were located in each unit. It might all just be an investigation or false alarm due to some hater's anonymous note. But I doubted it. I just had this feeling that Dave was hit. But Vince would find out. He wasn't no plastico.

The next day at mail call after la cuenta Vince provoked the cop by repeatedly asking him if he had any mail for him even before the cop had a chance to call out any names. The cop, a skinny, country type, got rattled by Vince's badgering and told him, "I'm giving you a direct order to shut up and let me call the mail."

Vince was like, "You can't tell me to shut up, motherfucker," and with that the cop ended mail call and called the LT on his walkie-talkie to tell the LT he had one for the bucket. That is how the cops carried it. Straight power trippers. It didn't matter if they were right or wrong.

The LT and the compound officers came down to the unit, handcuffed a smiling Vince, and escorted him to the hole.

I also found out when our unit was called to the chowhall that Leonardo had been locked up that afternoon before la cuenta. My homeboy, Mike from VA who locked on Leonardo's block, had told me.

Later, back on the unit, Fox the NY kid came over to my cell and told me that one of his homies saw the Cuban, Roberto, coming out of the Lt's office that afternoon. I was like, what the fuck, but I was not sure about stepping to the Cuban.

Fox said we should, though, so we cornered him in the Spanish TV room and hollered at him. "Yo Roberto, you got a shot or something, son?" Fox asked him.

"No way, bro, I had a piss test. Pinche ratas, tu sabes?" Answered Roberto.

"Damn, dude, did you flush?" I asked, knowing that he had been doing coke and the only way he would pass was if his piss came out absolutely clear like water. This was called flushing and was achieved by continually drinking water and pissing it out, thus flushing or cleaning your system out. Can't get a dirty out of pure water, you know.

"Si, Guero, tome mucha aqua," Roberto said.

"Sabes que, Leonardo got locked up," I told Roberto. Fox hit my leg like I shouldn't have told Roberto that but I was sure he knew and my suspicions were confirmed.

"Yeah, I heard. He's the Latin King, right?" Roberto asked as I wondered what kind of game this motherfucker was playing. Without answering his question I fired right back, "Vince should be out next week to let us know what's up with Dave. Holler at me later alright."

He nodded and we hit the rock, which is tapping fists, and the equivalent of a handshake in prison. I had my doubts about Roberto but I wasn't 100 percent sure. He was acting very nonchalant though, like he didn't want to fuck with me and Fox or something.

I told Fox that I'd holler at him and went to my cell. Luckily I had a joint that I copped off my homeboy Mike in the chow hall. I made sure my cellie, this Mexican, was not coming back to the cell anytime soon, put the shit sign up in the window-slit of the door, cracked the barred window of the cell, and sparked up the joint. My homeboy told me it was stoney. We would see.

As I lay on my bunk thinking, I watched the marijuana smoke swirl around as I exhaled it and it got sucked up into the vent. Thank God for the ventilation system, I thought as I finished the joint, all four hits of it. It was enough to get me stoned, and I puffed out a little baby powder to kill the weed smell. A lot of bullshit had happened and I was hoping it wouldn't get worse, but as I was to find out that was like hoping the chowhall food would be good, which it never was.

A couple of days later the FBI came on the compound, supposedly on the graveyard shift, and arrested the Puerto Rican cop Flores, right out of the unit he was working at. The midnight orderly told my homeboy Mike, who let me know the next morning at chow. Damn, I thought, that is way fucked up. And for the next week that was all anybody was talking about on the pound. There were crazy rumors flying around like the cop had an ounce of coke on him or some chiva but no one really knew. On the pound we just knew he was arrested by the motherfucking FBI. That shit was crazy.

Dave was locked up. Travieso was in the hole. Vince was in the hole and Larry, too. Leonardo, el magnate, was locked up. The Puerto Rican cop, who served as the drug pipeline for the compound, was arrested. Things were fucked up. All my peeps were under investigation or doing segregation time in the hole. I hoped that I wasn't next. So far I was under the SIS radar and I hoped I stayed that way. But I wondered who really knew what on the compound. I mean, I knew what I knew, but what did other people know? As far as I could see, all the major players were locked up. And the rumors on the pound were vicious. Some dudes were even saying Dave was the snitch and the Puerto Rican cop was an undercover DEA agent. You know how shit spreads. Blowing up and the like.

Gossip, innuendos, rumors—it's mostly all basura, but dudes love to talk shit. I guess they like the sound of their own voices.

Fox was hanging tight with his NY homeboys and in the yard I was sticking to the Virginia white boys and La Raza. Appearances are everything in prison, and if it seems like your own set or homies won't ride with you then you are an open target for rumors and the like. And usually once someone pins a jacket on you, it sticks, whether it's true or not. And it's hard to shake a bad tag, like the shit cons were saying about Dave. For real, they didn't know. It was all innuendo and speculation. But when you are not around to defend yourself the viciousness of prisoners comes out as they savage your character and say all types of fucked-up shit behind your back, thinking you will never come out of the hole to challenge their word or step to them. Dudes try to make themselves look big or tough or in the know at other prisoners' expense. And it is all just in the moment type of stuff. That's just how it is. Prisoners are brutal and backstabbing.

It's like when someone went to court, all these fake-ass motherfuckers on the pound would say the dude is a snitch going to testify and all that. But as soon as the dude gets back the same cats were there to offer him a cup of coffee, a cigarette, a pat on the back. Prison was supposed to be about honor and integrity and all that but sometimes it just all seems so twisted. Nobody had any paperwork on Dave, no proof that he snitched on anybody. But still, the shit flew and who was I to stop it?

I remember seeing Roberto in the yard, all decked out in Dave's money-green Champion sweatsuit and Dave's red and white Air Jordans, styling like he was the man or something. This Cubano was really brazen. He had probably started the rumors about Dave being a snitch. He was just fronting with his homeboys. Playing pool in the rec room and shit. His main man, this Cuban Chato, was holding court, telling all the other Cubans something. Jabbering away in rapid-fire español.

Supposedly Roberto was the subject, at least that was the way it looked from the laughter, pats on the back, and glances at Roberto. He was the center of attention. Big Willie status and all that.

I wanted to go over there and say what's up and ask him why he was all fronting on Dave instead of handling business like he was supposed to. But, to be honest, the big crowd of Cubans stopped me. Roberto would have felt the need to put on a show at my expense and I wasn't about to put myself in a situation where I got disrespected. In prison, that is just plain stupid. Because if someone disses you, you gotta get your respect. In whatever way you can. Even if it means shanking a motherfucker.

Shit on the yard was tense. The tension just hung in the air. It seemed like it was weighing me down, making it hard to breathe. Nobody was really sure what was happening, especially me. I just had this fucked-up feeling like something wasn't right. And the weed, it was scarce. It had dried up pretty quick. With all that had gone down and the compound so dry, convicts were putting two and two together. There was a lot of talk and a lot of questions. Dudes were constantly pulling me up, wanting to holler and the like. Asking me about Dave or about some moves they wanted to make. It was like with all the other players gone I was the man or something. Unfucking real. Cons were actually coming to me and checking if it was alright to get their hustle on. And for real, I didn't give a fuck. Dave had shit on lock but I wasn't running shit. I just told dudes to look out with some weed if they could. Because I wasn't a shot caller. I was just a kid from the suburbs, thrown into the turbulent and violent netherworld of prison.

A lot of dudes still owed money to Dave, though. I didn't know who all of them were. One day on the block a couple of days later I stepped to Roberto and asked him if Dave's money was straight. He told me, "Don't worry about that, Guero. I got it." But I wasn't sure what that meant.

Did it mean he was taking care of business for Dave or for himself? Later on I saw Roberto hollering at Fox so I checked him out that night.

"What's up, dude? What's up with the Cuban?" I asked Fox.

He told me that Roberto had given him an address to send the money he and his homies owed Dave for the weed. I was like, damn, maybe I got the Cuban wrong. But I didn't say anything. I asked Fox if he was gonna send the cheddar.

He said, "Look, son, it's bad business if I don't. Dave ain't sent out no kites and the Cuban was holding it down for him anyway, you heard."

I was like, alright, maybe the Cuban is straight. Maybe he is Dave's man. But in the twisted web that was being woven I felt trapped as the spider closed in to feed. Better safe then sorry though, I told myself. Let the dude play his hand out and maybe get trapped in his own web.

And as I found out Roberto was taking care of all Dave's business. I couldn't say shit for real because the Cuban was the one who Dave had holding it down before the DEA-style raid. I still wished I had someone to kick it with though. My homies from VA and La Raza were cool but they weren't my crew. I just laid low and tried to stay stoned; the Cuban even hooked me up a couple of times. It was about two weeks after the arrest of the cop and still no word form Vince or Dave. Dudes weren't bringing out any kites or nothing.

I stepped to the counselor for my unit, Mr. Newman, an ex-hippie-looking country dude who seemed way burnt out and asked him when Vince was coming out of the hole. He told me the unit team had referred Vince's incident report—or shot, as prisoners called them—to the discipline hearing officer and that the DHO hadn't seen him yet. I was like, damn, what the fuck is up with that? Me and Vince had expected the unit team to handle that bullshit shot but apparently the officer had wrote Vince up for creating a disturbance and inciting a riot. And those shots were 200 series and pretty serious as opposed to less serious or petty shots like insolence or disobeying a direct order which are 300 and 400 series shots. Bad luck for Vince.

I was really starting to believe that I had Roberto fucked up but then by chance I found something out. At dinner that night I saw my homeboy, Mike, kicking it with the Cuban, Chato, in the chowhall. That was strange because I didn't think my homeboy fucked with the Cuban who was Roberto's boy, and I knew them talking meant one of four things—my homeboy was buying drugs, getting some hooch, planning to do some tat work, or sizing dude up for a beatdown. That was just how Mike was.

Later on I copped a joint and went over to my homeboy's unit to kick it with him for an hour between the moves. I arrived at his cell expecting him to be doing some tat work but he was in there by himself drawing. "What's up, dog?" I said as I walked in his cell.

"Hey homeboy," he said as he looked up. I whipped out the joint, lit it up, and passed it to him after I took a hit.

"Damn, homie, you know I can't resist a joint. Especially when I'm coming down off this coke," Mike said.

Coke? I was surprised to hear that but I played it off, saying, "Let me find out you're making your own moves and shit."

"Naw, dog, it ain't that. I got the coke off that Cuban, Chato," Mike informed me. This was news indeed and with my original suspicions receding this bit of info piqued them up again. My stoned mind started rolling. "Damn, dog," I said. "What'd you do, a sendout?"

"Yeah, bro, I got a $100 piece, snorted it all myself, too. You know I'm a fiend," Mike said as his eyes bugged from the coke in a crazy gleam and a twisted smile plastered his face. My homie was a straight drug addict. He wasn't happy if he wasn't high or drunk. All he did was sling ink to pay for the drugs. And he had a reputation as the best inkslinger on the pound. Dudes said his work was like that and he had a real light hand. He could literally pick and choose who he wanted to tat

71

because dude had a waiting list and shit. He was that good. And if you weren't a solid dude you could forget it. Homeboy didn't tat no rats.

"Puerto Rico," I said, playing on the old joke I had with the white cons for the sendouts, knowing that was where the money was supposed to be going. My homeboy looked at me, all frazzled and strung out from the coke. "Naw bro, Chato gave me a Florida address."

Damn, I thought, what the fuck is up with that? What was Roberto up to? Selling coke which he had implied Dave had got busted with. And sending money to Florida, not the normal Puerto Rico drop? Dude was making a major power move, but if he was, then who snitched out the cop? I was stoned like a motherfucker but my mind was on one million like I was the one doing the coke.

I split on the 6:30 PM movement and went to the yard. I had to hit the track and think all this bullshit through. I didn't want to do anything stupid that might get a shank stuck in my gut. But shit was fucked up. And all my road dogs were in the hole taking the heat. Set up by either a cold, vicious power player or a snitch, or maybe both. I didn't know.

As I walked around the track I saw Fox on the weight pile with his boys. He called me over and we hit the rock. "What's up dog?" I said.

"You know," he replied, flexing a massive bicep for me and smiling his crazy smile, "getting my money, son."

"Damn kid," I said, "you got a holster for them guns?"

Fox laughed and shook his head then turned all serious like, "No way, son, but do you got some extra space in your locker?"

I took the bait, hook, line, and sinker, asking Fox, "Sure dude, what you wanna put there?"

Fox looked back at his homies on the weight bench, flexed his arms again and pointed at his biceps, "These, son."

As his homeboys broke out laughing I laughed too because Fox was my man. I clasped hands with him and bumped my chest to his. When I was close to him I said quietly, "Yo, dog, the address Roberto gave you, was it in Florida?"

He drew back and looked at me surprised. "Yeah, son, it was. Why? What's up?"

"I don't know for sure but I think I'm figuring it out. I'll holler at you back on the block after count, OK?" I resumed walking around the track.

"All right son, later," Fox hollered. All the pieces were fitting together for me. This Cuban was slick. He got rid of all the major players, stole their coke, and was now selling it and collecting all the outstanding debts and sending them to his people in Miami. The dude had balls. I would give him that. You just didn't fuck with Latin Kings like Leonardo and cats like Dave that way. Because it wasn't healthy and like they say, what comes around, goes around. And in prison when it is time to pay the piper sometimes you can end up paying with your life.

But one thing had me real fucked up. The cop. Somebody snitched him out and I couldn't figure out why. If the Cuban was making a power play why would he take out the meal ticket. Something just didn't fit. All of this was going through my mind as they called the move and I headed back to my unit. As I walked down the sidewalk I saw some Spanish dudes arguing in the entryway to my unit. A little scuffle ensued and two of the dudes, Boriquas from Leonardo's block I thought, split up the sidewalk past me walking rapidly. As I walked up to the door I saw a dude lying prone in the entryway with his head busted open, blood all in his black hair and gushing rapidly, a small pool forming on the waxed and buffed tile floor. I walked by quickly, not wanted to get jammed up, and went to my cell. But I knew who it was—the Cuban, Roberto.

PART 8: REVELATIONS

I knew the cop would go lock the door to the unit in a minute when the move was over and find Roberto crumpled in the entryway. The Cuban didn't look dead but he was fucked up. When the cop found him he would hit the deuces—that is what the prisoners called the body alarm on the cops walkie-talkie which signified "emergency."

I watched from the barred window in my cell, which faced the compound, as a bunch of officers, LT's and medical staff ran down to the unit in response to the deuces. They even brought the little golf cart ambulance. The flashing lights reflected through the window to my cell and bounced off the white walls of my cell in a kind of Grateful Dead-like light show. Too bad I wasn't on acid. As soon as they carted Roberto off to the hospital the cops would be locking down.

About 20 minutes later they did and started the interview process. The LT's and staff called us out cell by cell for our interviews concerning the incident. They sat the prisoners one at a time in the counselors', case managers', or unit manager's office and asked the standard questions: Do you know the person? Do you know what happened? Would you tell us if you knew?

Every convict knew the answers to this routine were no but after the interviewing staff member wrote your name, number, and answers down they would try to make small talk before they allowed you to leave. If they just shuffled you out quickly it would fuck it up for the snitches who would be in the office telling everything they knew about the incident or even making it up just to hear themselves talk. So the interviewing staff had to make it seem like everybody was telling them something to protect the snitches by keeping all prisoners in the office for a certain amount of time.

After my obligatory five minutes or so the interviewer said I could go and a C/O escorted me back to my cell and locked me in. My Mexican bunkie told me they busted open the

Cuban's head. I didn't ask who "they" were because I had a pretty good idea. I just told him, "Yeah, I heard," and got ready for bed because we were going to be locked down for the duration. But the doors would crack at breakfast.

The compound was buzzing the next morning as the news of the Cuban getting his dome split spread. My homeboy from VA, the inkslinger Mike, tracked me down to get the details. "I was coming in from rec and dude was crumpled there in the doorway with his head busted open and blood gushing out," I told him. I didn't say anything about the two Boriquas I saw making tracks, though. That wasn't anybody's business and I didn't want to generate any rumors that might end up with SIS and get dudes hemmed up. Because I knew that cats were probably dropping notes like crazy.

In a prison, whenever any major drama happens, the note droppers go crazy dropping notes. Some probably don't even know what the fuck happened but they want to put their two cents in to SIS. I couldn't tell you why because who knows what goes through the mind of a snitch? And prisoners are bad with the gossip, too. By the end of the day dudes on the pound were saying Roberto was in the infirmary, close to death and that Dave had sent a kite out from the hole telling La Raza to punish the Cuban. All types of crazy shit. So much that one of my carnalito's, Snake from Tejas, came and hollered at me on the block.

"Guero, que pasa, vato? Todo esta chevere?"

I told him, "Sabes que, shit is fucked up esse."

He slapped me on the back and flashed me the joint he had in his hand. "Quieres fumar, buey?" he inquired.

"Siempre," I replied as I led him to my cell.

"Check it out, vato," Snake said as he lit up the joint. "La Raza didn't have nothing to do with that bullshit, verdad?"

He handed me the burning joint which left smoke trails in the air. I watched as the smoke drifted in the dimly lit cell.

"Simon, esse," I answered, "Yo se." I took a hit of the joint and relaxed as the smoke slowly filled my lungs. A little marijuana break was definitely what I needed. Snake was right on time.

You know," he started again, "that these pinche putos on the pound are saying La Raza did that bullshit."

As I exhaled the smoke toward the vent and handed him the joint, I looked him straight in the eye, trying to judge what he was getting at. "Yeah, I know vato. Eso es pura mierda, tu lo sabes."

"All right, Guero. I'm glad tu entiendes," Snake said as he seemed to relax a little, puffing on the joint and passing it back to me for the last hit.

That is the thing with prison joints—four hits and the thing is gone. And that's ten bucks, too. But those two hits left me in heaven. I'm telling you, I was a big-time stoner. Snake got up to leave and hit the rock to indicate that everything was tranquilo. "Esse," I said as he walked out of my cell. "Maybe Vince will come out soon. I know he's gonna beat those bullshit shots."

Snake smiled and said, "Simon, esse, simon."

Indeed, Vince came out of the hole the next day. It was good to see him. He was my carnalito. Mi hermano, tu sabes. La Raza was also happy he was back and as soon as he hit the block Snake wanted to holler at him. I wanted to kick it with Vince also but I knew they had to get shit straight with La Raza. A lot of politics are involved in prison gangs and Vince probably had word from Travieso, who was the unofficial leader in this prison. As I saw Vince greeted by his carnals from La Raza I couldn't help but envy him because he was Mexican, a Chicano from Cali; he was La Raza and his gente showed love.

They have a saying in prison: "He stabbed you quicker then a Mexican." They say that because the esses have mucho corazon. They don't fuck around or fake it. They put in work. And dudes respect that. They got to because the vatos rolled fast and furious when shit jumped off. I respected La Raza because they carried themselves with strength, integrity and loyalty. And you hardly ever saw a Mexican snitch but when you did he was usually getting checked in or stuck by his own people. That was just how they handled their business. And when the drama came the Mexicans swarmed. They came in waves. It was like an attack of locusts.

Right before the 4:00 count Vince came by my cell. "Guero, Que onda buey?" He gave me a huge hug almost crushing me. "What the fuck is up, vato?"

"No manchas buey," I told him.

"Gimme a joint then, buey. Yo se tu tienes," Vince said.

I laughed at that; the same old Vince always ready for los drogas. "So what's up with Dave?" I asked.

Vince gave me a serious look. "Necesitamos hablar, Guero. Pero no ahora. We'll go to the yard later, all right? I need to see some vatos anyhow. But everything's cool, tu sabes?" Vince then flashed a big smile and flexed his rock-solid bicep. "See that, esse," he said. "Dos semanas in the hole and I'm still a beast. And I didn't do shit either. Just laid around and slept. I beat those pinche shots, too." Suddenly Vince reached into his pocket and pulled out a joint. "Light it up, buey," he said as he tossed it to me. And I was not one to argue.

Later that night in the yard, as me and Vince walked around the track, he gave me the 411. He said Dave and Leonardo figured out that Roberto put the fix on them and snitched out the cop, too. Vince said Leonardo was mad as fuck and ready to kill somebody. Dave was heated as well but was more worried about getting more time then anything else. He also told me that the cops only got 15 grams of coke so they figured that Roberto took half the coke he was holding for Dave for himself and put the other half back in Dave's cell when Dave went to his job assignment the next morning. It was all a set-up. Orchestrated by the Cuban. So the bust wasn't for the whole ounce, only about half, but it was still a lot by prison standards. As it stood, Dave, his bunkie Carlitos, Leonardo and

Larry were all under SIS investigation. Supposedly the US Attorneys office was preparing an indictment which also included the cop. Roberto was their star witness.

Damn, I thought. I always had that feeling about Roberto but I was never sure. I guess it's like they say, "Trust your guts, not your head." I was always making justifications for the dude when I should have trusted my instincts. We live and learn, though. And the dude was a viper. Who would have thought? I mean, he fooled us all, except for Leonardo. Somehow he knew.

I felt for Dave, though, since he got played by Roberto. And being played like that would have serious consequences for Dave. Not only with SIS and the feds but with Leonardo and the Latin Kings as well. Leonardo just didn't seem the forgiving type and Latin Kings were all over the system. And I didn't think one boriqua from Motown fancied his chances because he had got Leonardo seriously jammed up. But as we continued around the track I wondered what SIS really did know. 125 books of stamps, 15 grams of coke, a lot of bullshit dropped notes, and one snitch. It didn't seem like a very good case. And the cop would probably walk on hearsay because as far as I knew Roberto never dealt with the cop directly. But I knew one thing for sure—that cop would not be working for the Bureau of Prisons anymore. He might just end up with his own bid. But as a former guard he would get off light and do his sentence in a minimum-security camp. Dave and them would probably just have to do some serious hole time if they kept their mouths shut. But in the feds you never know how things will turn out or what people will say or do when the pressure mounts.

Dave had provided Vince with a list of outstanding debts on the compound with the request to collect them and get them sent to the Puerto Rico address. It wasn't chump change either. I guess Dave was trying to make it right for the cop and Leonardo. Dave always did have a big heart. I always thought a little more ruthlessness would have served Dave right but the boriqua was all heart, you know. Always trying to look out and hook a motherfucker up. Even when he was fucked up.

Vince was stepping to dudes on the yard who owed Dave cake. It was an effort in futility though, as the numerous cats Vince stepped too kept telling him that they had already squared up. "Some Florida address," they all kept telling him.

When Vince ran this by me I told him how the Cuban was collecting for Dave the last couple of weeks. Although I had my suspicions, at the time I didn't know he was the snitch. It appeared that Roberto had cleaned up a lot if not all the debts on the pound owed to Dave and had them all sent to an address in Miami. Vince started crossing names off the list and we figured Roberto had beat Dave for over 5 G's. But I guess for real he beat Leonardo for the money because Dave was just the front. Dave would not be happy and Leonardo would be furious. But that was Dave's problem, not ours.

Vince was angry as fuck, though. I guess he figured to skim some of the feria off the top for himself, and as the debt list dwindled so did Vince's prospects for some cheddar. "Fucking hell, Guero, that fucking Cuban. I would stick his ass right now if I could."

And I knew Vince would because he was not prone to idle threats. He was a thorough esse. Vato loco, tu sabes? The dude was a gangbanger from LA. Though not on the level of Travieso, he was still a bad motherfucker. Vicious in the extreme and not someone I would want to beef with. For real though, I was glad he was my carnal because I could tell he was full of rage for the way shit went down and looking for a reason to explode. Vince was known for his temper also. I always heard the black dudes saying, "Be careful around that amigo." And who knew what would set him off? I was just glad that Roberto was in the infirmary because if he was on the yard he would have been a dead man. Muerto, tu sabes? Not that I cared if the Cuban was dead, because I didn't. That pinche buey was a fucking snitch. But Vince was my dog. My carnal and I didn't want him to fuck up and catch a life bid for murder. He had two kids and a woman on the street who needed him. Plus he was short so he had a lot to lose. But vatos like Vince, for real, they didn't give a fuck. And to try to guess when and what he would do would be harder then smuggling a shank through a metal detector. And that was damn near impossible.

Back at the unit later on we hung out with Fox in the common area. He was holding court. "Damn, Vince, remember after that shit went down? When it was just you, me, Guero, and the Cuban in the cell? I told you, son. I called that. I told you it was someone in that room. I knew it, you heard? Ain't no faking it, son. I called that shit. You gotta give me props for that."

And Vince did, knocking fists with Fox. "Simon esse, you were right. I just wish you would have fingered that joker right there so I could have stuck his ass," Vince replied with a smirk.

I marveled at this vato. How the thought of violence brought a smile to his face. And this was my carnal. I seriously considered him a good dude—someone I would trust to get my back. Sometimes when I was stoned it didn't really seem like I was really there. In prison and all. It seemed like it was a dream or a movie or something. Was I really this dude sitting here talking about violence so easily? I had always considered myself a businessman, you know. Drug dealer. Entrepreneur. But my short time in prison had changed me, for the worse I believed. Because where I wouldn't consider violence before, now I was contemplating the idea of killing someone. I wasn't sure who but I knew someone deserved to die for all this bullshit. And in prison they say, "Boys fight—men kill." And I wanted to be a man. I had to prove it to myself, I guess.

Vince punched me in the shoulder. "Oye, Guero, que transas, buey? You're like looking into space, vato. What's up?"

He and Fox laughed, "Must be all that smoke," said Fox with a smile.

I laughed with them and said, "Naw, I'm cool. Just thinking, you know."

"Alright, esse," Vince said, "but don't be zoning out on me, OK?"

Then the cop shouted "Lockdown!" as the PA speaker blared, "Count time, Count time."

We exited the common area and returned to our rooms for the 10 PM count. I told Vince before he locked in, "Mira, carnal. I think I know who had the rest of the coke that Roberto took."

"What esse," Vince said all serious like. "What the fuck are you talking about, Guero."

As I made my way down the range I shouted back, "Despues de la cuenta, buey." As I locked in I contemplated if I wanted to go this route. If I told Vince about the coke my homeboy Mike had bought from the Cuban, Chato, I knew what he was going to want to do and I knew he would want me to do it with him. I just wasn't sure if it was something I was up to. At that moment I wished I had a joint to take the edge off but I didn't have shit. My bunkie was jabbering away at me in español about something, but I wasn't really paying attention as I slipped away into a dream-filled sleep.

Travieso...
Que pasa, carnal?
What's up?
Nada, Buey.
What do you think?
About what, Guero?
About the Cuban, Chato.
Well esse, you know what I think.
But what about me?
Well Guero you know what they say?
What's that vato?
Sometimes a man gotta be a man.
Thanks Travieso.
De nada, buey.

After the count my dream was ended abrubtly by Vince. Or was it a dream? I couldn't seem to remember once I was awake. "Damn, esse," I told Vince, "I was dreaming."

"Well fuck that, Guero. Tell me about the coke. Quien tiene?"

I ran it down to Vince about the coke my homeboy had bought from the Cuban and how he sent the money to the same Florida address. Fox had also told Vince about the Florida address so he was crazy mad.

"Pinche chingasos," Vince replied. "That rata got all the feria."

But Vince was scheming now. Chato was still on the pound. I told Vince how all the Cubans were fronting in rec. Roberto with Dave's sweats, sneakers, chain, and all that. The pinche plastico.

But Vince kept saying, "That pinche puto is still on the pound."

I knew he meant Chato and I also knew the time of reckoning was at hand.

"Mira, Guero, we gonna make our move tommorow. In rec, OK? That puto's been down there in the pool room almost everyday, right?"

As I nodded my head he continued. "Good. We'll go down on the rec move and wait. Is that shank still buried on the yard?" I nodded again. "Good, then tommorow is the day. Who the fuck does that Cuban think he's dealing with? We're gonna stick that motherfucker. This is how we're gonna do it."

Vince proceeded to lay out a plan. We would go to the on the rec move and post up at the corner pool table holding it down all night, playing 9-ball while we waited. I would go get the shank and stash it in the mop closet by the bathroom. Taped up behind the shelf in case any cop wanted to shakedown the mop closet. When the Cuban, Chato, went to the bathroom, we would follow, get the shank and go in the bathroom after him. Vince would enter first and distract him as I came in behind and stuck him.

A good enough plan for premeditated murder, I thought. If it even came to that. A lot of prison stabbings resulted only in minor flesh wounds, but you never know. It was all in the sticking and if you hit a vital organ the cat could die. The shank we had was serviceable. It was fashioned from die-cast metal bar that functioned as the frame of a chair. We had broken the chair up, thrown the plastic parts away, and made shanks out of the metal skeleton frame that supported the chair. By passing them through the fence to the vocational training shop we got them sharpened, then we got them passed back through the fence and buried them in the yard or taped them under the weight benches and bleachers. At one time we had about six shanks stashed in the yard but the cops had found them one by one in random searches with portable metal detectors and the like. Now there was only the one that I still knew about.

If I got the Cuban in the right place I figured he would be muerto.

Vince told me, "Get him right up in the back, esse. Drive the shank down into his ribs. Try to hit the back of the heart."

I heard all this almost surreally. I wasn't even sure if I was myself or if it was even me who was planning to do all this. It seemed like I was outside myself looking in. Everything was happening so fast. Like a frame-by-frame Charlie Chaplin movie.

The next day we went to the yard on the rec move and posted up at the corner pool table. I got the shank and stashed it. Then we waited. It seemed like hours. Each minute seemed an eternity. It was as if time had slowed to a crawl. Every time a prisoner entered the poolroom me and Vince looked up. We had our jackets stuffed with extra shirts hanging on the hooks above the benches that lined the walls of the poolroom. As time dragged to a stop I heard the PA blare, "the dining hall is now closed," and just at that moment Chato entered, flanked by a pair of Cubans. They went to a table on the far end of the room away from us that some brothers were holding for them.

We waited anxiously as the Cubans racked up and started to shoot pool. We were playing also but if anybody was watching our game they could tell we weren't interested in it. It seemed to be taking forever and then finally Chato walked back toward the bathroom by himself. Vince motioned me and I walked casually down the hall to the mop closet. I was calm, almost serene. I can do this, I thought. He deserves it. He helped that snitch fuck Dave over. Pinche puto. I retrieved the shank and saw Vince walking up the hall and into the bathroom. I heard him jabber in español to the Cuban, distracting him, and with a deep breath I entered the bathroom with the shank.

Vince was at the urinal and Chato was washing his hands at the sink. They both turned to look at me as I entered, and Chato's eyes went wide, almost popping out of his head as he saw the shank I was raising.

"Dale, carnal," Vince whispered as Chato put up his arms and backed up into the corner. I stood there with the shank raised. "Dale buey," Vince whispered again, a little louder, but I didn't do anything. I was frozen in place. As Chato realized this he made a move toward me but Vince caught him with a vicious right to the jaw that staggered him.

"Pinche buey, damme esso," Vince said as he snatched the shank and went to work.

It all happened so quick I hardly even noticed it. One minute I had the shank and the next Vince was sticking the Cuban in the chest. Again and again and again. Then Chato was on the floor of the bathroom bleeding from several wounds and Vince's arms, hands, and T-shirt were covered in blood. I moved back toward the wall as the blood crept toward my shoes. I heard this wheezing sound and as I looked down I noticed it was Chato trying to breathe. He must be drowning in his own blood, I thought. Vince snapped me out of my frozen state.

"Go get my chaqueta, buey." He ordered and I followed, creeping slowly out of the bathroom and down the hall to the poolroom thinking everybody must know what is going on. But as I casually and nonchalantly walked over to Vince's jacket hanging on the wall, nobody really even noticed me. It was all in my mind.

I met up with Vince again back in the mop closet where he washed off his arms, hands and upper torso. He had already shredded his blood-drenched t-shirt and flushed it down the toilet and also dragged Chato into the stall. Luckily, just as Vince put on his fresh t-shirt the PA blared, "Begin 10-minute move." I washed off the shank and taped it back behind the shelf in the mop closet, hoping it wouldn't be found. But it didn't matter because as soon as they found Chato there would be a lockdown. I was glad we had the chance to get out of the yard before they found him because whoever was in the yard would be there all night as staff took their names and started their investigation into the stabbing.

When they called the lockdown 30 minutes later, Vince and I had already showered and disposed of our clothes, which might have shown tiny blood drops under scrutiny.

"Lockdown," yelled the C/O. "Lock it up, guys." Vince smiled and gave me a nod as he locked in. When I was called for the interview I told them I didn't know what happened, I wouldn't tell them if I did know, and that I was in the unit the whole night reading in my cell. It seemed we had made a clean hit. I just hoped Vince would let me live it down.

PART 9: FREE AND CLEAR

"You fucked up, esse," Vince told me the next morning. "But you're still my carnal. What the fuck happened, though?"

I looked up at him, unsure of what to say. I knew how I felt but I didn't know how to describe it. I didn't want Vince to think I was scared, because it wasn't that. "I just couldn't do it, Vince," I said. "I wanted to but when I looked at him he just seemed so shook. Like a dog with a tail between his legs, you know. I was gonna do it but then it was like, damn, my arm won't fucking move. I like, froze up, you know? My bad, esse. I guess I wasn't mentally prepared. Entiendes?"

Vince took on a serious look and kind of glared down at the tile floor in the cell, shuffling his feet, and clasping his hands. "Damn, esse. That shit is deep and all," he said before punching me in the arm. It was hard, too. "But fuck that shit, vato. I know you ain't no coward. Next time you better do it."

I didn't know if that was a threat or not but I didn't take it like that because I didn't want no beef with Vince. That vato was vicious. With that settled we bounced to the chowhall to see what the word on the pound was about the stabbing and to hear if Chato was still alive. Vince told me on the way, "That Cuban is muerto, esse. I punished him."

But I wasn't so sure. I remembered that wheezy breathing sound like the Cuban was fighting for life, and as we walked I was thinking about what Vince said about next time. Could I do it? Would I? Was that what I was about? Fourteen inches of metal into the flesh. A killer. Vato loco and all that. I didn't know. I was just a kid from the suburbs. But in someway I knew that was no excuse because if I was down then I had to be down. Because in prison, la clicka was todos.

At the chowhall, all the prisoners were talking about the stabbing. I overhead some black dudes bullshitting in the chowline.

"Yo, G, did you hear about that Cuban? Damn," said a tall, skinny con.

"I can't call it man. You know niggas is crazy in here," answered the dude in front of him.

"I heard that amigo got punished," finished the tall, skinny prisoner.

"Word," said his partner as they got their trays and went to sit down.

Me and Vince got the lowdown from some other vatos. Supposedly Chato was in the infirmary with severe chest punctures, blood loss, and a collapsed lung but it seemed he would make it. Vince was mad as fuck because like he said, "That pinche buey might snitch, Guero." So now we were playing the waiting game to see if the Cuban fingered us for the stabbing. I doubted it because Vince was La Raza and they had a fierce reputation for retaliation on snitches and they were system wide.

I was another story, however. I might be marked out for revenge and for real, I didn't even get off. But the Cuban could finger me and leave Vince out of it. You never knew how shit would go down so now we began the wait. If they didn't lock us up in the next week or so we were probably cool. I was pretty sure nobody saw us but you never know. Dudes are always lurking on the low in prison. And Vince, he didn't even seem that put out. All he said was, "I can't fucking believe that pinche Cubano isn't muerto."

But I realized now that I would always have to worry about the revenge factor. I was a marked man. Could I ever feel comfortable around another Cuban? Vince was going home soon but I still had a lot of time to do. I would have to keep looking over my shoulder wondering if a shank was angling for my guts. Damn, I need a joint, I thought.

Vince saw me looking all fucked up like and said, "Don't worry, esse, that puto is gonna be in protective custody. They gonna transfer his bitch ass."

I felt a little reassured at that. Then, in a deadly serious tone, Vince added, "And if you ever see that pinche Cubano or his partner Roberto again, you don't ask any questions, Guero.

You stick the mother-fucker, OK Guero? For me, esse, you do it for me." Vince was looking all crazy with murder glinting in his eyes. He had a twisted smile on his face. This vato had an insatiable appetite for violence. But in prison, some dudes are just like that. Vato loco, tu sabes? You just had to learn to recognize them and I was just getting hip to this premise. Vince was my carnal but he was a dangerous dude to be around. Not necessarily for what he would do to me because he was my dog, but more so in the sense of what he could get me involved in.

I gotta keep it real, though. The vato kept your adrenaline running and I was becoming addicted to that rush. It was like the marijuana, but different. The weed was to escape, to dull the knowledge and reality of my incarceration. But Vince, he just made a motherfucker feel alive. Like in a dangerous, alert kind of way, because you never knew what was gonna happen with him. He was unpredictable like that. And since the stabbing Vince had been feeling good. He was on a serious rush. Walking on clouds and shit. The dude was strutting around like he was invincible. Vato firme, you know. And maybe in his mind he was.

A couple of days passed and Vince got a kite from Travieso. Vince told me that Travieso's disciplinary segregation time was up in 30 days. He would be back on the pound soon. Vince also told me that Leonardo had put the hit on Roberto but the boriquas had fucked up. Leonardo wanted Roberto muerto but his homeboys acted too fast. They couldn't get any shanks so they just punished dude with locks on a belt. They probably cracked his skull but he would heal. And when he came out of the infirmary he would be in PC too, probably going to testify at the grand jury and get Dave, Leonardo, Larry, and the cop indicted.

Vince also had some bad news. "Travieso said the FBI has been pulling Dave out for interviews. What do you think, Guero?"

I replied, "Dave ain't no pinche chota, tu sabes?"

"I know, but that shit is fucked up. If the motherfucking FBI came to see me I would tell them to fuck off. I wouldn't go sit in no pinche room with them. That shit looks bad, you know?" Vince pounded his fist into his hand for emphasis.

"It's probably nada," I told him, but I was thinking to myself, Dave, what the fuck are you doing?

Ever since the bust on Dave the pound had been pretty dry. I mean, shit was around but you had to go on a mission. When Dave had the compound on lock los drogas were everywhere. For the last year and a half the compound had been saturated with drugs. Heroin. Marijuana. Una poca coca. It was all good. Pero ahora, it had been almost a month and nobody had filled the vacuum. It was only a matter of time, though. Dudes were trying to come up.

The next day on the yard this Detroit cat, Dre, stepped to me. I had seen him around in the hobby craft. He was Dave's homie and supposedly fucked with Black Steve on the street. He was always hanging out with Dave in the yard and shit. "Yo, Guero, what's up?" I pounded fists with him.

"Look kid," he continued. "I got a little proposal for you. My homie got something in the works. Niggas trying to come up, you know. But niggas ain't trying to be on front street with all the bullshit right now. You wanna make some moves or what?"

That all depends, I thought. "What are you working with?"

"I'm talking OZ's," he said. "Of good bud. For $800 sendouts. Can you work with that?"

The fuck I could, I thought, but I played it all causal like. "Holla at me when that comes through, alright? We can do something," I said as I hit rocks with the brother, sealing the deal. I went to find Vince, who was playing dominoes with La Raza. I told him about the deal and he got that crazy smile on his face, "Back in business, right Guero?" He beamed.

That Sunday Dre brought me an ounce. I could tell he had already went through it though because he had it in papers of

20 caps each. I knew he had skimmed off the top because when me and Vince capped it all out it was short a couple of caps. But we didn't care. We were ready to smoke, to sell, and to collect commissary. A lot of drug dealing was just the thrill of the deal. The lifestyle, you know. Even in prison. Put it out, collect and smoke the profits.

Fox was making moves for me, doing sendouts, as was my homeboy Duncan, who was this loud, white-supremacist looking motherfucker from Roanoke, VA. Duncan was always bragging how he was straight out the trailer park. And I believed that spam-eating motherfucker. He was cool, though, and he carried much respect on the pound. He had a little crew of white boys who went hard. They were always checking in white dudes who were exposed as rats and robbing or extorting them too. They had some rigid ideas about race and were always like, "them fucking niggers," and all that. But the dude was solid and didn't start no drama. He just had certain beliefs. He was all about white pride. In prison there are a lot of white dudes like that but it's not like they are open racists. Because that would be stupid of them. They would be getting punished.

With blacks representing almost 65 percent of the prison population, whites and Latinos were outnumbered almost 2 to 1 with their combined 35 or so percent of the population. I always thought the white supremacist dudes were kind of closet racists because they fucked with blacks to their face and then called them "niggers" behind their backs. But I guess it is the same with some blacks and all that cracker shit.

Duncan was cool with me, though. He had some crazy religious beliefs also. He was into some odinest or creator-type shit. But in prison you learn to respect other peoples' beliefs because if you don't it might mean some serious drama. At one time Duncan had even tried to get me into all that stuff but I told him it wasn't my thing and he respected that. A lot of dudes find religion in prison. You know, born again Christians, Muslims, or whatever, but that wasn't me. I always figured that if the prison let Rastafarians smoke weed in religious services then the whole compound would be rastafari. That is just how things went. Prisoners became religious for all kinds of reasons like protection, acceptance, redemption, and maybe some actually had a real earth-shattering spiritual awakening. I don't know for real.

I had Fox and Duncan getting money sent to my girlfriend's address. She would then, in turn, send one lump of $800 to the address in Detroit that Dre gave me. Dre told me I had about two weeks leeway to get the money straight but I knew it wouldn't be a problem because I had it covered. My girl was holding me down. Actually she had all the cheddar I had left from my career on the street. It wasn't really a good representation of cash flow for all the years I was sentenced too, though. In fact, it was a bad match. I didn't have nearly enough to get me through my whole bid but I could splurge a little if needed.

I wasn't on big Willie status and for real, not even little Willie status, but I had un poco de feria. And as long as my girl stuck with me I was straight. But I had heard horror stories from other prisoners how their girls or baby's mamas had left them. Out of sight, out of mind, you know. They always told me I was crazy to leave my cake with a broad but maybe I hoped, just maybe, my girl was different.

As soon as the money hit for the first ounce Dre fronted me another. It was some of the only weed on the pound so it went quick. Me and Vince were smoking big time and had mucho commissary. We weren't going to the chowhall at all. We were eating on the unit. Beans and rice, nachos, burritos. We were styling. Just like old times. And we were looking out for La Raza, too. Hitting them off with caps and the like. Snake was hanging tight with us and smoking out. Because you know whoever has the drugs is the man and at the moment I was holding so I was the man. But I wasn't power tripping like Dave had. I just wanted to get my smoke on. I would look out and shit but I tried to keep it on the down low, even though my whole block was pretty much stoned. Me and Vince sold caps to the whole unit.

We even had our own little capping assembly line. It wasn't all elaborate like the scheme with Dave. It was just me and Vince capping up the weed and putting it into the envelope corner pockets that we cut out. We made smaller caps too because we were marijuana fiends and didn't have the sweet connect Dave had before. But dudes didn't complain because it was a seller's market and we were the ones holding.

But we weren't the only ones on the pound with weed. Some Kentucky boys were doing their thing also. Probably through the visit or something. I was pretty sure the Detroit cats were getting it through the V.I. Probably kiestering it, too. When the weed would hit I would take the Kentucky boys a couple of caps and trade for some of theirs. Just so me and Vince could have something different to smoke. Because smoking the same weed all the time gets old.

It had been a couple weeks since the stabbing and we felt like we were cool. It seemed Chato wasn't a snitch like his homeboy Roberto. He must have been planning his revenge, though. But as long as I was high I didn't give a fuck. No worries, no bothers, todos tranquilo, entiendes? Me and Vince were on some cartoon-like shit. Straight stoner status. Sleeping late, waking and baking, going to the yard, working out, and chilling. Every night we had this vato Flaco cooking for us. He would do the dishes and the whole nine yards. I just kicked down a couple joints. It was just commissary food, soups and the like, but Flaco could put it down, you know. Microwave cuisine. We were styling. At least in our own minds, that is.

And Travieso was coming out of the hole soon. I planned to surprise him with a cheech and chong-sized joint. I knew the vato would be jonesing for some heron, but the weed would have to do. Anyhow, me and Vince talked about it and decided we were gonna try to keep Travieso off the dope. Not that there was any around anyway. But Travieso was short. He had maybe a couple of months left and then that vato would be in la calle. He needed to make a clean break. So he could get his shit together. Wasn't any prison drug program helping him. There was too much drugs in the joint.

I would do what I could to help the vato but I knew you could only help those that helped themselves. Anything else was a lost cause. But I had to try, right? Travieso was my road dog. My carnalito. And the vato got mad respect. Just being around him was a buzz. On the pound dudes were always trying to holler at him. And dudes were always giving him shit—shoes, drugs, hooch, comida—whatever, you know. The vato was popular and had a serious reputation. And I was proud to be associated with him.

Travieso was getting ready to ride out and I wanted to make sure he was straight. Because the vato was a two-time felon. Next time it would be life. And nobody in prison wants to see a motherfucker get life. Especially his road dog. That is just a bad scene. Because what the fuck you got to look forward to if you got life? Nada—only endless days and nights in a netherworld of corruption and violence.

INTERLUDES 2

"The word nigger is itself offensive…nothing can redeem that word."

—Jack Henry Abbott

INTERLUDES V: BALD BULL

"Inmate!" the C/O yelled. "Get over here!"

The black prisoner slinked over to stand in front of the big, old, white, beer-bellied, bald and grey bearded correctional officer who was a known asshole on the compound.

"What are you doing with your shirt untucked on my compound, inmate?" asked the C/O in his countrified accent.

The prisoner started to tuck his shirt into his pants, cursing under his breath and wondering why he had been singled out for torment by the old timer C/O, who smirked, playing the game he'd played a million times.

"What's that, inmate? You got something stuck in your throat? I can't hear you," the C/O continued.

The prisoner mumbled a "no sir" and attempted to make his escape but the C/O who prisoners called Bald Bull wasn't having it.

"Inmate, I thought I just told you to tuck in your shirt. Are you disobeying a direct order?" The prisoner was clearly getting angry now but still attempted to bite his tongue, knowing that arguing or trying to reason with a correctional officer is a losing proposition.

"I tucked my shirt in, officer," the prisoner said as he turned around.

"Inmate, are you calling me a liar? I said, your shirt's still untucked. You better check again," the C/O said.

The prisoner went through the motions of tucking his shirt in again, this time getting the part in back that he missed before. "There, is that good, officer?" asked the prisoner.

Bald Bull looked the prisoner over and nodded, but as the prisoner tried to walk away, Bald Bull called him out yet again. "Inmate!" Bald Bull yelled. "I don't like your tone of voice. You're not being insolent toward me, are you? I can write an Incident Report for that. You're not trying to go to the hole are you inmate?"

"No sir," the prisoner said as he turned back to Bald Bull wondering when the fuck this asshole was gonna stop harassing him.

"What's the matter, inmate? You don't have your I.D. card? That's another shot right there. You're just stacking them up today, aren't you?"

The prisoner sighed, frustrated like, and said, "No sir. I mean, I forgot my I.D., officer." Thinking he's fucked, the prisoner accepted the fact that he might be going to the hole.

Bald Bull looked around contemplating. Back in the day I would have had some fun with this nigger, Bald Bull thought to himself, because he was from the old school. Beating prisoners down, fucking with them for fun, tormenting them, and harassing them. It was why he had taken this job in the first place. But now shit was different. Lieutenants always breathing down your neck, worrying about some stupid-ass paper work. Political correctness and all that bull-shit. Bald Bull didn't know why he stayed on. Only a couple of more years until retirement, he thought to himself. And these piss-poor niggers, he mused. They don't ever learn. Might as well line them up and shoot them. Worthless pieces of shit.

In the moment, however, Bald Bull had a job to do. As niggers went, he thought, this one in front of him wasn't too bad. A little lippy, but weren't they all? At least he wasn't no fucking amigo, cursing him out in Spanish and shit. Bald Bull didn't even know how to communicate with those fucking wetbacks.

"On your way, inmate," Bald Bull said as the prisoner walked away, not believing his luck. He escaped from the clutches of Bald Bull. It must be my lucky day, he thought.

Bald Bull scanned the compound to find his next victim. He had an itching to hit the deuces and slam some niggers' head into the ground. Let's see if I can provoke one of these ignorant motherfuckers, he thought to himself. "Inmate!" Bald Bull yelled at a different prisoner, and the whole ordeal began anew.

INTERLUDES VI: LOCKDOWN

Muthafucka ain't right. Making all that god damn noise, somebody should shank that crackhead. What the fuck is he doing anyhow? Nigga probably thinks I'm sleeping. At least the light ain't on. I would get up but the muthafucking doors locked shut, what the fuck time is it anyhow? I hate this lockdown shit. Why the fuck the bed shaking? What that nigga doing? "Yo, son, stop shaking the fucking bed, you heard. Let me find out you jacking off or something."

Nigga don't say nothing. Fuck, man, nigga ain't listening. Let me find out? Is that crackhead...fuck, he is—I can't believe it. That muthafucka is jacking off. What the fuck, he think he can disrespect me like that? Where the fuck is my shank? I'm gonna punish that kid. I gotta jump down off this top bunk, handle business.

"Yo, son, you think you can play me. Don't ever disrepect me, nigga."

I stabbed the fucka. He ain't jacking off no more. Kill this muthafucking crackhead...thinks he can disrespect me. God damn muthafucka. Stop screaming, fool. I'm killing your ass. Gotta stab you again and again. Is that your blood on me. punk ass muthafucka. What the fuck is wrong with you? Ain't screaming now, are you? What the fuck is that light? Shit, a flashlight, the C/O. Fuck, I got blood all over me. He hit the deuces.

Muthafucka I gotta get rid of this shank, but where? I gotta get rid of these clothes. What the fuck am I gonna do? Flashlights got me pegged. I'm fucked, trapped in here with this dead, bleeding disrespecting nigga.

INTERLUDES VII: WHIGGER

Kent was from Alexandria. He told people he was from the projects, but that was debatable. He seemed like a kid born with a silver spoon in his mouth. Anyway, he claimed D.C. like a lot of the Virginia and Maryland cats did. Because in the feds D.C. dudes had a reputation. I mean, it was the murder capital of the world at one point. So prisoners from the greater metropolitan area claimed D.C. It didn't matter if they were from outside the Beltway.

Kent was a young white kid. Don't get me wrong, he talked the talk and walked the walk. He was hip-hop to the core but he wasn't no black dude no matter how much he wanted to be. Still, he tried very hard to be down with the D.C. clique. His homeboys, he said. And they tolerated him, though they did make jokes at his expense and call him light skin to his face and cracker behind his back.

The white dudes on the pound shunned Kent. They called him whigger and nigger lover. Because in prison all lines are racial. Black and white are distinct groups with different sections to sit in in the chow hall, separate TV rooms, and even different phones.

But Kent didn't sweat it. He was who he was. And he acted like he was a white black dude. He couldn't help the color of his skin. It was what was in his soul that mattered. And for real, he wasn't a bad dude. Anybody who got to know him, black or white, could tell you that.

And with time, dudes on the block and pound accepted him for who he was. Well, at least most dudes did. There were always the extremists like the Nation of Islam cats and the white supremacist groups.

Kent was cool. He was down. He was a straight whigger. NWA, Tupac, Biggie and all that. The kid was a trooper. A soldier, you know. I used to talk to him. Try to figure him out and the like. But he kept it real. He was gangsta, you heard. Wasn't no faking it or fronting. That was just who he was.

I remember he used to tell me how his parents were all fucked up. About him being in prison. About him acting black. About him hustling, carrying guns, out in the streets and the like. But Kent told me he grew up on Yo! MTV Raps, Doug E. Fresh, BET, and Fresh Prince. And for real, his parents just didn't understand. He wasn't no wanna-be. He wasn't no studio gangsta. He wasn't no Urkel motherfucker. He was a pure soldier, straight and thorough. He would represent, he would bust his guns, carry a banger or whatever. He wanted cats to know he was about his. Light skin or not.

I took the man at his word. To each his own, right? Kent made it seem like he came up rough in the projects and shit but somehow I doubted it. I remember him getting plenty of yellow slips and packages with Polo t-shirts and drawers. The kid was styling. At least styling in prison, if you know what I mean.

His dad used to send him Charles Dickens books also and a bunch of other Signet Classics and we would read them and talk about them. It was funny to hear this hip-hop kid express his analogies on Oliver Twist and Great Expectations. But I could tell he dug the books. He always told me, "I never read no shit like this before, joe." For real though, I don't think he'd ever read before, period.

Then one day D.C. and North Carolina started beefing. There were several different fights in the gym and the different housing units. Shit was jumping off all over and that night a bunch of D.C. dudes got busted carrying shanks out to the yard. Kent was with them, riding. Holding his own shank and some other cats' shanks, too. He was going hard.

They threw Kent in the bucket and eventually he was transferred. I heard he ended up at USP Terre Haute. A rough place from what people said. Apparently Kent had some trouble up there. I heard that he was on the yard hanging with his homeboys from D.C. when another D.C. prisoner walked up.

The dude saw Kent, a white boy, hanging out with all the blacks, and due to Kent's youthfulness and slight build the dude took Kent for a gump. He sex-played Kent, tapping his ass and making references to Kent sucking his dick later. Some of the homies told dude he was outta line, that Kent wasn't no gump and that he had shit fucked up but the dude persisted, figuring he had a vic. Saying he would turn the white boy out.

Kent played it cool, though. I'm sure he was scared but he didn't let it show. He didn't react to the dude baiting him. But in his heart he knew he had to do something or he would end up getting raped and prostituted out by the D.C. dudes who were notorious for that type of shit. It was scandalous, really. They preyed on their own with a vengeance. So Kent didn't say nothing, but inside his head the wheels were turning. He played it humble. Like it was a misunderstanding. Like he was shook.

He walked away but in his heart he was burning up. Angry as fuck. But he was focused. He remained in control. Cool and calculating. He didn't give in to his anger and lose his shit; he directed his anger toward resolving the problem. He was gonna get his respect.

Kent calmly walked over to the put-put golf course they had in the yard, gave his inmate ID card, and got a golf club. He acted like he was playing put-put golf but all the time he was watching his homeboys who were laughing with dude.

Kent held the golf club close and walked back over to his homies. Some saw him and stepped back. They knew what was about to happen. They knew Kent wasn't no clown. But the one dude kept laughing like he didn't have a care in the world. Talking about how he was gonna go up in the white boy and make him his bitch. He was running at the mouth so much that he was oblivious to his surroundings.

Kent pulled the golf club back and swung, clocking the brother right on the head. Busting his dome. And Kent didn't stop there either. He punished dude. Beat him down. Broke his skull up and everything. Then he sat the golf club down and walked away, leaving the dude in a broken heap of blood and crushed bones.

Kent ended up in the bucket but he got his respect. Weren't no dudes trying to step to him and sex-play him again. And it turned out that the dude that got fucked up was a rat anyway. So after doing eight months in the hole Kent came back onto the compound as a sort of hero, with much love and respect.

The white dudes still looked at him as a whigger but the blacks and especially his homies accepted him completely. They called him Gangsta Kent and shit like that. Told him he was white on the outside but black on the inside. And Kent was cool with that. He was with his peoples, you know. He was bidding. In the feds and all that. Wasn't nothing to it. Whigger or whatever, Kent didn't care. He was just trying to be himself and do his time. Stay strong and keep it real. Because for real—what else can you do?

INTERLUDES VIII: THE CHECK-IN ARTIST

Jonesy hit the pound in the summer months. He said he transferred down from FCI-Raybrook. He was a weasly looking dude. The Grateful Dead-junkie type. Missing teeth, frazzled, long hair, boney, no money—the dude looked rough. But the white boys on the tier took him in. Felt sorry for him in a way. Plus the dude actually seemed alright. There wasn't no paperwork check or nothing like that but from the way he carried his self he seemed straight.

Jonesy blended in. Didn't make any noise or cause any drama. He got a job in the chow hall and started bringing dudes on the block food items. Hitting them off, you know. Nothing major. Sandwiches or an extra piece of chicken. A little food hustle, you know. For cigarettes and all. Like most prisoners, Jonesy did his bid on cigarettes and coffee. He was always jonesing for that nicotine or caffeine.

Dudes on the tier would hit him off. A pack of smokes here, some coffee there. You know, looking out and the like. Then one day another kid rolls in from Raybrook. He sees Jonesy and puts his name out on the pound. Talking smack and the like. He says Jonesy is a snitch and a check-in artist. And this white boy rolls with the Kensington crew. A set of hardknocks from Philly. They start putting the word out about Jonesy.

So dudes in the unit step to Jonesy. They like him so they give him the benefit of the doubt. They give him the chance to get his respect, and Jonesy says all that talk is some bullshit. He says the Kensington kid is a liar and that the kid was the one who checked in at Raybrook. But the Kensington crew ain't going for that. They call Jonesy out.

Neither Jonesy nor the Kensington kid will back off their claims, so the dudes from the block step to the Kensington crew and arrange a little one-on-one action in the bathroom at rec. The Kensington kid agrees because you know his people aren't letting him back out.

The dudes in the unit pump Jonesy up for the fight. It is set up like this: no weapons, no jump-ins, one on one. A couple of dudes from the block ride with Jonesy to get his back. The bathroom is cleared out and the two of them enter to handle their business. Dudes from the block are posted up to watch for the cops.

Jonesy and the kid have their little scrap which Jonesy gets the worst of. But it is nothing major. And it's over. The beef squashed as far as the dudes from the block are concerned. Since both dudes fought then that supposedly means they are OK in prison idealology. But where is the logic in that?

So life goes on. Football season rolls around and it turns out Jonesy is a massive gambling fiend. The dude keeps a parlay ticket in his hand. Somehow along the way he weasels himself into the butcher shop at the chow hall so he starts calling shots in the kitchen since he controls the meat hustle. He sets up contracts on the units with the big willies for cold cuts, hamburgers, chicken, and deli meats and cheeses. But for real, the dude can't get ahead.

He is living hand to mouth. With his gambling, cigarette, and coffee habits the dude is hit. He is constantly on broke status. Struggling to feed his addictions. So the dude starts running tickets and the like for the bookies. Handling a little action himself on the side. He becomes a major figure on the betting scene in the block as the months roll by. Different dudes on the block start getting locked up for gambling, but never Jonesy, and he is at the center of the action. He just keeps doing his thing. Hustling meat and cheese, running tickets, handling action, gambling, smoking, and drinking coffee. A low life, but prison is filled with those types.

And then one day Jonesy goes to the hole. A check-in, dudes on the block are saying. Supposedly Jonesy was taking betting action he couldn't handle. He was taking big bets and not turning them into the bookie. Keeping them himself and hoping dudes didn't hit. A typical crackhead move. But when you hustle like that it eventually will catch up with you. Karma, you know. It just so happened that on that one Sunday there were a whole lot of upsets and everybody hit. They were trying to get paid, but Jonesy couldn't pay them because he didn't turn the bets into the bookie and he had no bank to speak of. He thought he could pull a fast move by handling all his own action but dudes were trying to get theirs and Jonesy was broke. The dude wasn't about nothing.

So he lied. Said he would collect for them tomorrow after work. But Jonesy never came back from work. He got locked up for a bunch of turkeys. To cover his check-in he made a big move with some turkeys for show that he knew would get caught. But it was a straight check-in move. He knew he wasn't gonna get away with the turkey move. It was an attempt to save face. But dudes ain't stupid. They found out Jonesy owed a lot of money to many people and called his move for what it was—a punk-ass check-in move.

So now Jonesy is in the hole. Probably in Protective Custody snitching on motherfuckers and trying to make his break and transfer to another compound where the same thing will probably go down again, but maybe in a different fashion or set of circumstances.

But the crazy thing is, dudes on the block and in the prison were warned that Jonesy was no good. But the mind-set in prison these days is fucked up. Dudes are always looking for the best in a person instead of the worst. A leopard don't change his spots. A snitch is a snitch, a coward is a coward and a check-in artist will always be a no-good motherfucker.

DRUG DEALER

BOOK THREE

"You can't put your muscle on nobody cuz these dudes got cheese in their pockets."

—A black convict called Tank

PART 10: THE WAIT

"Holla at your boy, son," Fox said as he came into my cell. "Damn kid, doing big things," he continued, eye hustling the contents of my locker as I was putting a bag of commissary away. "Yo, let me get a bag of Doritos son, I don't think they'll all fit in there."

And he was right, too. My shit was on bling-bling status. And I still had about $250 worth of commissary to collect. It looked like I would be putting the bags all up under the bunk just like my man Dave used too. But it wasn't like I was blowing up. At least I kept telling myself that. But I gotta keep it real, I liked being the man. With the weed I was getting from Dre and the Detroit cats I was styling. Me and my man Vince, that is.

I tossed a bag of Doritos to Fox as he asked, "What's up with that $100 piece, son? Let me get that."

I sat down in the plastic, die-cast metal framed chair as commissary split from the net bag which fell open as I let go of it. Boxes of nutty bars, crackhead soups, AAA batteries, Pepsis, and bottles of vitamins scattered across the waxed and buffed tile floor of the cell, which shined like ice water. Dudes always thought the floor was wet and shit. Stopping at the door, not wanting to step on it. That was the good thing about my Mexican bunkie. He kept our cell immaculate.

I reached into my sock, kicking off one of my nouveau black Adidas indoor soccer joints to get at the packets of weed which I had stashed in my sock. They had slid underneath the bottom of my foot so it took some work on my part. I finally reached the four packets in my sock and handed one to Fox. "Damn dude, I thought that shit was gone for a minute," I told him as he laughed.

"Thanks, Guero. Dude says the money gonna be on the wire tonight. So check with your peeps and let me know. Because if it ain't straight I'll put down my press move, you heard," Fox said as he flexed his bicep, made a gully face, and laughed again, leaving my cell.

Earlier that day me and Vince had got a message from Dave and Larry telling us to be careful because shit was hot. Supposedly they had heard that we were moving weed through Dave's homeboys. I guess Dave didn't want us jammed up in the hole like him. Not that I was worried. And the action—the handling of the drugs, the collection of the commissary, making the moves—it was all good and had its own unique buzz. So I was on one million, you know. Drug dealer in the penitentiary. But it wasn't like I was all that. I just tried to be about my business.

I heard the PA announce the 6:30 PM move and I knew I had to meet my homeboy Mike the inkslinger who had some commissary for me, so I left all the shit on the floor and called Flaco to watch my cell while I went to collect. Because for real, I didn't trust none of the jokers on the unit. Where the fuck was Vince, I wondered, a little irritated. Motherfucker needs to give me a hand collecting this shit. But really it was all good. Word had just come out of the hole that Travieso would hit the pound next week so me and Vince were psyched. Dudes kept hollering at us, "What's up with your boy? He coming out?" Everybody wanted to be down with Travieso.

Vince had already told his bunkie that he had to cut out as soon as Travieso came out. It was no sweat though because dude didn't want beef with Vince. He was La Raza anyhow so he had to make way for Travieso. Because Travieso was his carnalito and the man so to speak, at least as far as dudes on the compound were concerned. All the vatos would be happy to see Travieso, even if it was only for a couple more months. Because the esse was short. His date was creeping up slowly and they had to give him un poco halfway house or something. I mean the vato had almost done a 10 piece. But with these prison people you never know because they are some busters for real. They might say Travieso is a danger to the community or some shit like that and use that as a basis to deny him halfway house. But I'm telling you when a man does 10 joints he needs some motherfucking halfway house to get used to la calle again. Throwing a dude who's done a long bid right back on the streets is like throwing him to the wolves. All types of shit can happen.

And for real, that is what all the prison people, judges, and probation officers want. They want dudes who just get out to violate so they can lock them up again. Recidivism, you know. That means job security.

"Homeboy," I said as I met Mike on the walk and shook his hand white-boy style.

"I got all the shit, Guero," he said. "But be careful, I heard that asshole compound officer, Briggs, is checking dudes receipts and taking bags of commissary if they don't have one."

Good looking out, I thought as I scoped the compound which was full of prisoners making moves like me, hollering at their boys, or going to rec and education. I spotted the compound officer Mike told me about harassing some black dudes and searching their rec bags for contraband. "Later, homeboy," I said as I made my way back to my unit while the asshole cop was busy.

Back in my cell I found Vince eating some Nutty Buddies. "Damn, esse, make yourself at home," I said sarcastically as I entered.

"Calmete buey," he said. "Sabes que, this other vato on la yarda told me that same shit we already heard from Dave and Larry."

I shrugged, not seeing the importance, but clearly Vince was perturbed. It didn't take much to set the esse off.

"Pinche Dave, how many motherfuckers he gonna send a message with? Putting our business all over the pound and shit. I wonder who told that boriqua anyway? I bet he still thinks he's running shit," Vince commented.

"He's just looking out, you know," I told Vince. "He wants us to be careful so we don't get jammed up like him."

"Well fuck that, Guero, ain't no motherfucker snitching on me. If they do, les puerto la madre."

I nodded my head. It was stupid to argue with Vince so I tended to agree with him unless it was something really important. I had other things on my mind anyhow. Like the big fat joint in my pocket. I took it out and lit it up, knowing we were cool because the cop working the unit was straight. He didn't do no rounds or nothing. Just stayed up in the office. He wasn't trying to sweat nobody, you know. Just do his eight hours all quiet like and split. Too bad more C/O's aren't like that, I thought. A lot of them are nosy fuckers. All up in your business and shit.

I took a couple of drags off the joint and passed it to Vince, who joked with me in an exaggerated surfer dude voice, "Don't be bogarting that joint, dude. Isn't that what you white dudes say?" He laughed and took a hit off the joint, almost coughing his guts up.

"The smoke, esse, don't waste the smoke," I told him in my best Mexican accent, clowning him as he clowned me. But it was all cool. He was my carnal, you know. Vato loco and all that. I was bidding, tu sabes. Stoned like Cheech and Chong. And stacked with mad commissary. It was a good day, I thought, as I took the joint and inhaled. Marijuana dreams filled my head as I laid back on my bunk all casual like, stoned and not really feeling like I was in prison.

The next Monday, Travieso came out the hole. Six motherfucking months that esse did. 24-hour lockdown, you know. For real, the hole sucks. But for vatos like Travieso that was how they did their time. He was looking fierce, too. All cut up. Told me and Vince he was doing 1000 pushups a day and I believed the esse. He looked like a pit bull. A Mexican pit bull, that is. That night La Raza threw a little fiesta for him in the block. Some burritos, nachos, some hooch, and a little weed tambien.

And you know I busted out the big joint, too. I rolled up two $100 pieces in one joint and gave it to Travieso. We retreated back to my cell with Vince and Snake to smoke it.

"Sabes que," Travieso told us, "I saw that pinche chota, el Cubano, en la hoyo. They put that motherfucker down on D-range, in PC."

"Does Dave know?" Vince asked.

"Simon," Travieso said, "I told him at rec the next day. Dave is up on A-range bunking with Carlitos. He's straight. But you heard about the FBI, right esse?"

"Que pasa con esso, vato?" Snake asked. "What's that boriqua doing?"

"He says they're just questioning him," Travieso answered. "But then again, you never know."

"Fuck that shit," Vince said. "Dave ain't no pinche chota."

"Tu nunca sabes buey, oiste?" Travieso replied. "Tu nunca sabes."

I was like, what the fuck, but I didn't say nothing. I just hit the joint.

"Que pasa con la lista buey? Tu no ganaste la feria ya?" Travieso asked.

"Charle buey, that pinche ratta got it all, vato?" Vince replied.

"Chingon, esse. Tu estas seguro? Check esta lista nueva," Travieso said as he took a list out of his pocket and gave it to Vince who studied all the names on it. "No esse. Es la misma. Todas la gente said they paid the Cuban."

Vince waded up the list and threw it in the toilet. "Then Dave and Leonardo got nothing. Dave is hit. That feria is all on him. Su palabra, tu sabes. That Cuban got him good, verdad?" Travieso said.

"Simon." We all said as we laughed, because it was funny in a way. In a very fucked up way, for real. But sometimes in prison you gotta laugh at fucked up shit, plus we were all stoned and Travieso was back on the pound. So it was all good.

PART 11: THE PLAN

Dudes on the pound were showing Travieso mad love. After a couple of days on the pound the vato had some new Air Jordans, a new Champion sweatsuit, much commissary, and was sporting a new Sony walkman with Koss PortaPro headphones. In prison parlance, the kid was styling. But he deserved it. The vato was gangsta, you know. Straight gutter. Dude didn't sell no wolf tickets, he handled his. And in prison, when you pump like that you get mad respect. Travieso carried it like a soldier. LA gangbanger and all that. And for real, dudes respected that. Plus the esse was humble. He would always help another con out if he could. But cross him or his ideals and you were hit. In prison the values of honor, respect and integrity were highly regarded and Travieso embodied them all.

"Qne onda, Guero," he said as he came into my cell.

"Que pasa, vato," I replied as I tapped fists with him and gave him a half-hug, prison style, bumping chests and shit.

"You ready to start a routine with me and Vince or what, buey?" Travieso asked.

I had jumped in with him and Vince before and I knew that they didn't fuck around on the weight pile. And being that I had been so lazy of late, smoking weed and collecting commissary—playing the role of the big man even if it was mostly in my head—I knew I had slipped up in my workouts. I also knew riding with them would get me back up to par. "Simon, esse. Estoy listo," I told him, almost cringing inside at the thought of the routine and the pain my muscles would feel. Travieso was ready to hit the street and he would be going hard. And Vince was just Vince, a beast. I wasn't no slouch either. Dudes on the pound considered me a go-hard white boy, but these two esses were in another class. I guess it was time to step it up, though. See if I could hang with the big dogs.

"Esse," Travieso said in a near whisper, "what the fuck was up with Dave? How did he let that Cubano play him like that?"

I could see Travieso struggling with the respect and friendship he had for Dave and his disdain for the whole situation. Travieso hated snitches, but more so he despised fools and in his eyes Dave had been played for a fool. "Sabes que, vato," I told Travieso, "when Black Steve left and you went to the hole Dave didn't have no support I guess." I was trying to be diplomatic about Dave but also honest with Travieso, so I was struggling with the context of my words. "Dave was like tripping, you know?" I continued. "He was always like, 'Yo, I run this compound. I'm calling the shots.' And all that shit, you know?"

Travieso looked at me all quizzical like, almost in disbelief. "That esse was saying all that shit?" he asked.

I nodded my head yes and I could tell Travieso couldn't believe it. He shook his head in resignation and kind of half-smiled, asking, "He was just telling you this shit?"

"Simon esse, but sometimes on la yarda when he was with his homeboys he would tell the new ones, 'I'm that man around here.' Crazy, verdad?" As I spoke Travieso shook his head some more. He was clearly fucked up by what he was hearing.

"Damn, Guero," he told me. "That vato fell off."

I agreed with him as we sat there for a minute saying nothing. Because really, what could you say? Dave had the pound on lock and he fell off. And now dudes were putting him on the burn, talking shit about him and even hanging a snitch jacket on him. That shit was wack, you know. But as I sat there thinking about it I concluded that Dave created that monster, you know. He became that dude. Power tripping and shit. Blinded by his own ego. Shit happens. I felt bad for Dave because he was my dog. But for real, what could you do? Nada, tu sabes. And Travieso knew that shit too. Like he said, Dave fell off. And that was that.

"Workcall, workcall. All inmates report to their assigned job detail," screeched the PA, prompting Travieso to say, "C'mon esse, vamos para la yarda."

I got my stuff ready and went to get a rec pass as Travieso got Vince. We stepped out on the pound in the hot summer sun and made for the yard.

"Damn, son," hollered Fox the NY hustler as he stopped us on the walk and we all hit rocks. "You esses are rolling deep," he said as we all laughed. "Going to get that money, right?"

Travieso nodded and said, "We gonna turn the white boy into a vato loco, you know."

Travieso and Vince shared a smile at that comment as Fox answered with a laugh, "I heard that, son. It's all good. Later." And he split toward the unit.

We made our way up the compound as prisoners shuffled off to their job assignments in UNICOR (the prison factory), facilities, education, or the chow hall. I was glad me and Vince worked in the unit as orderlies. We didn't really do much and had most of the day free. Travieso was still unassigned since he was just out the hole. As we went through the metal detector and entered rec I knew it was time to get busy.

"Dale buey, tres mas," Vince shouted as I strained to bench press the weight that was on the bar. "You got it buey, that's all you. Push it carnal, dale." Vince continued shouting encouragement. "Dos mas," he said. "I'm gonna ride with you."

And I was happy for that. I was only pressing 225lbs but it was killing me. Especially after a couple of sets. Vince spotted me on the last two reps and helped me put the bar back in the rack.

"Damn esse," he said. "You giving me an arm workout."

I glared at Vince for clowning me as Travieso said, "Calmete, Guero, stop maddogging Vince. Put another plate on."

Travieso laid down on the bench as me and Vince added a 45lb plate to each side. I went to get in position to spot Travieso's lift but he motioned me away, telling me, "No spot, Guero."

And then he pressed the 315lbs for 10 reps like it was nothing. I mean the vato was a beast, you know. Straight out the hole and benching 315. The esse wasn't no joke. Vince got up under that shit too and repped it for eight. Then they both looked at me like I would try, "You're crazy," I told them. "I'm through." That was the last set anyway and my muscles were spent. It was almost time for the 2:30 PM move so we got ready to go. I was drenched in sweat and tired like a motherfucker after working out for two hours with those vatos. I needed some food and a motherfucking joint, too. We finished up with a couple sets of sit-ups and when they called the move we bounced.

I saw my boy Duncan on the pound coming from the hospital and going back to UNICOR. "What's up dog?" he said as we hit rocks. He nodded to the vatos who walked on slowly. "Check it out, homeboy," he told me. "Can I get two hundreds later?"

I tried to think how much I had left. The smoke was addling my brains. "Yeah, I got you dog," I said. "I gotta check though."

"Alright, Guero, come see me at chow," he said as we hit rocks and went our separate ways.

I caught up to Travieso and Vince who said, "What's up with the skinhead, Guero?"

"He just wants some weed," I told them as they nodded, satisfied that everything was cool. At the block I jumped in the shower while Vince prepared some microwave comida for us. After we ate we chilled out in my cell and smoked a joint. Vince cruised to get some rest and Travieso started kicking it to me.

"Look Guero," he said, "you know I'm going home soon." I nodded because that was for real. Travieso continued, "and yo tengo nada, esse, nada. I'm trying to come up and I need you to help, oiste?"

I wasn't sure what Travieso was getting at but I had mad respect for the vato so I replied, "Tell me what's up esse?"

"I need to make a move, Guero," he told me. "Just one lick so I can get some feria, tu sabes?"

With that I had an idea what he was planning but I wasn't sure what part he wanted me to play. Travieso continued, "I ain't trying to hit the street broke, tu sabes. This is what I want to do. Let me lay it out to you, vato."

So Travieso let me know. He wanted to make a move for some heroin. Six grams to be exact. He would get his girl in East LA to get the tar for him at about $75 a gram, street price. And that same gram in prison would make $1200. Travieso wanted to control the whole thing from getting the heroin to packaging it to smuggling it into the prison to selling it in the prison. The vato didn't want to cut nobody in. He wanted to hit the street in style. The only problem was he needed someone to bring it in on the V.I. That was where me and my girl came in.

PART 12: THE MOVE

The way Travieso laid it out seemed pretty easy. Basically, his girl would get the tar and package it up in two balloons of three grams each. He told me he would make sure his girl got unbiodegradable balloons or condoms so that the plastic wouldn't dissolve in my stomach and let the heroin secrete out. Because six grams would definitely kill a motherfucker, and I wasn't trying to die. For real, I wasn't too keen on the move but Travieso was my dog and I wanted him to hit the streets with some cake.

I knew my girl would be against it but I would twist her arm. She would do it, at least I thought she would. The way Travieso told me it would go down seemed foolproof. Two balloons, three grams each; swallow one on the first kiss when my girl got there and swallow one when she left. Prison rules in the visiting room stipulated that prisoners could only hug and kiss their visitors once upon arrival and once upon departure. Kissing or hugging at any other time was forbidden. And if you violated the rules your visit would be terminated. No warnings and no second chances. At least that was how it was supposed to work. It all depended on who was working. Because I had heard of dudes getting laid, getting head and all types of shit in the visiting room. The thing was to just not front out the cop or let a C/O catch you out of pocket and you'd be straight. I didn't foresee any problems with the move and as long as Travieso's girl delivered, I believed it would be on.

I wouldn't even let my girl know what she was bringing. I'd let her think that it was some weed. What she didn't know couldn't hurt her and the less worried she was or less nervous and anxious she appeared the better. When I called her I just told her I needed her to come see me soon and that I was sending her a present and to make sure she told me all about it on the visit. My girl was a smart one so she would figure it out. Because with all the calls on the inmate phone system being monitored and recorded your messeges couldn't be direct. But there were ways around everything. As a convict you just had to figure them out. And my knowledge was growing everyday.

I just hoped my girl wouldn't lose her nerve. We had talked about making moves in some of her previous visits and for real, she didn't seem up to it. But I knew if I pressed she would come through. So I would put my press move down. On my girl, no doubt. Plus by this time Travieso already had everything in the works and I had given him my word. And in prison you only got two things. Your word and your balls.

Travieso told me to keep a lid on the move. He wanted everything on the downlow. He didn't even want Vince to know and for real, that is the best way. Because the less people that know the better. The quiet moves were always the best ones. I remembered back when Dave was doing everything on the low it was all good, but when he started getting sloppy and living large he contributed to his downfall. This was only a one time thing for me, to help out my carnal, but still I would do it right. I was still moving the weed for the Detroit cats also. It wasn't on the regular but they hit about once a month. It kept me busy at least.

I had Duncan, Fox, and Vince working most of that though, at least what I didn't give to my homeboy Mike the inkslinger. I just got the weed, broke it up, smoked out, made sure the money hit and collected commissary. It was all pretty easy. Just like this heroin lick will be, I thought. Travieso told me a third of the tar would be mine for bringing it in. I knew he would sell it for me too. But I figured to let Mike move it. He had a little taste for heron and knew a lot of junkies on the pound who would willingly give up that UNICOR check. So I figured I would be about two grand richer after the move. And that was definitely all good. Two grand for swallowing a couple of balloons. That's good cheddar in prison.

A couple of days later me and Travieso had the move all squared away and we were kicking it in my cell with Vince, smoking a joint. I could tell Vince and Travieso had been talking about something earlier because Travieso kept looking at me funny. All sideways out his face and shit. After we smoked the joint they both started laughing.

"What the fuck is so funny, vatos?" I asked them as they fell out again.

Travieso straightened up a little bit and told me, "I was asking Vince about the other Cuban, Chato, and how it all went down, and he told me." He looked at me all serious like and started laughing again,

"Let me find out, Guero." Vince kept laughing and started punching me in the shoulder.

Damn, these esses are clowning me, I thought. But for real, I didn't know what to say, so I didn't say anything. I just let them laugh at me. They were my carnalitos anyway.

"Damn, esse," Travieso said. "Why didn't you stick that motherfucker?"

I still didn't know what to say so I just shrugged my shoulders like I didn't know and Vince started laughing more. By this time I was getting kind of angry and feeling insecure, but what could I say?

Travieso continued, "Let me find out you were scared esse?" At this point, he and Vince stopped laughing. Actually, Travieso had to tell Vince to be quiet. "Well, esse," he said. "What was it?"

He was looking straight at me. Both of them were. I felt like I was a specimen under a microscope. I was looking at Vince and then at Travieso and said in a defiant tone. "I wasn't scared, vato. It was just..." I faltered and changed my tone to reflect my true feelings as they both looked on like predators on the hunt. Bloodthirsty and vicious.

"It was just, I never did no shit like that before. And I wasn't really ready to do it, you know. So I just..." I didn't get out what I was trying to say because Travieso cut me off mid-sentence.

"You just froze esse. I know. Vince told me." And with that hanging in the air the room grew quiet for a minute. They looked at me and I looked at my feet.

Then Vince put his finger to his lips to ask for silence, even though it was already deathly quiet. All we could hear was the continuous din from the common area. Vince put his cupped hand to his ear and whispered, "What's that?" He stood up and looked around and repeated, "What's that I hear?"

Me and Travieso were looking around like what the fuck. But Vince moved closer to me and looked at Travieso and then at me. "Can't you hear it esse?" I shook my head and looked askance at Travieso, but he had no answers for me. He was gonna let Vince play this out. Vince looked right at me then and lowered his cupped ear to my chest. "Don't you hear it, Guero?"

"Hear what?" I said. With that Vince looked me right in the face and said, "The screaming, Guero. It's the bitch inside of you screaming to get out."

When Vince said that shit, I snapped. The vato crossed the line. For real, I didn't even think about it. I just reacted. I punched the esse, my carnalito and a total vato loco, dead in the face. He grabbed me and we started wrestling around the cell but Travieso yelled at us and pulled us apart. "No manchas, bueys." He got in between both of us. I was breathing hard and hyped like a motherfucker, ready to go. In the moment you don't ever really consider the consequences of your actions. That is how a lot of dudes get jammed up.

But Travieso wasn't having any of it. I looked at Vince, who had a crazy glint in his eye. I noticed the blood dripping from his mouth. Burst his fucking mouth, I thought with a little feeling of pride. "Mira vatos," Travieso instructed. "We don't fight each other, alright?"

I didn't say shit, just shrugged myself out of his grasp. Vince stood up straight and puffed out his chest and told Travieso, "I was just testing him, esse." He looked at me and nodded, "I just wanted to see where your heart was at Guero. I knew you weren't no coward. And you proved it because a vato gotta be stupid to hit me." Then Vince smiled at me. "Stupid or have mucho corazon." Then he stepped right up to me and said, "Nice punch, buey. Canrnalitos verdad?"

I was still mad but I realized what Vince had done. The motherfucker was crazy but his intentions were good. Travieso stepped back and I gave Vince a hug.

"I'm sorry, buey," I told him.

He punched me in the shoulder, smiled and said, "I'm not, vato."

I didn't really know how to take that so I didn't say shit. Travieso looked at both of us and said with authority and finality, "Esta muerto, verdad?" Me and Vince both nodded and hit rocks on it. "Esse," Travieso said. "You better clean your lip up. It looks fucked up." Vince nodded and split to his cell. Travieso went with him and sent Flaco to get some ice and put it in a plastic bag so Vince's lip wouldn't swell up.

I was left there alone to think about what happened. I couldn't help but think that Vince had played me, but was that good or bad I wondered. And I also questioned if I had passed those vatos' test. Because I just had this feeling like it was all a set up. They were trying me. Testing my heart. I was mad at myself for the fact that my carnals felt they had to test me. I wasn't a chump. And in prison, proving you weren't some clown-ass buster was important. Because if other cons saw or perceived a weakness they would act on it. Everything was very predatory.

When Vince told Travieso about the botched stabbing Travieso must have sensed a weakness in me and I guess he felt, with the upcoming move and all, that he had to test me. Thinking about it now I realized Vince was just doing Travieso's dirty work. And I couldn't hold that against him. I mean, I punched him anyway. Drew first blood and the like. But I hope I showed Travieso what he was trying to see. Because when dudes started calling your character into question bad shit could happen. And my reputation was important to me as I was just starting out on my bid and didn't want to get a fucked-up jacket. Plus, keeping Travieso and Vince's respect was equally important to me because they were my road dogs.

About 10 minutes later Travieso came back to my cell. "Vince is gonna be alright. There won't be no mark or nothing," he told me. "You busted him good though," he laughed. "You did alright, you know. But don't be thinking about punching Vince no mas, esse. He would probably whup you."

I nodded, thinking the same thing myself. "But listen, esse, it's OK to be scared, tu sabes? I am scared all the time. But you got to admit it. Then you got to control it and conquer it, oiste? Fear is a good thing. It makes you cautious. So remember that, OK?"

PART 13: HOMECOMINGS

The next day, about two months after Dave went to the hole and they arrested the cop, Leonardo came out of the hole. I saw him walking back to his unit with a green military duffle bag slung over his shoulder. When the cops packed up a prisoner's property when they went to the hole they used the UNICOR-made green military duffle bags to transfer the prisoner's property to the property room in the hole where it would sit gathering dust until the prisoner got out. Because in the hole prisoners aren't allowed any personal property.

When I went back to the unit I gave Travieso the 411. He took the news nonchalantly but told me he would get Vince to step to Leonardo later to see what was up. But as it turned out Leonardo didn't wanna fuck with nobody. He was laying low. Supposedly they couldn't stick anything on him so SIS let him out. Probably to see what he would do, I thought. But it seemed Leonardo wasn't playing their game. He was blending into his environment. Not trying to straighten out anything or make any moves. For the moment at least. It was pretty smart of him, too. Because SIS probably had their undercover compound snitches watching him and ready to drop a note in a hot minute.

Vince stepped to Leonardo though, because for real, nobody was dodging Vince. Leonardo didn't say much, though. Either he wasn't saying or didn't know what was going on with Dave and his homeboy, the Puerto Rican cop. I figured he knew and just wasn't saying. The only thing he asked Vince was what happened to the money Dave owed him. Vince told Leonardo the truth. That the Cuban had collected it all. Vince told us the boriqua was mad but what could he do. The only person he could really blame was Dave and he was hemmed up in the hole taking the heat and possibly looking at an outside case. So Leonardo didn't say shit.

Vince told me and Travieso this later that night. And he also told us something else that surprised us. "Leonardo said that country boy Larry is coming out," Vince told us. Larry had been in the hole since before Travieso. A nice little stretch of about 7 months, I thought. Larry would be happy as shit to get out. I guess the SIS clowns couldn't tie him to Dave. It always worked best when dudes kept their mouths shut.

The SIS dudes aren't Sherlock Holmes and for real, neither is the FBI. They rely on snitches and if dudes keep their mouths shut then they have to do guesswork and make assumptions. Let the motherfuckers do their job is what I always thought. But nowadays you got so many dudes who just like to hear themselves talk. They make the DEA and FBI's jobs really easy. It must be like a cakewalk for them. And in prison, for the SIS LT's, it's the same. They got dudes beating down their doors to tell and dropping notes like crazy. For nothing, nothing at all.

If the code of silence, thieves honor and all that, was upheld, half the motherfuckers in prison wouldn't even be here. But you know there's always some pinche chota with cheese in his pocket who fucks it up for the real convicts. They'll be all over the compound, ear hustling and trying to act like they're down. Peeping out who is doing what and who hangs with who. For real, it is a dog eat dog world. Especially behind these fences.

But damn, I thought, my boy, motherfucking redneck, hick-ass Larry. The original tarheel was coming out. I still occupied the same cell, the corner one, we had shared before, so I had to make arrangements for my Mexican bunkie to split when Larry came out. It wouldn't be a problem though. I would just kick down some weed. But I was keeping that Mexican cleaning the room because he put it down. Put the esse on the payroll as they say. Big Willie status and all that. But not for real. Because I was on the low. Or at least that was what I liked to think. But you never really knew.

It wasn't like I had my ear on the prison grapevine. I was too busy getting stoned to go that route. For real, I didn't give a fuck what dudes on the pound thought. Well, for real, I did.

But I was stoned, you know. I had plans. I was making moves. I was safe and insulated in my little cocoon. I tried not to fuck with too many dudes. So I don't really know what the perception of me was on the yard. I knew I wasn't like Travieso and Vince but I walked the pound and the yard with those vatos. And they got mad love and respect. So I was down with all that in a way. And I had the weed connect so dudes were down with that. I just hoped I didn't have a reputation like Dave did. But I was kidding myself. Stoned delusions, you know. Because for real, I was smalltime. Dave had the compound on lock. I just had a little hustle.

I didn't really give a fuck anyway if dudes thought I was the man or what. I just hoped nobody was dropping no notes on me. Because I didn't need to get hemmed up like Dave. That would be fucked up, you know. I just wanted to be seen as a dude who handled mine because in prison perceptions are everything and I felt the perceptions about me were good. And if they weren't, I would handle that. Like a vato loco, tu sabes? Go hard white boy and all that. Or at least that is what I told myself, but sometimes in my cell at night when I laid there stoned, burnt out, and unable to sleep, I thought to myself, is the illusion real? Is it me? Am I a convict? A man's man? Because sometimes I felt like that young, scared white boy from the suburbs who first came in wide-eyed, entering the harsh reality and culture shock of the twisted and violent world of prison that I was now a semi-permanent resident of. Sometimes it seemed like the twilight zone or something. But for real, you just gotta live.

A couple of days later Larry came out the hole. I was happy to see him. "What's up dog?" I said as I greeted him when he came in the unit. I had seen him walking down the walk from the hole with two stuffed green military duffle bags bogging him down. He was scraggly looking, too. "Damn, Larry," I said. "You going hard or what?" He answered with a smile and threw one of the bags at me. And for real, the dude looked like Grizzly Adams. He was on viking status, you know. But Larry was my boy. We could relate. Not on all that country-type shit. But he was cool.

We walked up to the cell and Larry stashed all his stuff there until we could see the counselor and make the room change, moving him back in there. I gave my dog the bottom bunk back and everything. "Guero," he said, all exhausted like from struggling with the duffle bags, "have I got some shit to tell you."

I looked at him like, what the fuck, but Larry was drawing it out.

"You won't fucking believe what Dave found out about the Cuban, Roberto," Larry said.

I told Larry to hold up for now. "Vince and Travieso gotta hear this," I said. "But look, dog, get settled and cleaned up and the like. I know you wanna take a shower because you stink dude."

I laughed at this as Larry smelled his armpits. "Damn, Guero," he said. "It ain't that bad."

"I know," I told him, lying. "I'm joking. But for real, get in the shower dog. I'm gonna get you moved in here. And after count you can tell me, Vince, and Travieso what's up with the Cuban and the mother-fucking FBI, OK?"

"Alright, Guero," he said. "Thanks."

I left him there and went to find the counselor and get him to do the room change. Plus I hollered at Vince and Travieso telling them Larry had word from the hole.

Later on after la cuenta when Larry was all settled and cleaned up, Vince and Travieso came over to our cell and I rolled up a joint for the occasion. I knew Larry wouldn't smoke but that wouldn't stop me. Plus, me and Vince were jonesing to hear what Larry had to say. Travieso played it all cool. But he was like that. Suave, tu sabes?

As I went to light the joint, Travieso asked me, "What police is on, Guero?"

"It's that skinny, country hack. We're cool. He stays up in the office and it'll be chowtime in a minute so he'll be out front," I replied. Then I lit the joint as we all looked to Larry, who was about to tell us some crazy ass shit. And this would be just the beginning. Like dominoes, falling in a row. One after another. And in prison they call that jacking rec. Or in other words, some serious drama.

PART 14: THE TRUTH

The smoke from the joint was swirling. In my stoned mind the smoke appeared to be doing somersaults as it sucked up into the vent. Me and Vince were passing the joint, which I had put a $100 piece in, back and forth, because Travieso didn't want any and Larry didn't smoke. Larry started telling us how Dave was talking to the FBI, or as Dave told it, they were talking to him. Because he apparently told Larry that he wasn't telling them anything. Just listening. And Dave had a lawyer too, Larry said. Now this was news to us. We hadn't heard about all that.

And according to Dave, the FBI and his lawyer had told him all about the Cuban. Dave found out that Roberto had been working for the feds his whole bid. He had got sentenced to 20 years in the Miami federal courthouse, but during his seven years of incarceration he had worked his sentence down to the point where he was almost getting out. The Florida address that he had dudes on the pound sending money to was apparently a Miami DEA office.

Roberto was working with the original DEA agent from his case. Supposedly he had worked with this agent on two other cases while in prison. One in USP-Leavenworth and one in FCI-Memphis. In both cases it was the same routine. Roberto came in, scoped out the scene and made his move, with the DEA agent coordinating things on the outside with the local US Attorney's office. This way Roberto made cases for the local authorities through the DEA agent, who relayed the cooperation back to the US Attorney's in Miami, who subsequently put in Rule 35 motions to Roberto's sentencing judge for post-conviction sentence reductions.

This bust would be his third Rule 35 reduction and effectively would leave him with less then one year to do. Larry told us all this in about 10 minutes and we didn't say anything. I knew that Travieso and Vince were fucked up because I was. Roberto was a dirty dude, pinche chota and all

128

that, but to think that the feds worked like that? On that many different levels at once was scary. It just seemed a little far-fetched but Larry assured us that Dave had said both the FBI and his lawyer told him all this. So it had to be true and correct. But it was some fucked up shit. I mean, to think that a dude was a solid con and all the time he was working with the same motherfuckers who got him locked down in the first place. That shit was unreal. But in the world of first come, first serve federal justice it was becoming more and more prevalent.

The world of convicts was metamorphosizing into one of prisoners and inmates before my very eyes. I could honestly say that the War on Drugs killed the real convicts. The dudes I was hanging with were the last of a dying breed. I just couldn't believe that the Cuban could do that shit on two different compounds in the system and no word about his snitching followed him. I could tell Travieso couldn't believe that shit either. He was a deep thinker like me. Unlike Vince, who probably just felt like stabbing someone. Most likely Roberto.

After Larry told us all that everybody was quiet. I thought maybe it was the marijuana, but then I remembered that only Vince and me had smoked. So Larry and Travieso weren't even stoned, unless you count the contact buzz. But that couldn't account for much. Finally Travieso broke the silence. "Thanks Larry," he said. "Thanks for letting us know. But what is up with Dave? You were in the rec cage with him everyday. What's Dave up to with the lawyer and the FBI and shit?"

Larry didn't say anything for a minute. He kind of looked around the room searching for an answer. Then he said, "Travieso, you know what. I just couldn't tell you."

At that point I felt a kind of sadness descend on the cell, combined with disbelief. Finally Vince spoke up, jumping to his feet. "What are you saying, white boy? That Dave is a snitch? A pinche chota? I hope you aren't saying that, white boy."

Larry drew back at Vince's fierce outburst and Travieso stood also, "Calmete buey. El gavacho no dice esso. Calmete, esta bein."

Vince sat back down then, but as he did he said, "I just hope you aren't calling Dave a snitch. Because that's my carnal, oiste? Oiste esso, white boy?"

Clearly, Vince was disturbed. I think he was having a hard time dealing with all the relevant facts. He wasn't the brightest dude, but he was way street smart and loyal like a pit bull. Meaning he could turn on anybody at any moment. But I know he had a soft spot for Dave. Dave had looked out. I knew because me and Vince both were the recipients of Dave's goodwill for over a year. The dude took care of us, you know. So it was a fucked up thing to deal with. That somebody you liked, somebody who looked out for you, could be a snitch. But like they say, to each his own.

You can't live another man's life for him or tell him how to live it. But I could see Vince was having problems dealing with all his conflicting emotions. The dude was like a molotov cocktail. Ready to explode. And for real, I wasn't sure what would set him off or if I even wanted to be around. I knew that was fucked up of me, being that he was my carnalito and all, but all this bullshit had me thinking about what I was doing, who I was hanging around with and the direction my life was taking. I was just praying to God that I wouldn't get trapped and find myself jammed up in some drama of someone else's making. Because in prison one false step could lead to death or a life bid and neither of those were things I aspired to.

Travieso shook Larry's hand and got up to leave. Vince hit rocks with me and went with him.

"Oh yeah," Larry said as they were walking out the cell. "The cops fucked up the other day and put Roberto in the cage with Carlitos, Dave's Cuban cellie, at rec. And before the cops took Roberto's cuffs off, Carlitos whaled on him. It wasn't pretty. He had Roberto on the ground and kicked the shit out of him."

Vince smiled at this with a murderous glint in his eyes and Travieso kind of half-smiled also, saying, "That Cubano deserved that and more, verdad?"

Larry and I nodded in agreement as Travieso continued out of the cell. Vince lingered a minute and asked Larry, "Did he punish him?"

"Yeah," Larry said. "Roberto's face was all fucked up. His eye was swelling up too."

"Orale vato," Vince smiled as he jumped back into the cell to his rocks with Larry who almost shit his pants for a minute thinking Vince was gonna smash him. I laughed at Vince because for real, that vato was insane. Vince told me later and split.

I jumped up on the top bunk and read my *Don Diva* magzine. It had a story on this Harlem hustler, Kevin chiles, who'd done time in the feds. Larry got up and made a crackhead soup. "You know what, Guero," he began. "Those esses are crazy."

What an understatement I thought to myself. Then I told him, "Yeah, I know, dude. Loco."

INTERLUDES 3

*"The normal attitude among men in society is that it is
a great shame and dishonor to have experienced what it feels
like to be a woman."*

—Jack Henry Abbott

INTERLUDES IX: THE STORY OF LITTLE SHORTY

Dude was a midget. I mean for real, he was tiny. Maybe five feet tall and about a buck-twenty-five. He looked like someone's little brother. But the kid was in the penitentiary, you heard. Ain't no faking it. He was doing time. And shorty was street, you know. He walked it and talked it. Straight gangsta, or at least that is what he wanted dudes to think. He didn't take no static. Or at least he was fronting like that.

Little shorty was Dominicano. Washington Heights, you heard. He was a baller, as in basketballer. Kid had game for a little dude. He could handle the rock, let's put it like that. He was basically a little hip-hop kid. Trying to live the life and play the game. He liked to smoke blunts and drink hooch. He was like most young cats in prison today. Thought he was about something, you know. Hating, talking about that Benz he never had, that bling-bling, the dime pieces, the cheddar— but dudes could tell Shorty wasn't no player. He was probably a crackhead. But he was doing time in the feds.

He did his thing on the compound. Hustling a little weed, a little hooch, some kitchen moves—Shorty had his hand in everything, trying to come up. The kid was trying to put in work. Get his respect and shit, you know. But dudes carried Little Shorty. They equated his size with his manhood and Shorty didn't buck. He didn't have no cut card. He wasn't built like that. So he played the part. He acted a clown.

This old head, Gaps, who came down from the hot house, took the kid under his wing. Gaps had already done 20 years straight or something. He was an old-time hustler. Ran a cigarette store and loan-shark business on the block. What a lot of dudes didn't know though was that Gaps was an old gump from way back. Dude was a predator, who cut his teeth in the halls of one of the toughest penitentiaries in the federal system, USP Leavenworth. But he was discreet. Kept his shit on the low.

But dudes knew. They whispered about him. Whenever a new young dude came in and Gaps pushed up on him all smiling and the like playing the daddy role prisoners would give the youngster a jewel. Watch out, they would say, he's a gump. But only if they liked the new guy. If he was a snitch or clown or punk nobody gave a fuck. And then sometimes dudes just slipped through the cracks, you know. A clown like Little Shorty, who everybody dissed and carried, was a perfect mark for old Gaps.

So Gaps started putting his game down. Laying the bait and reeling Little Shorty in. First Gaps started getting Little Shorty to cook for him. They would eat together and shit. Dudes would joke and say, "Look, there goes Gap's boy." But for real, dudes did not give a fuck. Little Shorty was a clown and there were rumors on the pound that he was a snitch, too. But you never know. In prison you just try to stay away from dudes like that.

But Shorty could still ball for a little dude so he played on the block's B-League team and smoked out with dudes. A little weed, you know, or drank some hooch. Shorty was bidding, you heard. He liked to hang out with his boys playing cards or dominoes and watching videos. And in prison there are a lot of dudes like that who enjoy similar pursuits. So Shorty was down, in a way at least. When certain prisoners became familiar with you that tended to accept you on a certain level even if there were rumors about your integrity or manhood. But these same prisoners who Shorty kicked it with were probably questionable themselves. Snitches tend to band together. But Gaps, the old head, he was just looking for a piece of ass. And Shorty was his prime target.

Dudes on the block started talking about how Little Shorty came up. Gaps started buying him commissary and paying for his hooch and weed. A regular sugar daddy, you know. He had his boy sitting by him every night. Cooking, eating, doing the dishes, his laundry, and all that. Little Shorty was Gap's manservant, cook, maid, and who knew what else. Dudes kept whispering, "Gaps is fucking Little Shorty," but you never know for sure. And there are a lot of haters in prison. Probably just jealous of Shorty's good fortune. Maybe Gaps was just looking out for his adopted son. But dudes who had done time knew. They had seen it before.

Finally Little Shorty—who was broke like a joke—went to commissary and bought new sneaks, a new sweatsuit, and a new radio plus big willie headphones. Dudes were like, what? He got yellow slips like that? Shorty must be putting in work. Getting his back tore out or something. But wasn't nothing in the open so dudes just whispered. Gossip and rumors, you know.

The old head, Gaps, must have upped the ante but who knows, it was their business, so dudes stayed out of it. Little Shorty had come up, dudes said. Found himself a sugar daddy. Ain't no shame in that, if you're a punk that is. That is what punks do—take it in the ass. Little Shorty must have found his calling.

Months rolled by and Little Shorty was benefiting from the fruits of his labor. He was on Big Willie status and all. But were the pair of shoes, the sweatsuit, a radio, worth it for taking it in the ass? To each his own, right? Little Shorty was bidding, you heard. He was getting his. Anyway he could.

Then one day a bus rolled in and Little Shorty's uncle was on it. Now supposedly, Little Shorty was scared to death of his uncle because when he found out his uncle was on the pound he checked the fuck in. And it came out that Shorty indeed was a snitch. He had snitched on his own uncle. His uncle was going around the compound showing paperwork on Little Shorty. How he had testified against him for a 5K1 and all that shit.

Now Gaps wasn't happy. You could see he was put out. He lost his fuckboy so all the old gumps on the pound commiserated with him. It would turn out that Gaps was bummed out about something more then losing his fuckboy, but that would come out later. At the moment though all the prisoners just thought Gaps was a sentimental old gump.

Dudes who came out the hole brought word that Shorty was the orderly in the hole, running cigarettes and the like. He kept telling other prisoners that he was coming back to the pound. But he was faking for real. It didn't seem his uncle was going anywhere and him and Shorty had a separation. After a couple of months Shorty's uncle found out about the fuckboy shit. Not only was his nephew a snitch, he knew that of course, but his nephew was a punkboy too. Taking it up the ass.

Now this was more then Shorty's uncle could handle. He was still dealing with the snitch factor. Now to find out that his own flesh and blood, his sister's son, was a motherfucking gump. That was it. It was more then his Latin pride could handle. Shorty's family was already having problems because of his snitching but now his uncle was about to blow the lid off.

Somehow, word got to Shorty's mom on the street (probably through the uncle) that Shorty was a maricon. She freaked out and started writing Shorty and pressing him about it. Supposedly Shorty denied it at first but then confessed to his mother that he got turned out and sold his ass. In the midst of them writing back and forth a midnight officer in the hole who screened the mail read about Shorty getting fucked. The C/O reported this to the SIS LT who investigated all prison occurrences involving drugs, stabbings, and rape cases. They started monitoring Shorty's mail and correspondence with his mother since the whole story was coming out as Shorty tried to explain it to his moms.

Then the SIS LT went to the hole and pulled Little Shorty into a conference room and laid it all out to him. Thinking he had a potential rape case on his hands. With a little pressure the SIS LT broke Shorty. He was already a snitch so it probably didn't take much pressure. Sure enough, Shorty spilled the beans, telling the SIS LT how Gaps was his daddy and all that.

Even when he found out that he didn't have a rape case, the SIS LT kept investigating because he figured something was probably up. Little Shorty was a tiny dude and was probably intimidated by and scared of Gaps. So as a routine matter of the investigation he ran both their inmate profiles and checked their commissary accounts. The SIS LT was surprised to find that right before Little Shorty had checked in he received a money order for $1000 dollars.

When the SIS LT confronted Shorty with this, Shorty told him that his daddy Gaps had got the money sent to him. That same day Gaps was locked up for investigation. Shorty the snitch had struck again. Snitching out his daddy. But when word of these events hit the pound about a week after Gaps got locked up dudes were like damn, Little Shorty's a trick. The little fuckboy played the old gump for a $1000 dollars.

But by writing and corresponding with his mother about the gump shit Little Shorty had played himself. He could have got over like he had planned and got the transfer because of the separation with his uncle. But he had to blab it all out to his mom. Once a snitch, always a snitch.

And what's worse, the old gump, Gaps, is probably in a criminal investigation now. Paying for sex and the like, you know. Shorty will probably testify against his daddy but the feds will probably keep the money—evidence, you heard. That is how the feds roll.

And little Shorty, What can you say? He was taking it in the ass and tried to come up. But because of his inability to stop snitching he lost the only come up he had, the $1000 dollars. Little Shorty tried to make a move and you gotta respect that. But for real he played himself and the clown is a double negative, as in a snitch and a gump, and ain't no prisoner respecting that.

But Shorty isn't through. He'll be on another compound soon. Probably taking it up the ass while he tries to run another scam, and snitching on whoever when things get rough. People don't change and Little Shorty is hit. Being a fuckboy is bad, and being a snitch is worse, but to be both? A snitching fuckboy? Now that is fucked up. But Shorty got a jacket now and he can't shake that. Wherever he goes in the system, word will follow about who and what he is, so he won't be able to live it down. When Little Shorty looks in the mirror, I wonder what he sees?

INTERLUDES X: THE KID

The kid is in the yard. He knows what he's gotta do. Six inches of steel in his hand. It's time to become a man. Can't let no motherfucker disrespect you in here. This is the penitentiary, son. Can't let no motherfucker take your ass. It's time for retribution, time for blood. Where is that buttfucking, god damn, piece of shit rapist anyway? Motherfuckers gonna pay now. It's bleeding time. Gonna get buttfucked with a shank. Six inches of steel up his ass. Motherfucking homo piece of shit.

The kid looks around. Sees the fuckface on the weight pile. Hanging with his road dogs. Like he's all that. Laughing. Acting tough. Holding court. The kid is blind with fury. He's gonna do this. He ain't no punk. So what if he got raped—he's gonna get his respect. Prison style.

The buttfucker sees the kid coming. He notes the menace in the kid's eyes. He motions to his road dogs. Points at the kid. He yells out loud, "Come to daddy, bitch."

The kid walks over, tense and shaking with rage. Tears in his eye. The group of cons sees the shank in the kid's death white grip and back off, leaving the buttfucker to fend for himself.

The kid lunges forward, trying to stab his shank into the buttfucker's gut. The old con buttfucker slaps away the kid's hand and his shank—his ticket to salvation. Six inches of steel clatters away, coming to lie next to a 55-pound dumbbell. The kid is shocked. A group of prisoners has gathered round to watch the scene. The drama which passes for entertainment in the pen. As the kid scurries onto the ground, trying to grab the shank, the old con buttfucker slaps him hard across the face.

The kid lies prone on the ground and wipes the blood from his nose with his t-shirt.

"Get the fuck back to the cell, bitch," says the old con as he turns back to finishing his workout.

The fuckboy—brutally defeated—goes back to his cell.

INTERLUDES XI: GUMPS

I had known this dude B from a previous spot I was at. I did three years with the dude. He was a solid type of guy, go-hard and all that. From North Carolina. Rooted for the Tar Heels. Wasn't no Duke fan. Not many of them are. Air Jordan, Stackhouse and Vinsanity, you know. Anyway, this dude was a typical Carolina dude. Played sports and the like. I never heard nothing bad about the dude. He transferred to a different prison. I transferred to a different prison. The years passed. Then I transferred again and ran into him at this new spot I was at.

It wasn't like dude was my best friend or nothing. I just knew him and he was a solid con. Not no fucking snitch or nothing. And in the feds that's a good resume. Well in any prison, really. So when I ran into him again he was still going hard, playing sports and the like. He also ran a little store on the block, selling stuff from the commissary on a 2-for-1 basis. That is, borrow one and pay two back. Normal prison economics.

Since I knew him he would give me stuff on credit and cut me breaks if I needed something but couldn't get to the commissary. From being around me for three years previously he knew I wasn't no sucker and was good for the money. Plus he would sell me stamps and mackerels—the prison's currency—at a discount rate if I sent the money directly to his account from the street.

Like I said, he was a trustworthy dude. Not a grimy cat like a lot of dudes you meet in the feds who want something for nothing and think they are straight con men or something. I thought dude was straight, even though back when I'd first hit the pound I heard some whispers about him. Supposedly, when B was at the low he got busted fucking a gump or something and they sent him back up to the medium. That was the word but I wasn't going for that. I was like, no way, dude ain't like that. And the whispers never grew so I just thought it was idle chatter or bad gossip. All of that goes around in the feds. It's like a bunch of women spreading rumors sometimes.

So the years passed again and I kept doing business with dude. Buying stamps and mac's, getting stuff from his store, and bullshitting about sports with the dude, because he went hard on sports like I did. Betting, playing, watching or whatever. That was how we did our time.

B was getting short, though, and one of his aunts from North Carolina hooked him up with a pen pal. One of her friends, I guess. He started corresponding with this lady who was about 15 years older then him. Writing, calling and shit. But the chick had him open for real. He used to get this colored paper, pay a dude to draw some artwork on it, and then pay me to type a letter on it to her from him. I was up in the legal library all the time and I normally didn't type for other people but considering I had known the dude like 7 years I made an exception.

He would write the letter out and give me the special paper to type his words on. And I could tell B was flipping for the broad because he would be laying it on thick in the letters. Talking about, he loved the old heifer and shit. And heifer she was because he showed me a picture. I even said to him once, "Damn, B, you in love or what?"

"No way," he told me. "I'm just playing her."

Yeah, right, I thought, but it wasn't my business. I was just the typist, you know. So this went on for a minute, and then it just stopped. B didn't ask me to type no more letters. I thought about it for a second but it was his business so I didn't say nothing. You can't be getting all up in people's business in here. It's bad etiquette.

It wasn't even a month later that I noticed this gump hanging out in B's cell every time I went to pick up some stamps. I passed it off as a coincidence at first because dude was running a store and a gump's money is as good as anyones. But then dudes on the block started hollering, like, "Yo playa, What's up with your boy? B got that gump all up in his room."

I didn't want to believe it, but then again, you never know in prison. And they say that after 10 years, it's all legal. So I gave dude the benefit of the doubt and kept messing with him on the stamps and mac thing. But it wasn't long before B fell all the way off.

I remember one day I was on the block looking for him. I went to his cell but another dude pulled me up and told me B changed cells. Supposedly he moved from a two-man cell to a three-man cell, which was practically unheard of. And to top it all off, B moved into the three-man with the gump.

I couldn't fucking believe it. It was time for me to step the fuck back. I ain't got nothing against gay people but I wasn't trying to be associated with no gump-ass motherfucker, you know. It's not like I was prejudiced or anything. It's their thing, you know. But it is bad business. And the thing was, I had known dude a long time and given him the benefit of the doubt. We were cool. We'd done time together. Played football, basketball, and softball. Battled, you know. Go hard prison sports. I respected dude and to learn that he fell off like that when he was short just fucked me up.

A couple of months later I transferred to a new spot and my last images of B were of him all coupled up with his gump, walking around the track and shit like a couple. I still said what's up but I had a fucked up feeling in my gut because this dude B was straight until the prison life had broken him down and now a dude I considered my roaddog was a motherfucking gump.

This dude Scrappy from Ohio started telling me a story.

"You know Lou, right? My homie. The one that be balling all the time?" I told him yeah, I knew the cat he was talking about.

"Well check this out, that nigga was my homie, right. My boy. He was looking out ever since I hit the pound. Smoking me out and shit. We stayed stoned down on the block. I could never figure out were the nigga was getting the weed, though. But I didn't say shit. I knew the nigga wasn't getting no yellow slips or no visits either, so I was like, what the fuck is up with this nigga? But it was all good cuz I was stoned, right? And the nigga was good at ball—always dropping 30 and shit—so I figured something must be up. The nigga got a hustle."

"But for real, I didn't know what the hustle was. Then one day we chillin' on the block and that nigga Will, you know, the one that be coaching the basketball team and shit."

Yeah, I nodded my head,

"And he be working up in the law library. I know the dude."

I had talked to the dude a lot, up in the law library. He was a good dude, I thought. Wasn't no knucklehead.

"Well check this out," Scrappy said. "Me and Lou was on the block, stoned and shit, and Will came up and said some real foul shit to Lou. Straight sex played him and shit and then walked away. Talking about whenever the motherfucker nigga was ready to suck his dick he'd be waiting in the cell. I was like, what the fuck? I mean, Lou was my boy. The nigga been getting me high for months. I was like, 'what's up with that nigga, homie? We gotta put in some work or what? Because that man seriously disrespected you. You gotta handle that. You can't let no nigga come at you like that, ever.'"

"Lou looked all stupid and told me, 'No man, he just playing.' I was like, damn, but I was stoned and the nigga wasn't talking to me so I let it go. Then I remembered one day Lou had this big bag of commissary and he'd just come out of Will's cell. I stepped to Lou like, 'What's up with that nigga?'

And Lou just shook his head and said, 'I gotta get mines somehow, nigga. Ain't nobody sending no yellow slips. I'm taking care of mines.' And I was like, damn. My homie is a motherfucking gump."

Scrappy shook his head in resignation. "And then I started thinking," he continued. "I was adding shit up and putting two and two together. I remembered all the times that Will would be checking Lou and pressing up on him. I figured it was because Will was his basketball coach. But that shit was because Lou was Will's motherfucking fuck boy. Sucking his dick and shit. Goddamn motherfucking undercover homo-thugs. I couldn't believe that shit."

This black muslim dude from New Jersey I did time with used to regale me with stories about the shit that went down in Jersey's rough state prisons. He had done a 10-year bid in the 80's and early 90's at Rahway, the most vicious pen in the state, and the way he told it, shit was off the hook.

He told me the weirdest shit he ever saw was what happened to this Indian dude in the pen. The way he told it, the Indian dude was a straight killer. Had a life sentence and wasn't scared to stick a motherfucker or cut him up. The Indian dude had the respect and fear of the whole compound . And wouldn't nobody fuck with him. As dude told it, the Indian guy was built like that. Thorough, you know. A true soldier. Hardman. Tough guy. Whatever you what to call it. The dude was like that. Been killing and stomping motherfuckers in the pen for almost 10 years.

Then, all of a sudden, without no warning, the Indian dude changed the game. He started getting all feminine and shit. Putting kool aid on his lips. Shaving off all his facial and body hair, pulling his hair back, tying his shirt up, and wearing tight pants. Almost a total transformation, overnight.

Dudes in the prison were tripping. The straight killer had turned gump. He transformed into a queen just like that. Dude told me he didn't understand how some shit like that happened so one time he stepped to the Indian dude and asked him what the fuck happened. The Indian dude told him he was just sick of it all and wanted some love in his life. He wanted to be dominated, he said. My buddy started to laugh but then he was like, fuck that, this dude's still a killer. So he stopped laughing before the Indian dude took offense. And when the Muslim dude left the state and came into the feds the Indian dude was still flamin' and looking for a man, but his past reputation as a psycho killer scared off most of his potential suitors.

INTERLUDES XII: TAR BABY

Big Foot was a bully. Of course he thought he was straight gangsta. A playa from way back. But you know how that goes. Big Foot was a large dude, easily 6'5" and 230 pounds. He was an old head, been down for a minute, and black as night. He had been through the wars. He had his gump, he had his hustle, and he had his bitch. Or at least a female staff member he thought of as his bitch.

Big Foot worked in education and that is where his girl, the College and Literacy coordinator Ms. Jones, worked. Big Foot doted on his lady. Always up in her office. Watering the plants. Vacuuming her carpet. Big Foot was in love for real. Ms. Jones could do no wrong in his eyes, cop or not.

But on the other end was Big Foot's gump, Cookie. Because a brother had to get his some way. And plus, as the saying went, after 10 years, it was all legal. So Foot was punishing the gump but in no way did he consider himself a faggot. He was a ladies man. And Ms. Jones from education was his muse.

Cookie was jealous as shit of Ms. Jones and the time Foot spent with her. Because whenever they weren't together Cookie knew Big Foot was all up in education with Ms. Jones. Cookie hated that bitch. Smiling at her man and shit. Keeping him away. Cookie would have liked to smack that little petite bitch.

Big Foot wouldn't hear none of it. If Cookie opened her mouth about Ms. Jones, Big Foot would bitch slap Cookie. And Cookie wasn't trying to get slapped up. She didn't get down like that. She was trying to suck some dick. So Cookie didn't say shit. She just hung out and followed Big Foot around, doing whatever he said. Like some puppy dog following its master. For almost two years Big Foot worked for Ms. Jones and hung out with his gump, Cookie, on the side. To him he had the best of both worlds. Though for real, he despised the gump. Big Foot was a Christian. But still a man had to keep it real. And Big Foot was bidding.

Ms. Jones grew real accustomed to Big Foot. He made himself indispensable. Ms. Jones was just a home girl for real. Straight outta Motown. Grew up in the projects and all. An around the way girl, you know. And she liked Big Foot. She imagined his big strong black hands holding her little self. It was a fantasy that she had formed in her mind. But she was a practical girl and a fantasy was all that it would be.

But when she looked at Big Foot she saw something else too. She was from the hood. She knew what was up. How the government was still enslaving the black man. It was all a conspiracy, she thought. And she had a reputation among the staff for speaking her mind. A wild card so to speak. But she never pushed the envelope far enough to lose her job. She knew the limits.

She made a lot of scenes though. Arguing with her white boss, the supervisor of education. Even threatening her a couple of times. She got warnings from the AW but she was like, fuck those crackers.

And she kept seeing money when she looked at Big Foot so eventually she took him into her confidence and asked the big black convict if he wanted to make some cake. She was trying to come up and she hated the system for real anyhow. And with her job she had an opportunity to come up and buck the system at the same time. So for these reasons she made her proposition.

Big Foot was taken aback at first. Thinking it was a set-up or that Ms. Jones was a skeezer, but finally she convinced him she was serious. She queried Big Foot about the particulars of the prison drug trade while she was formulating a plan in her mind. She decided she would bring in some heroin. Since she was from the hood she didn't figure she would have any problem hooking up and Big Foot assured her that he could move it and get money sent to her in a street-to-street transaction to avoid any complications. Ms. Jones thought she was all in.

Big Foot couldn't believe his luck. It wasn't a week later and he had the tar. He made his gump, Cookie, hold it and business was good because Big Foot knew all the junkies. In fact he was a junkie himself, albeit a closet one. Just like he was a closet gump. Big Foot kept his business on the down low. But there was nothing he liked more than nodding off on a heroin buzz while the gump sucked him off. He would imagine Cookie was Ms. Jones. With her fine juicy lips wrapped around his manhood.

This business was going on for awhile but then Cookie got careless and got busted with some of the tar. She was putting her business on front street and somebody snitched her out. The cops pulled Big Foot in, too, putting him under investigation with Cookie.

The SIS LT's were sweating them something fierce trying to figure out where the heroin was coming from. A lot of notes had been dropped and they figured they had their man in Big Foot. But neither Foot nor Cookie got visits so the SIS LT's were crazy to find out where the dope was coming from.

Because Ms. Jones had burned a lot of bridges with the administration and due to her connection with Big Foot, the SIS LT's started investigating her as well. But Ms. Jones wasn't going for it and Big Foot was a convict so nothing came of it. The investigation produced only suspicions.

And Big Foot made sure Cookie's mouth stayed shut. Cookie took the charge and they let Big Foot out of the hole.

But the cops put a twist in the game because they had their suspicions on where the dope was coming from. They had the supervisor of education tell Big Foot that he wouldn't be able to work for Ms. Jones anymore and furthermore that he couldn't even go into education. He was on education restriction.

This fucked the game up a bit. So Big Foot tried to send different dudes to Ms. Jones but she wasn't playing that. She was feeling the heat and didn't like it one bit. She trusted Big Foot but she didn't trust the gump when she got wind of the whole story. And she wasn't sure how much Big Foot had told the gump.

The SIS LT's had their snitches watching Ms. Jones overtime. Cookie was still in the hole and Big Foot was banned from education. The SIS LT's were pressing Cookie as well, trying to break her gump ass and get her to spill the beans. Cookie wasn't telling but the SIS LT's weren't that interested in Big Foot any more. They had gathered enough information to be sure that Ms. Jones had brought in the heroin and they had a hard-on to bust her. Cookie figured it was her chance to get rid of the bitch once and for all and have Big Foot's attention all to herself.

Big Foot had laid out the whole deal to her over the months so she knew the 411 and she decided to get her revenge and snitch on the bitch who mesmerized her man. The LT's hushed the whole affair up. Ms. Jones was offered the opportunity to resign and she did rather then face charges. Cookie was released to the pound and ran back to her man. Big Foot was fucked up by the whole deal but at least he could still get his dick sucked, he thought.

The heroin dried up on the pound but it wasn't long before some other prisoner started making moves to fill the vacuum. Because for real, it's a never-ending cycle. They call it the war on drugs but the government can't even keep the drugs out of their own prisons. And when one of their own gets busted bringing drugs in they get a slap on the wrist and are shown the door. But don't let it be a prisoner or a free world person who gets caught, because they'll get sentenced to a decade or more. The devil has many mansions.

DRUG DEALER

BOOK FOUR

"Anger can change back into happiness. Rage can change back into joy. But dead men do not return to the living."
—Sun Tzu

PART 15: CONSEQUENCES

"What you working with, son?" Fox asked me as he walked into my cell.

"I got four hundreds left, dog," I answered.

"Let me get that," he said as I dug into my sock and pulled out the four fat packets of weed and handed them to him. "Is it the same shit?" he asked.

"You know it, dude. Straight-commercial-brick-shit."

"Damn, son, you'd think that since these cats is going through all the trouble of smuggling weed into the prison that they'd at least get some chronic, you heard," Fox said dejectedly, pouting like only a true stoner could.

"I know what you mean bro, I feel you," I told him as we both nodded our heads understanding that we were a different breed of stoner. Connoisseurs.

"You want a send-out for these?" He asked. I said yes as he confirmed my girl's address. "Alright, Guero, inside of two weeks. Word is bond." And with that we hit rocks, sealing the deal. Fox split.

No sooner did Fox leave then Vince entered, telling me, "You will not fucking believe this."

And at once I could tell it was something way fucked up.

It was almost lunchtime and I was just waking up, but I knew Vince had probably been in the yard all morning. Something had gone down and I was about to get the 411.

"The Puerto Rican cop was indicted, Guero," Vince said. "This country dude told me his people read it in this morning's paper. He came right out to rec and told me and Travieso."

Damn, I thought, that was bad news. And I knew worse was coming.

"That shit is all over the pound, Guero," Vince said. "And dudes are saying Dave told. Nobody will tell me directly or say who started that rumor but everybody is saying that." Vince continued, "The country vato said he would check with his people about exactly what the article said when he calls his wife back later. Can you fucking believe that shit?"

Vince was exasperated. I could tell he was in some serious shock. I just hoped he kept his cool and didn't flip out or anything. I was surprised too, but I figured something like that might happen. I just wasn't sure when.

Vince continued talking, "Guero, can you believe that all these pinche putos who Dave looked out for and showed mad love to are now talking shit about him? I mean, they don't even know for real. They are just talking shit. The no good pinche bueys," Vince said with an air of disgust. "Damn," he continued, "I can't stand these backstabbing motherfuckers."

"Fuck those culeros," I said, trying to pacify Vince. "They don't know what's up. Dudes on this pound just like to jump on a man when he is down, you know. We'll find out what is up and straighten it out, tu sabes."

"Yeah, maybe," he said, slightly mollified. "You got a joint or what, Guero?" he asked me.

"Ain't no question, carnal," I said as I reached into my pocket and threw a toothpick-sized joint at him.

As he sparked it up he told me, "Damn, Guero. I just can't believe how quick these no good motherfuckers flip the script, you know? It's like Dave was everybody's man and now all these dudes just want to talk shit. They don't got no paper work, no proof, nada, tu sabes. Todo esto es mierda. Dave ain't no snitch. And if anyone tells me he is to my face I'm gonna bust their mouth. That's my word carnal, me entiendes?"

I nodded my head as he hit the joint and passed it to me. Wake and bake, I thought. But other then the high, the morning—or should I say afternoon—was off to a bad start. It had only been a week since Larry got out of the hole and shit was fucked up already.

I caught Larry in the chow hall and after I went through the line I sat down at the table next to him. Burger and fries today. Motherfucking McDonald's, or at least as close as I was coming to getting it.

As Larry started jabbering low and rapidly into my ear I glanced around the chow hall, which was partitioned into two sections with rows of four-person cafeteria style tables on each side. The side on the left was the black side and the right was the white side. Of course this was unofficial, but it was a prison norm. Whites and Spanish just didn't sit on the black side and rarely went through the line on that side. You did see some blacks on the white side, though, and also in the white line. I always wondered about this strange set-up with its overtly racist tone. But for the life of me I couldn't understand who was more racist. I guess the whites and Spanish were because you hardly ever saw them on the black side. But then again maybe that was just how it was. In prison your skin color identifies you. Boundaries are set and not crossed. It seemed you either flew the white flag or the black one. There was no in between unless you considered the Spanish, but they always tended to side with the whites in almost everything. That is just how it was.

It did always seem to me that blacks dominated the prisons in a numerical sense. Maybe that was why you saw some blacks on the white side. Or maybe they were just the ostracized blacks. I never really looked into it. In the penitentiary it was not smart to go asking question or to start philosophical debates. Especially where race was concerned. That was a serious no-no. Like if a white dude called a black dude "nigger" to his face. Those were fighting words and seriously disrespectful. And yet the blacks called each other "niggas" and the whites called them that behind their backs. And the Spanish, they had their own words for the blacks and probably said them right in front of the American brothers who didn't understand español. So it was all fucked up in a way. Contradictions on top of contradictions. A mirror of the real world I guess.

Another thing I thought about as I sat there stoned and ate my Mickey D's-style lunch was what in prison they called standing mainline. Everyday at lunch all the prison administration staff, like the warden, assistant wardens, captain, SIS LT's, department heads, unit teams, and supervisors all stood at mainline as the prisoners were fed. This was so prisoners that had problems or issues could address them with the appropriate staff member or with the higher ups and decision makers.

But for real, the staff was only interested in talking to each other. It must have been like their impromptu social hour because they were so busy chatting amongst themselves that they couldn't be bothered with talking to inmates. The warden stressed "zero tolerance" also and if you tried to talk to him he would interrogate you about who you had talked to previously. And if you didn't follow the chain of command to the letter he would have the custody LT and C/O's escort you to the hole. I always thought that was real fucked up. But nobody cared what I thought.

So I was kind of daydreaming, looking at the executive staff and thinking how weak and pathetic they appeared and wondering what type of person would want to work in a prison anyway when Larry, who had been going on excitedly, punched me in the arm as I ate my french fries.

"Guero, are you listening or what," he exclaimed. He looked at me sideways as I continued to eat, imagining that I was at McDonald's. The warden did kind of look like the Ronald McDonald clown, I thought. And the SIS LT could have been the Hamburgler...then Larry hit my arm again.

"Guero," he continued. "What the fuck? Snap back into reality there buddy. You're zoning like a motherfucker. Did you hear what I told you? They indicted the Puerto Rican cop." I finished my burger and turned to look at him.

"I heard, dog," I said. "And what is this shit that Dave told?"

"That's the word on the pound, Guero," he replied. "Dudes are saying that shit is fucked up and that Dave is a snitch. Just look around, everybody is talking about it," Larry said and gestured to the whole cafeteria.

I glanced around and opened my ears to the din and discovered that Larry was right. The whole chow hall was buzzing about Dave. I caught comments like, "That hot motherfucker," "bitch-ass nigga," and "word is Dave's a snitch." It was crazy. I knew by the end of the day the belief that Dave was a snitch would be an accepted fact. That was bad news for him because in the feds when somebody hung a jacket on you and it fit it most likely would stick. And Dave had quite a few years left on his sentence. About 14 to be exact. And that snitch label would be hanging around his neck like a noose.

Dave was my friend, though, and I didn't want to hear it. Dudes were all trying to holler at me and shit, asking me what was up with my boy and if it was true or not as if I could give confirmation, but I didn't feel like dealing with it so I retreated back to my unit. I knew Larry and Vince were dealing with the same thing and it was not a good M.O. to be associated with a snitch so I tried to distance myself. When dudes stepped to me asking about Dave I just told them I didn't know. I hadn't seen any paperwork but in the feds you never know I told them. I just knew I wasn't gonna get in no beef over whether Dave was a snitch or not especially when I was so unsure myself and for real the evidence was stacked against Dave. It didn't look good but who knew? Only the US Attorneys I guess. And anyway I had other things to think about. Like my upcoming visit. Where the fuck is Travieso, I wondered.

PART 16: THE VISIT

The Detroit cats weren't doing anything. And there was no weed left on the pound. I had moved the last OZ Dre and his homeboy gave me and when I went to re-up they said wasn't nothing happening for a minute. So for the moment I was chilling. I had some smoke for my head, you know, personal and the like, but shop was shut down. The NY kid, Fox, my homeboy Mike the inkslinger and Duncan the skinhead didn't like it but that was how shit went down in the drug business. When the connect dried up, business stopped.

But I had something in the works. Only it wouldn't be involving weed or Fox and Duncan. They didn't fuck with no tar. They were straight weedheads. Stoners, you know. They were basically hustling to stay high like me. And for the little extras also. A locker full of commissary didn't hurt. And for real, unless your money was long you had to hustle in prison. The motherfuckers only pay you like $15 a month and even if you work in the factory you might only get $200 or so. So everybody in prison had their little hustle. Be it ironing and washing clothes, cleaning rooms, shining boots, running food, doing tattoos, making hooch or selling drugs. But heroin was a different thing altogether. Dudes went hard for some good dope.

I let my homeboy Mike know that some tar would be coming through. He was a big-time junkie and would be lining up all the other junkies for when the dope hit. All those dudes would be getting their works ready or trying to find out who was holding a set. Some of the junkies on the pound kept a set of works handy so when the heroin hit they would be in the mix loaning out their works for a shot here and there. That way they didn't have to shell out the $50 or $100 it took to get a paper. These dudes were crazy for real, sharing needles and everything. I guess they weren't sweating hepatitis C or HIV but they should have been because that shit ran rampant in prison. Sometimes I would see prisoners just wasting away and then one day they would be gone. To the medical facility, I guess, or more to the point, dead. I could never understand why a dude would take the risk of being infected by using a dirty needle but I guess that is the power of the drug. The hold that it has over them. And what could I say, I was a marijuana addict. But still, in my mind it was different. To each his own as they say.

I saw Travieso after the count. We talked a little bit about the ongoing Dave situation and what dudes on the pound were saying but like me, Travieso wanted to wash his hands of the matter. He was short, real short, and he was more interested in making some cake before he hit the street then what the fuck was going on with Dave. His eyes were on the street—not the prison.

Travieso told me everything on his end was set. My girl should have received the package by now. I hadn't called her since last Saturday and I knew she was coming to visit this Friday. All I had to do was call to confirm. She would be driving from St. Louis, about a six-hour trip, but she was used to making it as she visited me at least once every three or four months. My girl was a sweetheart and I was a lucky man, as all the prisoners whose girls had split at the first sign of trouble let me know.

I knew my girl would be nervous about the visit. I just hoped every thing went smoothly. I kept telling myself it would be like Travieso said, "Just two balloons, carnal. Nice and easy. Nothing to worry about." But still, it was something I had never done before. What if the balloons broke, I thought? What if I got busted? What if my girl got nervous? A lot of bullshit was running through my head but I wouldn't get cold feet. I was committed. I didn't want to look bad in front of Travieso. I had a lot of respect for that vato, and I would have rather got busted then tell him that I got cold feet.

That type of shit happened too much in the joint anyhow. Shit would get all set up. The drugs were sent. The trip paid for and then the prisoner or his visitors would lose their nerve.

And sometimes there would be a price to be paid. Dudes got fucked up when they didn't deliver. I didn't think Travieso would stab me but I didn't want to find out. Sometimes dudes put all their hopes on one thing and when it didn't happen they got irrational. Let's put it this way: when dudes break their words in prison they are held accountable. And I had no intention of breaking my word. Fuck the consequences. Fuck what my girl thought. And fuck my stomach. I just hoped I could pull it off.

I called my girl later that night. She confirmed that she got the letter from Cali and that she would see me that Friday. Everything was set. I told her I would just see her then because I had no intentions of calling her again, which would just give her an opportunity to back out or say something suspicious over the phone. And they did record all the conversations plus listened periodically so you had to be real careful. It was Tuesday so it was all good. I would be straight in four days.

I went and found Travieso.

"Que pasa?" he said.

"She got it," I told him.

"Mira, Guero," he said all conspiratorially. "No digas nada a nadie. Me entiendes? Don't say nothing to nobody."

I nodded my head, fully understanding the importance of secrecy. By letting dudes know what was up word could reach the wrong ears. That was how prisoners ended up in the dry cell. All it took was one dropped note and boom—you would be escorted from the visiting room to the dry cell, where you would have to shit for three days and have the shit inspected by the LT's for balloons. And if they found balloons in your shit you might be looking at an outside case for yourself and your visitor.

But prisoners still took the risk. The money was too good. One gram of heroin was worth $1000 in prison. And it sold fast because junkies were always gonna come up with the money, either by gambling for it, stealing it or working in UNICOR, the prison factory. And some junkies were big-time drug dealers on the street so their money was long to begin with. And when the heroin hit they would be fiending, spending thousands of dollars to maintain that buzz.

On the Thursday before my visit I saw my homeboy Mike on the yard.

"You got it yet?" he asked me, all eager like.

I thought back to what Travieso said and realized that I had fucked up by informing my homeboy about the heroin so I played him. "Naw dude, that shit ain't happening for a couple of weeks yet. At the end of the month, I think." I could see the disappointment in his junkie face,

"Damn, Guero," he said "you made it seem like that shit was jumping off soon."

"My bad, dog," I told him. Glad that I could rectify my mistake. But dude was hyped for real. I guess he could feel the heroin flowing into his blood already. I never did heroin and I didn't plan to. They said once you did it you were hooked. And I wasn't trying to be no junkie. I already had one habit and that was enough for me.

Mike hit rocks with me and headed back to the poker tables. Not only was he a junkie but he was a compulsive gambler. Parlay tickets, poker, spades, dominos—dude would gamble on anything. Luckily he could tattoo his ass off because he wasn't a hustler and he wasn't a real gambler either. It seemed all he did was lose. And of course, he did a lot of drugs. He was consumption man. That was just how he did his time.

I knew when I stepped to him on Monday or Tuesday with the tar he would be happy as fuck. And I knew his money was straight too. Because junkie or not, Mike was a solid con. I was glad he was my homeboy. He represented for Virginia. White pride and all that. Not that I was down with all that racist shit but I could recognize, you know. A man is a man no matter what his color or personal views. As long as he wasn't a snitch and his word was good he would be respected. That's just how it was.

Friday morning came and they called me for the V.I. I went to see Travieso before I went,

"Just be cool, Guero," he told me. "Act normal."

We pounded rocks and off I went.

The C/O in the visiting room took my ID card and patted me down. Then I went into the visiting room and saw my girl. Damn, she's beautiful, I thought. And she's here to see me. She didn't look nervous at all. Actually she was beaming. Happy to see me I guessed. I went and hugged her tightly and as she kissed me I felt her push a balloon into my mouth with her tongue. I quickly swallowed it as I embraced her again and then we sat down.

"Did I do it right?" she asked with a smile.

"Yeah, honey, but I didn't think you were gonna do it now, right off. We still got tomorrow, you know?"

"Well, I just wanted to get it taken care of. I got the other one, too. I'll do it when I leave. But anyways, how are you baby? I miss you so much."

And with that I slipped into another world for a couple of hours. The prison netherworld of corruption and violence was the furthest thing from my mind as I stared into those deep and beautiful brown eyes and curvy smile which held me enraptured.

We spent the visit eating, talking, laughing and reminiscing. Damn how I wanted to hold her, but that was against policy. And there weren't any conjugal visits either. So I was hit. One kiss and hug on arrival and one kiss and hug on departure. Anything else and the visit would end prematurely. When it got near to closing time my girl slipped into the bathroom and when she came back she kissed me hard on the lips and slipped the second balloon into my mouth which I swallowed. As I swallowed it I was thinking how easy it was all going down. Just like Travieso had said.

I walked my girl to the reception desk where she checked out, promising to return tomorrow. I watched as the C/O's at the desk eyed my girl longingly, probably wondering why a lot of the prisoners, the so-called felons and criminals, had such pretty girls while they, "the hard-working, law-abiding prison guards," couldn't even get laid. I laughed as I imagined their thoughts and that got me a hard look from the guard as I was led back to the strip search room and stripped of all my clothes, which the C/O shook out and ran his hands over, checking for contraband.

He then did the strip search routine, "Open up your mouth, lift up your tongue, run your hands through your hair, let me see behind your ears, show me your hands, put your hands straight up in the air, turn around, show me the bottom of your foot, wiggle your toes, the other foot now, bend over, spread your cheeks, cough, get dressed."

I was all inspected and cleared to go with two balloons of heroin in my stomach. So much for the security measures. Just say no, I laughed to myself as I headed back toward my unit.

PART 17: THE SCORE

I went to the visit again on Saturday but I cut out early. I felt weird sticking around the scene of the crime, so to speak, with two balloons of heroin still in my stomach. The whole night before Travieso was pressing me to shit the balloons out. I shit once but no balloons. But I made sure to eat a lot of junk food in the visit and filled my girl in on the money I would be getting sent her way. Then I thanked her for coming, kissed her again and split.

She was kind of upset because she had driven so far but I wasn't trying to hang out. I loved my girl and everything but hanging out in the visiting room was like being stranded in a bus station waiting area. Plus the no-touching, no-kissing policy sucked. I was trying to have sex. I had heard of dudes doing it but I didn't see where or how in that visiting room. It seemed like a sure bust. I just wish I could've gotten a blowjob or something, you know. My girl would have been up for it. She was a real trooper.

As I kissed her goodbye I promised to call her later that night to make sure she made it home safely. As she checked out and left I made my way to the strip search room and got stripped out. As I was putting my clothes back on I momentarily panicked. What if the balloons broke I thought? Six grams of heroin in my stomach would kill me. I had heard of dudes turning blue and shit. But I shook it off. I trusted Travieso and he trusted his people to wrap the dope up right. Plus it had been over 24 hours since I swallowed the first balloon and I felt alright. But I really had to shit. All that vending machine food was digesting fast.

Back at the unit I kicked Larry out of the cell and got down to business. I kept telling myself, "don't flush, don't flush." Because if I did the balloons would be down the drain and Travieso would be irate. So I just sat there and shit, smelling it and all. It was some nasty smelling shit for real. When I was done I got some plastic gloves that I had saved just for this occasion out of my locker and went to work. I found the first balloon but couldn't locate the second so I washed up and flushed the remains down the toilet.

It wasn't a minute later that Travieso was there sweating the balloons. When I held up the one he smiled like a fat kid eating cake.

"Dame esso, buey. Did you rinse it off?"

I nodded and handed him the balloon, but before he grabbed it I closed my hand. "Mira, carnal," I told him. "This is to sell, right?"

The big smile he had on his face quickly disappeared. I didn't mean to check him like that but he was my carnalito. And he was a junkie. Right is right, so I wanted to make sure that Travieso had his priorities straight. He would have to remain strong to avoid the temptation to shoot up. I saw it in his eyes, too. He wanted the heroin. He needed it in his blood but he had given me his word that he wouldn't do none. That this score was for sale only. To make a little loot to hit the street with. So that he could go out in style and not have to be begging his family for clothes and shit. I wouldn't have done the move otherwise. I was concerned about Travieso's future. I was hoping he would land on his feet this time. He needed to have a future without heroin, without crime and without prison. Or he was done, for real. Three time loser, you know. If this vato fucked up again he was looking at life.

He seemed to be considering something for a moment. His life, I guess, and what it was worth. I was just trying to reinforce what he was trying to accomplish here with this move. And from everything we had discussed, getting high wasn't it. And it seemed that he was reinforcing all this to himself because the glaze from his eyes receded a bit and he said, "Thanks, carnal. This chiva is to sell. I'm through being a slave to that drug."

Feeling relieved, I hit rocks with him and gave him the balloon. We quickly set up to get working and break the tar up. We placed it in papers. Travieso carefully divided it up so that each $100 paper was the same. I got Larry to post up on the tier and watch for the five-0 while Travieso and I got to work.

We used the little aluminum foil-like paper from cigarette packs to wrap the heroin in, as it was moist. We had 3 grams in the first balloon which were divided into 36 one hundred dollar pieces. I told Travieso to keep it all as I would get my 2 grams from the next balloon. I could tell he was anxious to get it sold. I'm sure he didn't like holding all that heroin. I just hoped he didn't have any works handy.

It was almost count time so Travieso left.

When Larry came back he asked me, "What is that all about, Guero?"

I told him I was making some moves. When I told him it was with some dope he said, "Be careful, buddy." I assured him I would be. Larry had been a little overcautious since he came out of the hole. I guess the six months or so SHU time had left him a little shook. I told him not to sweat it as we got locked in for the count.

Later on I shit out the other balloon and me and Travieso broke it up the same way. I had my two grams now. Twenty four hundred dollar pieces.

At dinnertime Travieso cruised and stayed on the yard until recall, making moves the whole time. I was just chilling. I decided I would go and see my homeboy Mike the next day and let him put the dope on the market. Travieso wanted to sell it for me but I told him I had it covered. I knew he didn't fuck with my homeboy Mike and the Virginia crew, so I was straight. I knew Mike would be hollering at me anyway as soon as he found out heroin was on the pound. He might have even already done a taste tester of the shit Travieso put out because I knew he kept a rig. I figured he would be over bright and early when they called chow and if not, I would be.

Before lockdown me and Travieso were kicking it with Larry when Vince came over. "Damn vatos," he said. "Where the fuck you all been?"

"Making moves, tu sabes, vato," Travieso told him.

"Yo se," Vince said. "Pero, when can a motherfucker get down with you all?"

"Ahora, esse," I told him. "Que queires?"

"I know you all are holding but I ain't looking para esso. Pero quiero fumar buey, que pasa?" Vince answered, looking at me hopefully.

"You know I got you dog. Mira." And with that I flipped a joint to him.

"Damn esse, you're right on time. Sabes que, yo estaba hablando con Leonardo hoy. El dice que necesita hablar con nosotros."

"Oh yeah," Travieso replied. "Cuando?"

"El digo, manana," Vince answered.

"Bet," Travieso told him. "Set it up."

Vince nodded and lit the joint. As he passed it to me I was thinking, what the fuck does Leonardo want? Did he hear about the heroin? Did he want a piece of the action? You never knew in the pen. When dudes thought they were entitled to something shit could jump off. And for real, I knew Travieso wasn't having none of that. Whatever was up, I knew tomorrow would be an interesting day.

PART 18: THE BEEF

I got up when the doors cracked the next morning. I had to go see my homeboy Mike. I knew he would be pressed to see me. No sooner had I put on my khakis and brushed my teeth than the PA blared, "compound open for the morning meal." I stashed 12 papers of heroin in my sock and hit the pound, leaving the other 12 papers stashed in my mattress.

Dudes were shuffling out of their rooms groggily and making a beeline for the chow hall. In the mornings prisoners didn't really greet or talk to each other that much. At 6 AM dudes were more interested in that first cup of coffee you know. Most of the prisoners ate breakfast and then got ready for work call which was at about 7:30 AM.

So everybody was heading for chow. I wasn't a big eater—at least not in the chow hall—but meal times were the perfect cover to conduct illicit business because everyone was gathered in one place. I found Mike scarfing down some French Toast. When he saw me he knew what was up.

"You got it," he said as I sat down next to him.

I just nodded my head. No sense in putting our business on front street. I ate one of the French Toasts and gave Mike the other one. After I washed it down with some milk, we cruised. I could tell Mike was ready to get down.

We went back to his unit, which was the furthest opposite from mine. It was still early and the compound would be open until last call for chow at about 7 AM, so I was kicking back with my homie for a minute to handle the move.

Mike found his bunkie in the TV room watching Sportscenter with all the other gambling addicts who were trying to see if they hit that four-pick. You could here them hollering, "Did the Bulls cover? How many did Jordan get?" Dudes on the pound went hard on all different types of things. You would hear them talking about "my team this" and "my team that" like they were actually associated with the sports team they claimed in some way. Mike told his bunkie that he would be using the room for a minute and asked him to keep an eye out for the hack.

As we entered Mike's cell he put up the shit sign to cover the little 2' by 4" slotted window. "What you got dog?" He was eager.

"I got the tar, homeboy," I told him. "I need sendouts to my girl's address. Can you handle that?"

"How much you got?" he asked.

"Twelve hundred dollar papers," I told him. "I need a thousand to hit inside a week. The other two are yours, off the top. Alright? You got it or what?"

"I think I can manage that, homeboy," he said with a wink. "Who else are you giving it too?"

"Nobody," I told him. "Only you, but the Mexicans got four grams of the same dope so the shit is on the pound. When you move these I got some more for you. Same deal, OK?"

"Alright, dog, that's straight. Thanks for giving me the lowdown," Mike said. "I copped a taste last night. The shit is good. This is the same shit, right?"

"Yeah," I told him.

"Good then," he replied. "I know some old country boys from Carolina who don't fuck with no Mexicans and love to shoot dope. Their money is good, too. This will go quick. When can you hit me off with the other?"

"Whenever. Later tonight, tomorrow morning, let me know," I answered. "I got it stashed so it's cool. Just get the money straight. Alright, homeboy?"

"Don't worry," he told me. "I got you, dog. Later, alright?"

"Yeah later bro. Be careful." We hit rocks and I cruised, knowing Mike wanted to get down right then. He was a straight junkie but the man was also a convict who handled his. He was a solid dude.

As I walked back to my unit I noticed the sun rising in the sky. The morning air was brisk. I could tell it would be a nice spring day. I looked to the hills and forest that dotted the landscape outside the prison fences and wondered how it would feel to be free.

My thoughts were interrupted by gunshots reverberating in the distance. Just the shooting range, I reminded myself. The cops were always practicing with their guns. The better to shoot prisoners who tried to escape, I thought. Not like anyone ever tried. Where would you go? We were in bumfuck, the sticks, you know. On top of a motherfucking mountain in Klan country was how the brothers told it. The feds always built the prisons in rural, out of the way places. Out of sight, out of mind, was their objective.

As the gunshots echoed I thought that the feds probably figured having the shooting ranges close to the prison would reinforce the concept that the C/O's would shoot to kill if they had to. It was all a little psychological game they played. Like pitting prisoner against prisoner. Black against white. Divide and conquer. That was how they kept control. Because for real, if 1,200 men decided to take over, they could. But in prison, unity was the last thing on any convict's mind. Dudes were trying to make power plays, get their hustle on and get their respect. Because it didn't pay to fight for a cause. Dudes just wanted to get fucked up.

Drugs, gambling, coffee, cigarettes, hooch, gumps and violence—those were the things that prison life revolved around. And those were the things that prisoners beefed over. And the administration made sure there was just enough to fight over. That was how they maintained control, by keeping prisoners at each others' throats. It was a sad state to exist in.

Imagine a reality that dictated violence, cruelty and corruption? But in a strange twist also inspired courageousness, loyalty and honor? Sounds like a war zone, and that's exactly what being in prison was like. Like there are two sides to every coin there were two facets to every situation in prison. You just had to be careful who you sided with.

When I went back to my unit I saw Larry up on the tier in the lookout position. Apparently something was up. I walked quickly to my cell as Larry nodded at me. Leonardo was arguing with Vince and Travieso. "Que pasa?" I said as I walked in.

"Que onda, carnal?" Travieso said as I nodded to Vince and Leonardo.

"Mira, Leonardo was just telling us about Dave and Roberto," Travieso told me.

"Sabes que," Leonardo said. "I told motherfucking Dave that Roberto was no good. I told him so. Pero esa cabron no me escucho. Y ahora tu vistes lo que paso."

Vince and Travieso just nodded. I could tell Leonardo was angry like a motherfucker. It seemed that since he couldn't confront Dave he was trying to pass the blame. At least he wasn't here about the heroin, I thought. I just hoped everybody played it cool. Because shit could get ugly real quick and all the dudes in this room besides me were accustomed to violence. Leonardo was definitely in his feelings. And rightly so—his homeboy and connect, the Puerto Rican cop, was indicted by the feds. Maybe Leonardo thought he was next.

"Mira, I told that fucking gordito that Roberto was no good. I told him, me entiendes? And now that puto is fucking snitching, oiste? He is fucking snitching. God damn motherfucking cabron. He better not snitch on me. I'll kill his motherfucking snitch ass," fumed Leonardo.

Clearly the boriqua was losing his shit and I knew he better tread carefully because even though he was Latin King he was by himself in a room with two vato locos de Califas. La Raza, tu sabes. Wasn't no faking or fronting about it. I looked to Travieso, who remained cool. But Vince was another story. The esse was like an M-80, ready to explode. I could see the rage consuming him. I just hoped he kept his mouth shut. But it wasn't to be.

"Mira, buey," Vince said. "You can't come in here hablando mierda. I ain't seen no paperwork on Dave and until

I do nobody can call him a snitch. Not to my motherfucking face, me entiendes?"

Leonardo tensed for a moment and I swore it was on. The silence was tremendous as the two met glares. But Travieso, ever the cool one, put his hands up and stepped in front of Vince.

"Oye, carnalitos, I don't know if Dave is un pinche chota or not. But I do know there's no pinche chotas en este cuarto," said Travieso. "Verdad?" Travieso looked Leonardo in the eyes and then turned to Vince as they both nodded.

"Mira, tambien—we got no beefs here. Nada. Nothing, entiendes? Para que? Por Dave, who might be a snitch? Now Vince, I'm not saying he is because I don't know, but is it worth it? We don't need no drama, entiendes?" Travieso asked and Vince nodded. Leonardo was still tense like a wild boar but the moment seemed to have passed.

"Now look, Leonardo, esta bien, verdad? Todo esta tranquilo," Travieso continued. "Esta muerto, verdad?"

Leonardo shook his head and said, "Mira, estoy bein contigo pero fucking Dave is hit. Cuando yo lo veo, esta muerto. Me entiendes?" Leonardo turned to leave as he said this but before he went out the cell he turned and faced Vince. In his Spanish-accented ingles, Leonardo said, "and you, vato loco, if you get in my way, you are dead, too."

Vince's eyes went wide and he made a move for Leonardo that Travieso and I quickly blocked. Leonardo laughed as he went out the door, never once looking back over his shoulder.

Vince was saying, "I'll kill that motherfucker." But Travieso pushed him back into the chair and I shut the door to the cell.

"Mira, carnal," Travieso said. "Fuck that boriqua. Esto no es nada. We're short, carnal, entiendes? He's not. So don't blow it. We're short, homeboy."

But Vince looked at him like he was crazy. "He disrespected me, esse. You didn't see. You heard him, right Guero? He disrespected me. I gotta go get him."

"No vato, you don't," Travieso said while he shook his head. Vince looked to me but I shook my head as well. "Vato," Travieso continued, "what you gotta do is go home to your family. Fuck that Latin King. Entiendes buey?"

Travieso put both of his hands on Vince's shoulders and pushed   him   back   into   the   chair.   "Entiendes?"

PART 19: DEPARTURES

The next day Vince beat the shit out of a little back dude in the laundry room. Supposedly Shorty put his clothes in the washer before Vince, who had been next in line. As they dragged Vince to the hole all cuffed up he kept yelling, "Don't jump line, motherfucker, don't jump line."

I was kind of glad Vince went to the hole because now the beef with Leonardo wouldn't escalate. Me and Travieso figured Vince might do 30-60 days because he had been in a lot of fights and for real he punished Shorty. Hopefully the dude wouldn't press charges. I knew Shorty and he was pretty straight so I didn't think that would happen, but he probably would get transferred. And for real he was just in the wrong place at the wrong time. Sometimes I felt that Vince did some real immature and stupid stuff and this was one of those times.

By the time Vince got out of the hole Travieso would be gone. Back to Cali and all that. They gave my man six months halfway house. He was outta here. He had sent his package slip out to get his release clothes sent in and everything. It was all good. And as far as I could tell he hadn't shot any dope. Things were on the up and up. And I knew he was set to clear four grand on the heroin move so he would be straight when he hit the street. Travieso was getting excited, I could tell. We just chilled out everyday and kicked it. Walking the yard and working out. My carnal was going hard.

"Sabes que, Guero, I can't wait to get some panoche," he told me. "Tu sabes, a real woman. I'm gonna punish my girl, Guero. And then I'm gonna look up some otra heynas and punish them also. I'm gonna be a fucking machine, vato, tu sabes?"

I told him I was happy for him. "Eight years, Guero," Travieso continued. "Ocho pinche anos en prison. Charlie buey. I'm going home. La calle vato, verdad?"

"Simon, vato," I told him. "And fuck some chicks for me OK, carnal? When you're fucking them, tell them, 'this is for Guero.' Make them scream my name, esse."

"Oirala vato. You're loco," Travieso said, looking at me like I was nuts. "I'm not gonna say that shit. You're wack, vato. How many years you got left anyway?"

"Muchos años, buey," I said with a laugh. "Punish those ruckas, carnal. Tell 'em, 'this is for my carnalito Guero who is in the feds.'"

"Charlie, buey. Callate," he laughed.

About a week later I saw Leonardo in the chow hall. "Mira, Guero," he told me. "I got no beef with you or los mexicanos."

I nodded, accepting his statement, before he continued. "Tell them esta muerto. I'm transferring anyway. I packed out today."

Well, that was a motherfucking surprise.

"Pero escuchas, if you ever see that snitch Dave tell him I said he's a dead man, entiendes? Dile esso, Ok?"

I nodded and shook Leonardo's hand. Who was I to tell him his business? Plus, that boriqua gave me the creeps. He was vicious I knew and a snake also. For real, I was glad he was transferring. He put me on edge.

Later that day I saw my homeboy Mike in the yard. He told me all my money should be straight and to let him know. He also told me that he was getting transferred, too. The feds were opening a new joint up in West Virginia and the BOP was transferring a lot of the Virginia dudes up there. He said I might be on the list later. Mike was gonna be on the first bus up there. Probably leaving in a couple of weeks. "But you know how that goes," he said. Here today, gone tomorrow. Diesel therapy and all that.

Damn, I thought. My homeboy was transferring. Travieso was going home. Shit was changing up. But for real that was how the feds kept it. They liked to shuffle prisoners around to keep things in flux. I wondered when I would be getting on that bus. This joint was sweet but so much shit had happened and I hadn't even completed two calendars yet. I was seriously thinking about all the shit I was getting into. And that Cuban, Chato, kept playing on my mind. Would I ever be able to feel safe in the system again? I would have to be constantly looking over my shoulder and watching out for Cubans. That shit was crazy.

I continued walking around the track with my homeboy Mike until they called the move, then I bounced, telling my homie later and looking for Travieso. He would be doing his merry go-round soon. The vato had six days and a wake-up left.

Travieso was chilling in his cell. As I looked in I thought for a minute that the vato was nodding. I hoped he didn't dip into the heroin. You know what they say, "Don't get high on your own supply." As I knocked on Travieso's cell door that NWA song, "Dopeman, Dopeman," played in my mind. I just hoped Travieso hadn't broke weak. He needed to get that monkey off his back. Especially since he was about to hit the streets.

As I entered Travieso sprang up. He was just dozing, I thought, instantly relieved. "Que pasa carnal," I said.

"No manchas buey," he said. "Yo estaba dormiendo. Que transa?"

"Todo bien, vato," I replied. "What you trying to do? Sleep away your last week?"

"Tu sabes esse," he said with a laugh. He got up and shook my hand. "Una semana mas," he said. "Pinche Guero. No lo puedo creer."

"Es la neta, carnal," I told him. "You're going home, vato, and don't be coming back 'cause I don't wanna see your ugly face."

"Damn, esse, it's like that," he said, smiling because he knew I was fronting on him. "But check it, esse, you handling yours? You got paid or what?"

"Tu lo sabes, buey," I answered, knowing most of my two grand had already hit.

Travieso slapped my shoulder and gave me a half-hug, prison style. "Six grand in two weeks, vato. That ain't bad business, verdad?"

"Simon," I answered, knowing that I would miss this vato, who had become like a brother to me. We identified in a lot of different ways. It didn't matter that he was from the barrio and me from the suburbs. He didn't hold that against me. He was my carnalito for real. Damn, only six more days, I thought.

Travieso told me that Leonardo had stepped to him also and he told what Leonardo had said. I confirmed that he said the same shit to me.

"Mira, carnal, stay away from vatos like Leonardo," Travieso said. "They are bad news for real. Nothing but trouble. And be careful around Vince, too, because he is loco tu sabes?"

"You got a lot of time, esse," he continued. "And you need to choose your friends carefully. Don't let no knuckleheads drag you down to their level. You're smart, esse, so use your brain. Don't fall into no trap or let no vatos influence you and the like. Be your own man, esse, me entiendes?"

"Simon," I told him. "And thanks for keeping it real. I appreciate it." I gave him another half hug knowing that this vato was a real good dude. There weren't many real convicts left but Travieso definitely qualified. I don't know what else you could say. But in prison, dudes recognized. Like they say, real recognizes real.

A week later Travieso was history. I walked him to R and D that morning. He would be catching a bus back out to Cali. Like a 36-hour ride. At least he would have time to think. He gave me his grandmother's address in East LA and told me to write. As he left I gave him a hug and told him, "Stay away from the tar, vato, me entiendes?"

He looked at me, all reflective with his LA gangbanger grill, gritted his face and said, "Simon esse, hasta luego." And with that, Travieso cut out.

INTERLUDES 4

"In prison people invariably mistake kindness for weakness."

—George Jackson

INTERLUDES XIII: SHAKEDOWN BILLY

Shakedown Billy was a little round motherfucker. He looked like Humpty Dumpty in a uniform. He took his job seriously, too. Either that or he was just a nosey fucker. When he was on the block he'd be shaking down cells his whole shift. The motherfucker would be up in there going through all of a prisoner's personal belongings and shit, looking for God knows what. He would have a big green duffle bag with him too, because no doubt, he was taking something. He could always find something that didn't fit his profile of what a prisoner should have. And by the end of his shift, that duffle bag would be full of prisoners' stuff.

And don't try to get it back either, because Shakedown Billy ain't hearing it. His rote response when a prisoner complained was, "You should've thought of that before you got locked up!" And if he had a beef with a prisoner, then that dude was hit. Shakedown Billy would ransack his cell. Dudes would go back to their cells thinking a motherfuckin' tornado tore through it. They would be like, "Damn, C/O, you can't take the shit I bought from commissary." And Shakedown Billy would be like, "You got a receipt?" After the prisoner shook his head no, Shakedown Billy would conclude, "then how do I know you bought it? You could've stolen it. You are a prisoner, right?"

That was just how Shakedown Billy carried it. He had it in his mind that all prisoners were scum and when he worked a unit, he enjoyed nothing more than going through some scum's locker and personal belongings. He would read prisoners' letters, look at their pictures, and examine every little crevice and corner searching for contraband, i.e. shanks, drugs, wine, money, etc. Because Shakedown Billy was looking for the big score, the big bust, he wanted to be recognized by his peers as an efficient and skilled correctional officer. His whole life was his job and vice-versa. But secretly, Shakedown Billy's fellow officers laughed at him behind his back, and even worse, the prisoners ridiculed him to his face. "You fat, Humpty Dumpty-looking motherfucker," someone would yell from the tier as Shakedown Billy was taking count.

"You bitch-ass, shakin' down cocksucker!!"

Shakedown Billy ignored the insults as he counted, but in his mind he was already marking out the area where the voices came from and planning his next series of shakedowns.

The count cleared and Shakedown Billy popped the doors. As he went back to his office, unlocked the door and went to open it, his hand came away with a wad of shit on it. Shakedown Billy grimaced, but that was ok, he thought. "These fuckers wanna play games, I got some games for them," he said to himself.

He got his shakedown bag and went to the area where he heard the voices coming from. He knocked on the door of cell number 230, awakening the prisoner who was sleeping on the bottom of the triple bunk. "Shakedown," Billy said. The prisoner, Jimmy, rolled his eyes, got up, and exited the cell.

Jimmy and his two bunkies stood outside the cell for half an hour as Shakedown Billy ripped their cell apart. He took a lot of inconsequential things like spoons from the chow hall, bread, apples, old magazines, extra blankets, paper towels, cleanser, government pens, and the like. No biggie. Routine shit that prisoners would just steal back because for real, it was all a game. Prisoners steal it, cops repossess it and prisoners steal it back again. No harm, no foul.

But Shakedown Billy fucked up. In his zest and in his anger he had taken Jimmy's sketchpad and pencils. Jimmy was an artist and spent his time working on his art. In his sketchpad he had close to a year's worth of work. When he found it was missing, he reacted calmly, approaching Shakedown Billy with respect. "Excuse me, C/O, I think you took something by accident," said Jimmy.

"Oh yeah," Shakedown Billy sneered. "What was that?"

"My sketchpad and pencils. That's my work. I'm an artist. I bought the materials through recreation. Here's the receipt."

Jimmy knew the routine so he had the receipts ready and handed them to the C/O.

Shakedown Billy took the receipts, examined them, and then handed them back to Jimmy. "Well, you know, I confiscated your stuff because I thought it was tattoo material. That's what it looked like to me. But here, let me see." Shakedown Billy rustled through the bag and pulled out the sketching pad, ripping it in two as he removed it from the bag.

"Oops! Oh, here it is. I guess you can have it back. I can't find the pencils though. I guess you're hit."

Jimmy watched in disbelief as Shakedown Billy handed him the torn and tattered sketch pad. Jimmy was enraged. He knew who hollered out to Shakedown Billy during the count, but Jimmy was no snitch. He couldn't believe his artwork was destroyed, though. Without thinking, Jimmy acted. He wheeled around and punched Shakedown Billy in the throat. The fat C/O didn't stand a chance as the well-conditioned prisoner pounded him to the ground. Jimmy then ripped up his sketch pad and showered the remains onto Shakedown Billy.

The unit erupted in noise as the beating transpired. *"That's what you get, you fat motherfucker!"*
"Maybe you'll stop fuckin' with peoples shit, asshole!!"
"How's it feel, faggot?"
"About time someone beat that cracker's ass."

Shakedown Billy laid there on the floor, not believing what just happened as the insults poured in. Realizing the attack was over, he hit the deuces and talked into his walkie-talkie.

"Officer down, I've been assaulted!"

At first, control couldn't learn anything with all the prisoners going wild. Jimmy walked to his room to a tumult of cheering. In the eyes of the prisoners, he was a hero. But Jimmy knew there'd be a price to pay. He sat at the top of the stairs and awaited the inevitable. There wasn't no getting away. He was in prison and knew he was going to the hole.

After the assault, Shakedown Billy got three months off, with pay. Jimmy got 24-hour lockdown and 18 months added to his sentence. But Jimmy's fists made their impression on Shakedown Billy. When he came back to work, he still shook down. He was too nosey not to, and his job justified his nosiness. But prisoners noticed that Shakedown Billy took a lot more care with people's stuff whenever he shook down after that.

INTERLUDES XIV: CATFISH

"Fuck you, punk," snarled the gnarly-looking, big-lipped, no-toothed, smashed-nose motherfucker. The dude thought he was tough or something I guess. But he should of known better. He'd gotten his ass whupped like three times over the last couple of months but some dudes never learn.

Catfish was a straight crackhead. He wasn't no tough guy but he wasn't no snitch, neither. He was a gnarly, old, crusty brother that had probably smoked too much crack and just didn't give a fuck. He had a bad habit of cussing motherfuckers out and throwing punk or bitch around like it was nothing. The dude had problems watching what he said. And in the penitentiary saying the wrong thing to the wrong person could get you fucked up.

A lot of dudes accepted Catfish for what he was and let his shit slide. Others just didn't fuck with his crackhead-ass. Then again, some dudes just weren't about to get disrespected or called out their names by some old, gnarly-looking crack fiend. Catfish stayed in some drama because he couldn't watch his mouth.

One day on his job assignment in the kitchen, Catfish was mopping up in the dining hall. He sloshed some water on a young Muslim brother's boots who was kicking it at a table before the noon meal.

"Yo, my man, watch where you mopping," the young Muslim brother said.

Catfish looked down at the dude's boots and told him, "Ain't nothing but water, nigga, chill the fuck out."

The young Muslim brother took offense but he saw that Catfish was an old head and he remembered the old prison maxim: don't fuck with an old head, because if you whup him, dudes are gonna say you picked on an old man and if he whips you, dudes are gonna say you're a chump. It's a no-win situation so it's better just to leave it alone. Remembering this, the young Muslim brother tried to be polite. He took the humble route. "I understand it's water, my brother. But please don't splash it on my boots. If you need me to move so you can mop the floor, just say the word."

The young cat was proud of himself for handling the situation righteously but Catfish, crackhead motherfucker that he was, wasn't having none of it. "Fuck you, punk. I don't care if your bitch-ass moves or not. You need to shut the fuck up and let a nigga work," snarled Catfish as he continued mopping.

The young Muslim brother sat there stunned as a couple of other kitchen workers looked over. The young cat felt seriously disrespected and thought, old head or not, dude was in the wrong. He had to make amends. "Yo, my man, old head," said the young Muslim. Catfish turned around, big lips snarling, hot breath ranking, to eye the brother. "You need to watch your mouth. I don't appreciate the way you're coming at me."

Catfish gave the brother the once over and snarled out his crusty, no-toothed mouth, "Fuck you, punk. Get mines or be mines." The young dude couldn't hesitate any longer. He answered Catfish with a straight right to the face, busting open Catfish's left eye and knocking him the fuck out.

I tried, thought the young brother, as Catfish laid sprawled out on the wet floor, eye bleeding and swelling up like a grapefruit.

The kitchen workers scrambled over to gawk as the cop hit the deuces. The compound C/O's ran in, handcuffed dude,

and took Catfish to the PA. Catfish spent a month in the hole
and then came back out on the pound. So did the Muslim
brother, so I guessed they made their peace. Catfish took a lot
of ribbing for getting knocked the fuck out but he didn't care.
He was actually pretty quiet; humbled or ashamed, I don't
know. He watched his mouth for the first couple of weeks after
he got out. But it didn't last.

A month later and Catfish had gotten all his old bluster
back. "Crackhead courage," they call it. Walking around like
he was a bad ass, talking shit and the like. The counselor gave
him a job as a unit orderly. Felt sorry for him, I guess. But the
job couldn't have been a more perfect fit—they made Catfish
the unit garbage man. He talked garbage out of his mouth and
now he emptied the trashcans also. He was pure garbage, you
know.

So everything was chilling, the normal routine on the
block, you know. Dudes playing cards, spades, tunk, gin, and
the like. And don't get it fucked up, Catfish was a card fiend.
Since he was a unit orderly he'd be on the block playing all
day. One day he was playing spades with some young New
York cats and during the game Catfish got rowdy and started
talking shit.

"Fuck you, punk," Catfish said to D, one of the dudes
playing cards with him.

Now D was a no-nonsense young brother. He was quiet
and respectful, but he went hard, like New York cats do. Not
really the type of dude to fuck with.

"What'd you say, Catfish?" D asked him, thinking
maybe he didn't hear the gnarly old motherfucker right.

"Did I stutter, nigga? I said fuck you, punk. With your
non-card playing ass," Catfish snarled.

D didn't fuck around. He flipped the table over onto
Catfish, grabbed him and then it was WWF time. D, who
was a well-built dude, slung Catfish around and slammed his
head into the corner of the flipped over wooden table. Wood
splintered and smashed as Catfish's forehead was gashed.

Blood flowed and spurted onto the floor as cards lay scattered and wood chips scattered.

"Oh fuck," Catfish moaned as he put his shirt to his head to stop the blood flow. The other unit orderlies got mops and buckets of water to mop up the blood before the cop saw. Luckily, the cop was out front bullshitting with some other C/O's. Some of D's homeboys calmed him down so he didn't kill Catfish, who went up to his cell to get cleaned up. Catfish had a big cut on his forehead, though, and it would need stitches. So he concocted this story about how he hit his head on the locker door when he was bending over to get something. The C/O bought it and sent Catfish to the PA, who wrote out an injury report and stitched up the cut. Nobody went to he hole but the whole block was talking about Catfish and his big mouth and the WWF time that happened on day watch in the common area.

I don't know what Catfish thought. Maybe he figured he got away with something. Maybe he thought he showed mad heart. Who knows what goes on in the mind of a crackhead? It was a big joke on the block, though. Dudes kept asking, why does Catfish keep trying to fight when he can't? Why don't he shut the fuck up? When he gonna learn?

After that D incident his balls got even bigger. I guess he felt that since he got his ass beat and didn't go to the hole that he was big shit. I'll give him one thing, though—he wasn't no snitch. And that was saying a lot in the feds. But what was Catfish? Tough guy? No way. Shot caller? In his dreams. Baller? Give me a break. He was just an old, crusty crackhead who talked sideways out his mouth. A big-mouth motherfucker who couldn't back up his own shit.

Shit was chill for a couple of weeks after that. But then Catfish shot his mouth off again and got his head busted. This time it was another NY kid called Cash. I don't even know what it was about but dudes said that Catfish tried to sucker punch the kid but kid ducked and clocked Catfish in the side of the head. Catfish fell and busted his head on the side of a table again. Catfish had some bad luck with tables and the C/O wasn't buying the locker routine again so Catfish went right to the hole after the PA patched him up.

The Lieutenants locked the unit down and went cell by cell inspecting everybody's fists and looking for any signs or marks of a scuffle. They knew Catfish was fighting somebody, but for real, dude had a habit of fighting table corners.

They didn't get Cash in the sweep but they locked him up later that evening. Somebody dropped a note. I guess they wanted Catfish to stay in the hole. But he got out again and went right back to his old tricks. Playing cards, talking shit, and acting tough.

"Fuck you, punk," he said across the card table and boom—it was on again. I couldn't help but think that it wouldn't be long until somebody stuck him. In prison you can only press your luck so many times. And Catfish's luck was about to run out. Because everybody knew there was no way he would watch his mouth. All it would take was the wrong word to the wrong person at the wrong time.

INTERLUDES XV: GANJA, MON!

The cops were sweating Skinner Dread. Somebody probably dropped a note on him. Twice in one week they shook him down. And I don't mean no routine shakedown, either; they were looking for drugs. They had Skinner Dread all up in the room buck naked, looking up his ass and shit, giving him a strip search. They probably were all inspecting his long-ass dreads and shit, looking for contraband, but Skinner Dread wasn't sweating it. He was a rasta man.

"Bumberclut, dem white devils me search me whole life, bloodclut," he said. And Skinner Dread was smooth, too. He smoked some weed and didn't even hide it. He'd be all up in the unit, eyes bloodshot, laughing his head off. "Rasclaat, mon," he'd holler. "Gimme a cigarette."

Most of the time somebody would hook Skinner Dread up because everybody liked him. He was international. He fucked with the Muslims, the Puerto Ricans, the white boys, the Italians, the blacks, and most of the other Spanish too. Dread was a little wiry dude with thick dreads that went down to his waist. He commanded respect, too. Supposedly he was a killer on the street. Down with the notorious Shower Posse. But who knew?

I liked Skinner Dread. He would say to me, "White boy, when you gonna smoke some ganja with me?" I would always shake my head and laugh, telling Dread there were too many snitches in this joint. I loved to smoke some weed, but this FCI joint was vicious, you know what I mean? It was a snitch culture where a solid con couldn't get a break and I didn't want to put myself at risk. I told Dread he should be careful, but he just laughed.

"Fuck dem," he said. "Snitches and policeman to boot, me smoke when I want. Me never stop for dem."

I could respect that but I just hoped Dread didn't go down because he was obviously a target and the cops were trying to bust him. And nowadays in the feds they were giving out more time and casing dudes up for a little bit of marijuana. And I'm talking about a little bit.

When you roll a joint on the street, the shake that is left over that you nonchalantly brush into the ashtray is like $25 worth in here. It's like a micro drug economy. But dudes buy it and Dreads like Skinner control the market because for real, he lived on marijuana.

Skinner Dread didn't fuck around, either. He was known to be quick with a shank or his feet if a dispute arose. I'd heard he could whip that shit right outta his dreads and cut somebody up something proper. I always thought he hid the ganja up in his dreads also. I used to wonder if when he was stoned he forgot which dread the weed was stashed in. Could you imagine the dude going through all his locks searching for the weed. "Me know it here somewhere, bloodclaat!"

But anyway, Skinner Dread was chill. He played cards on the unit, dominoes, smoked, gambled. He liked to stay busy.

The cat would play some soccer too. "Starballer" is what they called him. He would do all types of tricks with the ball and make dudes look silly, like Allan Iverson with a soccer ball. When he got the ball at his feet all the other Jamaicans would start hollering, "star time, star time."

But he was getting it bad all the time. The cops kept searching him. Ripping his cell apart. Pissing him. They had a target placed on Skinner Dread's back.

"Dem white devils got dem a conspiracy theory," he'd say. "But dem no get nothin' from me."

Someone in the administration did definitely have a hard-on for Skinner Dread. One afternoon I saw Skinner Dread flash by me, running. Soon after came a couple of cops. The next thing I knew they had Skinner Dread posted up, escorting him to the middle offices on the unit. Skinner Dread was yelling something fierce. "Get off me, white devils."

Through the windows and the door to the middle you could see Skinner Dread struggling with three cops. He popped one in the face during his struggles. One of the cops hit the deuces and a couple of minutes later the calvary came rushing in. Skinner Dread was hit. They had him all hemmed up. He was taken to the hole amid a crowd of cops.

Immediately, rumors started swirling around the yard. "Skinner Dread was holding," "He's gonna catch an outside case," "The cops whupped his ass," "He gave one of the cops a black eye," "So and so snitched him out," "He had a half ounce of ganja in his dreads."

That was the way prison rumors went. Gossip, really. Drama. But nobody really knew what happened. I figured it was harassment, but they could have found some weed. I mean, the man made no secret about it—he flaunted it in their faces. I thought that was maybe the last the compound would see of Skinner Dread. He'd probably get transferred or cased up or something. But six months later, Skinner Dread was back on the pound.

"They don't get me for nothing, mon," Dread said, proclaiming his innocence. "Bloodclaat white devils, always harassing the black man."

Dudes on the pound were happy to see Dread back out. Like I said, he was a popular dude. International, you know.

I pounded rocks with Dread and said, "You gonna lay off that herb now, right?"

Skinner Dread looked at me all serious, like I offended his honor or something. "Never dat, mon," he said. "Never dat, bloodclaat."

INTERLUDES XVI: BARRACHO

Gallo was a Mexican; a Chicano, really, straight out of Cali. He talked English like an American but he was fluent in español also. He was a little dude. Maybe about 5 feet tall and a buck-twenty-five. Nobody was trying him though because short or not, he was about his business. He was also called, "Rooster," which is the English equivalent of "Gallo." Maybe he fancied himself a little fighting cock, I don't know, but he was straight. Not feared, but respected, you know.

But the vato liked to drink and I guess he thought he was a thief or something. Ain't nothing new—most of the Mexicans will steal in a heartbeat. It's because they don't got nothing. In the feds on an INS charge doing three to five just for being in the country, making $15 a month ain't a lot to call home on. Much less live on.

So Gallo was a drunk and a little sneak thief. Scoping out the unit to see who he could hit. You could see him up on the tier in the morning, watching who went where, and what cells were empty, and the like. He would just chill and drink his coffee or do some push-ups. Most of the time he was stealing to pay off his wine debts. That is when he didn't make the hooch himself. Every weekend you would see him smiling. Drunk off his ass and walking around the unit in the little direct way he had. Like he was going somewhere important. He really didn't bother nobody, so dudes never really messed with him. He kept to himself and only associated with the Mexicans on the block and on the pound.

I remember this one time when they cleared the unit for a shakedown, and there was little Gallo with his big jacket on. It was hot as fuck outside too. The middle of summer. But Gallo had a bag of wine up his jacket. He wasn't leaving nothing to chance. Weren't no cops finding his hooch. It was so obvious, though. Dudes were laughing about it, but little Gallo blended in with the crowd and made his way back into the unit after the shakedown.

I guess he started drinking straight off when he got back in. Because later that night he was plastered, walking around the tier in his socks and singing mariachi songs. For real, he didn't give a fuck. The only thing was the cop saw him and knew straight up what the deal was. But he didn't confront Gallo, he called it in to the LT's office.

Somebody overheard him on the phone and went and told Gallo what was up. Gallo figured that they were coming to breathalize him and he was punch drunk, so he wasn't trying to blow in no tube. It wasn't a couple of minutes later that two lieutenants and some custody staff barged in the unit and up the stairs to Gallo's cell. The only thing was, Gallo wasn't there. The cops looked all around the unit, searched every room, and still no Gallo. As it turned out, the little motherfucker had squeezed up under the bunk, which was a feat considering the cells had triple bunks with the bottom one no more then a foot off the floor.

I don't know how the LT's figured out he was under the bunk—maybe he busted ass or something—but the next thing you know all the cops were rushing into Gallo's open cell while the LT was trying to pull Gallo out from under the bed. The LT had Gallo's leg as he fought to stay under the bed. As soon as the cops pulled him out he started wrestling with them. It was little Gallo versus five cops and he was giving them problems. I guess in his drinking state he had the strength of the Incredible Midget because it took the cops several minutes to subdue him. When they finally did he was marched out of the unit, handcuffed and in his socks, still fighting and resisting the cops as they pulled and carried him down the stairs, up the compound, and into the hole.

I heard later that they had beat the shit outta the little dude. You never know for sure in here with the rumors and all, but I wouldn't put it past the cops. Time went on, the routine returned, and dudes kept bidding. I even forgot about the little dude, figuring he'd been transferred or something. But 18 months later, Gallo walked out of the hole and back into the unit.

"Damn, esse," I told him. "Where the fuck you been?"

The little vato got a lot of respect when he came back on the pound, and all the Mexicans were glad to see him. 18 months, I thought. That is a motherfucking stretch in 24-hour lockdown.

Gallo was a little out there before but now he was a bug. 18 months in the hole will do that to a motherfucker. I asked him about the hooch; if he was still trying to go. He looked at me with his crooked grin and told me he "gave up drinking." I guess they beat it out of him. Who knows? But hole time like that can seriously fuck up your head. I haven't heard of him stealing nothing either but I still see him up on the tier early in the morning scoping shit out. I wonder what he's up to? Planning a heist or just thinking about it?

DRUG DEALER

BOOK FIVE

"I do not need what the devil alone can give me if I have a few drugs."

—Jack Henry Abbott

PART 20: MORE BALLOONS

"What type of time you on, son?" Fox the NY hustler said as he entered my cell.

"Chillin', you know," I answered. But for real, I was bumming. Shit wasn't the same. The pound was just different.

"Damn, son," said Fox. "You all fucked up cause your mans and them gone."

"Naw, dog, for real, I'm happy. For Travieso and shit. You know Vince will probably be back out next week or something. And Dave...well, you know what's up with that," I said, squinching up my face. Just talking bout the Dave situation fucked me up. It left a sour, bitter taste in my mouth.

"Yo, son, check it, don't none of that bullshit reflect on you, you heard. I know Dave was your man, I liked the cat too, but shit happens you know. You can't account for another man's actions, you heard," Fox said. "Every man is responsible to himself. You gotta keep it real and be true to your word. Death before dishonor, you heard. But some niggas ain't built like that. And they get exposed, you heard," Fox continued, giving me a crazy chesire cat grin and punching me in the arm.

"Anyways, son. Can a nigga get stoned or what?"

I looked at him like, motherfucker I knew you wanted something, but my man Fox was grinning like a cartoon. Dude was clowning me. But not really, I thought. He was my dog. And even though my weed supply, my personal stash, was getting low, I could still look out. I fished the baggie out of my sock and flipped it to him. "Roll it up, dog," I told him.

"Alright, son," he replied. "But we doing it New York style, you heard. We getting blunted."

And with that, Fox pulled out a Black and Mild cigar and freaked it, putting a good amount of marijuana back in with the tobacco.

"Damn, esse, don't be using all my smoke," I told him, fronting as he took the bait.

"Yo, kid, why I gotta be an esse?" he said.

"Well, you know, being that I'm a cracker, I can't be calling you nigga, right?" I replied.

Fox screwed his face all up, looking serious for a minute and said all gully, "Who you calling nigga, white boy?"

We both broke out laughing at that, knowing that we were down. That racial shit was out the door with us. But it was an inside joke. It wasn't nothing to be taken out on the pound. Because other dudes wouldn't understand. If Fox's homeboys heard me calling him a nigga they would be in their feelinqs quick and would press him to straighten me out. They would be like, "Yo, you better check that cracker."

But Fox was cool with me and knew I would never step over that boundary and put him on front street like that. It just wasn't good prison etiquette. There was a fine line between joking and seriousness. And you had to realize when you could joke and when you couldn't because convicts didn't like dudes who were on some serious clown-type shit. In prison you had to learn to decipher when the time to joke was or you could wind up with a shank in you back. Because when it came down to it, beefs were largely geographical and drawn along gang lines. And when the drama got thick all that friendship shit gets thrown out the window. Two dudes might be tight but if dude is beefing with your homie, you rolling with your homie even if he's the one in the wrong.

But wasn't no shit jumping off like that. Me and Fox were just getting high. We were on joke time, clowning you know. Wasn't no harm in that. We fired up the blunt and burned it. I had smoked a lot of blunts before but most of the white cons didn't go for it. They would be like, "that's some nigga shit." I guess it was just a hip-hop thing. Even the vatos I hung out with like Travieso and Vince weren't down with the blunt thing. But I liked it. It gave the weed a smooth taste and it burned slow.

Fox bounced when we finished the blunt. We hit rocks as he left, telling me, "good lookin'."

Not a minute later Snake knocked on my door with this other vato who was wearing bus clothes and apparently had just got off the bus.

"Que pasa, buey?" Snake said as he sniffed the air. I nodded to him and the other vato as they entered the cell. Now that Travieso was gone and Vince was in the hole, Snake was the ranking member of La Raza. He was from Tejas but was still down. La Raza was more of a Mexican thing than a geographical thing anyway. Because there were a lot of Mexican prison gangs like the Paisas, the Neros, the Surenos, the Mexican mafia, the Texas syndicate, la Nietas, and the Nortenos. But in the feds all that regional shit was out the window because they had these vatos all over the place. So in a lot of joints, especially the mediums, it was just La Raza.

And from what I'd seen in the last week since Travieso left, Snake was calling the shots. Not that he had any shots to call because the drugs had dried up, but he was the man. And who knew? Shit was bound to start jumping again. I was down for whatever.

"Mira, buey," Snake said. "This is my homie Brian."

I hit rocks with dude. He looked more like a suburbanite then a vato loco but he was definitely Mexican.

"Brian just rolled in from El Reno," Snake continued. El Reno in Oklahoma was the big transit hub in the BOP. Whenever you transferred or went to court or anything you usually went through El Reno.

"In transit, verdad?" I said as Brian nodded.

"Simon, that shit sucked, esse."

Snake asked me if I was holding. I figured what the fuck. I was stoned but another wouldn't hurt. Like they say, smoke 'em if you got 'em. I busted it out and they sat down, chilling. I was glad it was Friday night. Late night, too. My Bunkie Larry would be in the TV room all night watching movies. He was go hard when it came to flicks. So I settled in for a serious stoner session with Snake and Brian.

Brian seemed cool. He was young like me. First time in prison. He had caught a case selling weight to a DEA agent. He was a student at the University of Tennessee when he got busted but he grew up in Texas. San Antonio to be exact. Same as Snake. Apparently Snake was a legend in San Antonio and Brian couldn't believe his luck when he hit the pound and ran into him. Not that he knew Snake from the street but apparently everyone in the barrio had heard of dude due to his balling.

This was all new to me. I knew Snake had been down awhile. He was finishing up a seven-year bid for marijuana distribution, but I didn't know the particulars. To Brian he seemed an idol. Snake was chilling, puffing on the joint as Brian told me of Snake's exploits in la calle.

"Damn, Snake," I said. "I didn't know it was like that."

"Sabes que, buey," he said, "Estaba todos." We all laughed at this, stoned as we were on our second joint. They both got quiet then for a minute and I knew something was up. Snake motioned for Brian to say something.

"Guero is cool, buey. Dile." My ears perked up because it sounded like something might be going down.

"I got a girl," Brian started. "She goes to the University of Tennessee also and I was thinking about getting her to bring me some weed when she visits. Snake said you might be able to tell me what's up here and how the visiting room is."

Damn right, I thought. Good thing, too, because I was at the end of my personal. "Es facil, buey," I told him. "This visiting room is sweet. You gonna kiester it or go with balloons?"

He looked at me kind of weird when I said that. I guess he didn't like the kiester idea. I can't say that I did either but that was the way a lot of dudes went. And I was just throwing it out there to see what type of time dude was on. There wasn't no way I would kiester any weed but you could get an ounce in at a time by doing it like that. I guess it just depended on how motivated you were for money or smoke. In the joint dudes would get a lot of the gumps to kiester shit for them but hard-core cons did it, too. So it wasn't anything disgraceful, just a personal preference.

"Balloons," Brian told me as he looked to Snake for approval.

I guessed that if Snake said kiester he might of kiestered, but I didn't know for real. I laid it all out to them exactly as Travieso had laid it out to me. I knew Snake had been down and probably knew all this but he must not have been privy to any moves at this prison and he must have known after the fact that I pulled the move off for Travieso. Now he must have wanted Brian to get firsthand knowledge.

At the 12 PM count they bounced. Brian told me he was in the 12-man common area. That sucked, I thought. But that's what usually happened when dudes came in off the bus—they did their bids in the common area until a two-man cell came open. I hit rocks with them and told Brian to holler if he needed anything. I knew Snake had the kid under his thumb but I was determined to get a piece of the action even if it was only some smoke for myself.

Tennessee was the next state over so Brian could get a lot of visits. I hope the girl loves him, I thought. And better yet, I hope she has some friends. My stoned brain started spinning as I thought of the possibilities. A honey to visit and more balloons. I hoped I wasn't being too greedy. But in my stoned mind it was all good.

"Fucking hell, Guero," Larry said as he came in the cell for count. "You're missing some good movies, dog. They're playing *Terminator 2*."

Larry sniffed the air. "It smells like weed, bunkie. Where's the powder?" With that, Larry deodorized the room. But I didn't care. I was high and dreaming. In la-la land, tu sabes?

PART 21: SCHEMING

The next day I was on the yard with my homeboys, Mike the ink slinger and Duncan the skinhead. They were pressing me about some weed.

"Damn, homeboy," Duncan said. "What's up with the smoke?"

"No hay nada, buey," I said, not realizing who I was talking to.

"Fucking hell, Mike," began Duncan through gritted teeth. "What is up with this white boy talking Spanish all the time? Is he a wanna-be Mexican or what? Hello, hello, homeboy: can we get some conversation in English please? This is America, right? Speak English or die. That's what is wrong with this fucking country. Too many immigrants and niggers."

Mike hit me in the arm. "What's up with the weed, Guero? Kick down, dog."

Fuck these motherfuckers, I thought. I was scheming on how to get some dope and all these crazy motherfuckers were doing was bothering me. "Look, homeboys," I said. "I don't got shit. I'm trying to figure out how to come up so leave me the fuck alone." Then I remembered I had a toothpick-sized joint in my sock which I fished out and gave to Mike.

"That's what the fuck I'm talking about, dog," Duncan said, still gritting his face at me. Mike told me thanks and they cruised to walk the track and fire up the joint.

I was left alone with my thoughts. I had to get in with that new vato, Snake's homeboy Brian. Something told me that he would be my come up. I was hoping I could convince him to get one of his girl's friends to visit me so we could double dip with the balloons, so to speak, but I barely knew the dude so I didn't want to approach him too directly. Plus, I didn't really like Snake. He seemed like such a wanna-be, un plastico, in comparison with Travieso and Vince, who were vatos firme.

But I guessed he was calling the shots and had Brian under his wing. I would just have to figure out an angle.

La Raza was hanging deep over by the handball courts so I went over to kick it. Snake was playing handball, stripped to the waist and sweating. His numerous jailhouse tattoos gleaming in the sunlight. I saw Brian kicking the soccer ball around with some other Mexicans so I joined them.

"What's up, vato?" I said to Brian. He acknowledged me and kicked me the ball, which I promptly juggled for a minute before passing it back.

"You got it like that," said Brian, impressed with my soccer skills. I nodded at the other Mexicans.

"Este Guero juega bien," one of the vatos said.

"Orale," Brian said while he juggled the ball with his head, laughing the whole time.

It wasn't long before Brian was getting his hustle on. His girl came up faithfully every weekend. And by Sunday or Monday night Brian was holding. It wasn't no bullshit either. His girl was bringing him the chronic. Kind bud, you know. First class stoner weed. On the street I used to get a lot of nice homegrown out of Kentucky and Tennessee so I had figured that Brian's girl would bring him some good weed but you never knew.

It seemed that Brian was everybody's new best friend but Snake had that kid on lock. Everything was going through him. I was buying $100 pieces and the like which were the only weight they were selling. I was doing like five or six sendouts a week but I couldn't turn a profit. I was burning money, hustling backwards as they called it. It was some good smoke but for real I wanted to be in the mix, making moves and the like. I was trying to add to my bank, not deplete it, and I still had a long bid to go. At this rate I figured there was no way what little money I had would last. This customer shit was fucked up. But I guessed I would just have to bide my time. I was hooking dudes up like Fox, Duncan and Mike, you know, holding them down. But I was just doing that on the GP. I wasn't even making any smoke off it.

Snake knew that the weed was the bomb so he was bleeding motherfuckers. Plus, at the time it was the only ticket on the pound. So Snake and La Raza had the compound in a chokehold. Everybody was trying to get some of that chronic but for real, there just wasn't enough to go around. That caused some bad feelings but that was Snake's problem. He was the one calling the shots. Nobody knew about the kid Brian. And that was for the best because if somebody knew they might try to lay a serious press game down on the kid and then La Raza would retaliate to protect their interest. So it was best for Brian to remain in the shadows of the prison's razor-wire fences because if he tried to make his own moves without being established shit could get ugly.

I actually don't think the kid Brian understood the severity of the prison politics that were going on around him. That was probably for the best as well. It seemed he was getting used by La Raza but what could I say, they were his people and he was using them for protection also. And prison was just a big clusterfuck of use or get used. It like how dudes come in scared to death and end up joining the Muslim community or Christian community. For real, they are just looking for some strength in numbers. And a lot of them are rats, too, so they think they can hide out under the wings of some righteous religious brothers. Gangs are the same way. I guess Brian felt he needed that strength or back up.

One day Brian was kicking it on the unit with this black kid he had come in on the bus with. He was getting the kid high and the like, just hanging on the block, you know. This black kid was staying in the upstairs common area, a 12-man room just like the one Brian was in downstairs. In our unit they put all the new black guys in the upstairs common area and all the new white and Spanish prisoners in the downstairs 12-man room. The new dudes would stay in the common area until a

2-man room opened up, which happened when someone transferred, went to court, or went to the hole.

Brian and the black kid had been on the pound almost a month when the black kid got robbed. Somebody went into the 12-man room and busted open his locker, cleaning him out. And the thieves knew what they were doing because they had scoped dude out and waited until he went to the store and bought new sneaks, sweats, and everything. Needless to say the black kid was fucked up and so was Brian because that was his man. Supposedly they had been in the county together before being sentenced by the feds.

Brian went right to Snake to find out how to help his man but Snake told Brian not to fuck with it. A lot of times when new dudes came in their stuff got stolen. Any unaffiliated prisoner was fair game. Odds also increased if the thieves thought their mark wouldn't do anything. Dudes didn't try to steal from a killer or someone who they thought would handle their business.

It seems every unit has a couple of thieves who like to lie in wait and check out every new dude who comes in looking for a mark. If it seems the dude is about something or is somehow affiliated with convicts already there, like Brian and La Raza, the thieves leave them alone. But when they see a dude like Brian's man who was unaffiliated, didn't really know anyone and was a little slight of stature, they strike.

Me and Snake had been on the block for a minute so we knew who all the thieves were. There was a Mexican, Pelon, who stole his ass off. For real, a lot of time he sold the stuff he stole to me, Travieso or Dave (before he went to the hole). But he didn't steal from any black guys. Only Spanish and white. Most of the times dudes only preyed on their own races. So I was talking to Snake about it the next day and we figured P-Nut and Mo-Mo, two black orderlies who were known sneak thieves, had ripped off the kid's shit.

In prison there were two ways to take someone's shit. One way was the direct, manly approach—just take it. "Rough it off," was what they called it. That's what a real man did. The cowards were sneak thieves. They stole on the low. Most convicts didn't have a problem with dudes who stole from the man-like the kitchen, commissary, rec, chapel or whatever. That was government shit. But dudes looked down on sneak thieves. They were the worst, preying on their own tribe.

But if the dude they ripped off didn't do anything then he was considered to be the chump that the sneak thieves played him for. Brian kept telling Snake that his man was no chump so Snake told Brian about P-Nut and Mo-Mo. About another week went by and one night while I was in the common area on the phone I saw the black kid that Brian came with run up on P-nut and clock him. And then it was on. The two dudes were boxing right in the middle of the common area.

The cop came out of the office and took a seat to watch the fight as convicts gathered on the tiers, cheering. This C/O was a redneck, country type who didn't really give a fuck so he didn't hit the deuces. The deuces were what the cops hit when there was a disturbance. It was an emergency call button on their two-way radio that would call the calvary to the unit for disturbances like fights, riots or whatever. But this cop was too interested in watching the dudes slug it out just like the whole unit was. It was like entertainment. The prison news network, you know.

It was a pretty evenly matched fight. Both dudes were skinny black dudes. Like lightweights or something, and they were throwing down. They were pummeling each other. The weird thing was that they were just boxing. Neither one attempted to wrestle the other one down to the ground or nothing. From watching and being in a lot of fights I knew that most fights ended up on the ground, but these two brothers were doing their Sugar Ray Leonard impersonations. Dancing around and boxing. Putting on a show for real. Gladiator style, you know?

The whole block was watching and cheering. It was crazy. Dudes were on the tiers yelling their heads off. Taking bets or whatever. The fight was a great tension reliever for those watching. As I hung up the phone (it was impossible to hear my girl anyway) I saw Snake and Brian up on the tier with their boots on. And Snake was yelling, "That's for Steven, that's for Steven." I was thinking, Who the fuck is Steven when I realized he was saying stealing, not Steven. It was just his Mexican accent. I don't know why they had their boots on. Maybe they were fitting to help Brian's man and stomp P-nut.

The fighters were tiring and then finally P-Nut, the sneak thief, got knocked down and the whole block erupted. As Brian's man jumped on him the cop finally hit the deuces and the block flooded with C/O's and LT's who broke up the fight, handcuffed the combatants, took them to the hole, and locked the unit down. Both dudes looked battered but neither was seriously hurt.

After we were locked down me and Larry talked about the fight, pointing out punches we might have missed and analyzing the match like we were some boxing analysts or something. I filled Larry in on how P-Nut had most likely stole dude's shit and Larry summed up every convict's feelings when he said, "Served him right then. Fucking sneak thief. He should have stabbed his ass."

PART 22: OUT OF THE HOLE

A week after the fight, Vince came out of the hole. I was glad to see his crazy ass. He told me the black dude he punished signed a seperatee and wouldn't be coming back on the pound until Vince went home. But that wouldn't be long. It just depended on how much halfway house the unit team put Vince in for. The vato was getting short.

"Mira, Guero," he said. "I saw that pinche Dave."

"Oh yeah," I said. "Que pasa con el?"

Vince kind of gnashed his teeth and scrunched up his face and said, "That boriqua had the nerve to tell me that I owe him money. He was like, 'Donde esta la feria?' And I was like, what money? And that boriqua said, 'The money you were supposed to collect for me. Tu tienes la lista.'"

I was checking Vince out as he talked and I could tell he was fucked up. He continued, "I told Dave that Roberto got all that money. Oh yeah, they transferred that puto tambien. But Dave kept saying that he knew I collected some of the feria. I was like, whatever, fuck you. Then the boriqua told me I better get his money straight."

I was like, damn, Dave must be tripping.

"You know, he's the orderly too," Vince said. "Painting cells and the like. That motherfucker was all up in front of my door everyday pulling that cell gangsta shit. I finally told him that I didn't have any of his fucking money and that he was a fucking snitch anyway so he better shut the fuck up."

Vince threw up his hands as I was taking it all in. Then he finished by telling me, "Dave flipped when I called him a snitch. He started yelling, 'I ain't no fucking snitch! You lucky you in that cell motherfucker. You a snitch and a thief you bitch motherfucker.' I was like, damn, this boriqua is tripping. I told him to go out to rec if he wanted to deal with something but the motherfucker never went out and never came back on my tier. Then they let me out this morning. I had 15 days left, too. Fucked up, verdad?"

I nodded my head. Dave had tried to flip the script on Vince and Vince seemed kind of dumbfounded. Like he couldn't believe the whole scenario. But that goes to show how dudes flip when the pressure gets to them. I didn't know the whole story or circumstances but it seemed from what Vince said that Dave had seriously fell off his game. And I was now convinced that he was a snitch.

They had put Vince in the 12-man common area with the new kid Brian so I let Vince know the whole scoop about the weed and everything.

"Damn, Guero," he said. "I just talked to Snake and he didn't say nada about that." I guessed that Snake wanted that hustle to himself but I doubted he could hold Vince off. For real, everybody was scared shitless of Vince and for good reason, too. The dude had no conscious. I told Vince my idea of getting Brian to get one of his girlfriend's amigos to visit me and hit me off. Vince liked the idea and said since Snake had the kid on lock and didn't want to cut him in on that he would convince Brian and Snake to roll with my idea so that he and I get in on some of the action. It was all good and I knew Vince would muscle in on the move. He just had to make arrangements.

"Chingow, Guero," Vince said. "I fucking miss Travieso. He was straight cuando se fue, verdad?"

"Simon, esse," I told him. "He left with over four grand waiting for him. I got his abuela's address if you want it."

"Esso buey," Vince said. "You know I'm gonna get with that vato en la calle."

"Es todo, buey," I said, feeling the same. I just hoped that Travieso would keep his shit together. Everything was stacked against him in the streets. Ex-convict, gangbanger, tattoos, criminal record, junkie, two-time loser—it would be hard for him to make it but I held out hope that my carnal would make it. "You're getting short too, esse," I told Vince.

"Tu lo sabes, buey," he laughed. "Tu lo sabes. Let's smoke some of that kind bud you been telling me about. Estoy listo. A fumar buey."

I pulled a packet out of my sock and rolled up a fattie. At least by prison standards it was a fattie. Fox, the NY kid, came over to my cell to check Vince out and we smoked out. Chilling, stoned to the bone, and on some cartoon-like shit. Just another day chilling in federal prison, I thought.

The next day I found out my homeboy Mike the inkslinger had packed out. He would be on his way to the new joint in WVA inside a week. He told me to get up there if I could. I gave his junkie-ass a hug and wished him the best. He told me to look out for our homeboy Duncan on the weed tip and all the other Virginia boys too.

I saw Duncan on the yard later and he was trying to sell me on getting a job with him in UNICOR, the prison factory. He tried to convince me that he could get me right in his section at a high pay grade and that his boss was cool. I told him I didn't know. I wasn't sure about all that work shit. Plus I had heard a lot of dudes say that it was the prison factories like UNICOR that enabled the feds to build so many new prisons.

Duncan also told me that they were making his unit, Whitley B, into the UNICOR unit because it was the closest to the factory and that all the UNICOR workers would be moving up there. I let him know I would consider it but I wasn't sold on the idea. We hit rocks and I bounced on the 7:30 PM move.

Vince found me later that night. He told me that he put the press move down on Brian and Snake and that Brian would be hooking me up with an address to send a visiting list to. Vince was fucked up on some hooch too and invited me down to the 12-man common area.

It seemed La Raza had taken over the room because it was full of Mexicans drinking hooch, burning joints and lounging on the bunkbeds. It was a little party. The vatos were partying and jabbering away in Spanglish. Just my speed, I thought. Vince pulled me over to sit between him and Brian. Brian was showing the esses pictures of his girl and the college life. He showed me a picture of a cute honey.

"That's your girl," I said.

"No vato, that's your girl," he told me. I nodded my head as I understood.

"You gotta write her and send her a visiting list," he continued. To get a visit a prisoner had to send the visitor a form that they filled in and sent back to the prison so that they could be approved. The prison did an NCIC check to make sure the visitor wasn't a convicted felon because the feds didn't want any free-world criminals coming to visit the incarcerated criminals. It was one of their so-called crime preventive measures, I guess.

Brian gave me the girl's address. Her name was Carley, 19 years old and a student at the University of Tennessee like Brian's girlfriend. Finally I would be able to get my hustle on again. And it wasn't a moment too soon because I was out of weed.

"Brian," I said. "Let me get some smoke man. No tengo nada."

Brian nodded, "Alright, I got you. But wait 'til later cuz I got the weed stashed in the light." He looked up, letting me know his stash spot. I hit rocks with him and Vince and went back to my cell to write Carley and send her that visiting list. Brian assured me that she would know what was up so everything was straight.

And it was straight. A couple of weeks later I was in the visiting room with Carley, Brian and his girl swallowing balloons of kind bud. Vince's last two months on the compound were a haze as I stayed stoned on the chronic. Me, Brian, Vince and Snake hustled the weed, getting mad sendouts and smoked like fiends, chilling in the yard for most of the day in the hot summer sun. Todo estaba tranquillo. I was hooking Fox and Duncan up and still smoking out. My girl was piling up the sendouts for me and Vince. I was in the VI every weekend with Carley who was a cute girl but for real was only a means to an end. I mean, I would of hit it if I could have, but no way was she replacing my main girl. Balloons and proximity notwithstanding.

PART 23: INTERRUPTED

Vince, Brian, and Snake were bullshitting and playing cutthroat in the common area. As I walked up I caught the tail end of the conversation and heard Snake telling them how the case manager just put him in for halfway house. That was a surprise to me. I mean, I knew Vince was about to go home but Snake, too? It seemed all my carnalitos were leaving.

"It's like that, simon buey?" I said to Snake when I walked up.

"Like what, vato?" He answered.

"You bouncing on the low, or what?" I said.

"No buey, it's not like that. I just don't put my business on front street. Plus I was gonna try to sneak outta here without paying you that feria, buey," Snake joked.

"Simon, esse," I said playing along. "You better get my feria straight or boom-boom." I formed my hand and fingers into a gun and shot it, blowing the imaginary smoke away. As I did this Brian crept up behind me with his own imaginary guns.

"Damn, vato," Snake said. "You a gangsta, but my homie got the drop on you so you better drop your piece."

I looked around and saw Brian, putting up my hands in mock surrender.

"You got me, vato," I laughed. "I guess you will be leaving without paying me that feria." We all laughed some more and hit rocks all around.

I sat down at the table with them. "Chingow, buey. Travieso left, now you and Vince. You're all leaving a motherfucker all by his lonesome."

"It's time to go, buey," Snake said. "We did our time. You just beginning. You got my homie here to ride with, though." Snake motioned at Brian and said, "You all the new breed. The youngsters. Up and coming, tu sabes?"

"Simon, buey." I said. "And we riding, too. That motherfucking chronic." We all laughed some more as I hit rocks with Brian.

Vince told me the case manager also put him in for halfway house so he was outta there soon. I was happy my carnals were going home but I would miss them and for real, I didn't even like Snake. But he was vato loco, La Raza, you know, and I was down.

A minute later this dread came up to the table. "Hey Brian, mon," he said. "What's up with the ganja, mon? Give us some."

Snake and Vince looked at Brian like, what the fuck? Brian got all squeamish, like he didn't know what to say. I was thinking that this Jamaican had bad etiquette because I knew Vince, Snake, and I didn't fuck with him on that level. We were all waiting for Brian to say something and when he didn't Vince told the dread, "Ain't no buds here, mon," mocking dude's accent.

The dread looked Vince straight in the eyes and said, "Me no talking to you mon, me be talking to Brian. What's up, mon? Gives us a joint, mon?"

I could tell that Vince couldn't believe that shit. He jumped up and smashed the dread right in his face. Blood splattered from his nose. Dude didn't even know what hit him. He fell back holding his hands up and said, "Me just want some bud, mon. Me no want problems, mon. No problems amigos."

The dread was on the ground, trying to stop the blood gushing from his nose. I grabbed Vince before he could do anymore damage and looked around to see if the cop saw. Luckily the cop was up in his office and didn't see anything. A couple of dudes on the block were checking the scene out but turned away as I looked their way. I yelled at Vince to come on and motioned for Snake and Brian to come with us. We ended up in my cell.

"What the fuck was that Jamaican about, Brian?" Vince shouted. "You been running your mouth or what?"

With Vince bearing into him it seemed Brian was trying to melt into the wall. Snake whacked him on the head.

"Que pasa, buey?" he said.

Brian kind of shrank down and weakly said, "I smoked a joint with the dread the other day. But I didn't think he would be asking me for more."

"A la verga, buey," Snake said. "Tu eres un burro. Don't fuck with no mayates like that carnal. You hook them up once and they'll be begging like a dog, me entienedes buey?"

Brian looked chastised after receiving the tongue lashing and Vince was staring murder at him. It just goes to show how quick shit can jump off in prison. Over nothing, for real. And I knew it was on. I was trying to figure out how to diffuse the situation.

I looked out the cell and saw the couple of Jamaicans that lived on the block gathering up around the dread. If I didn't think quick some serious drama was about to jump off. I knew Vince wasn't backing down from nobody. Short timer or not.

"Damn, esses," I said. "We gotta make this right, verdad?"

"Fuck those mayates," Vince said all agitated.

"No Vince, we got to make amends. We don't need no drama. You're going home and Snake too. Let me handle this, alright?" I said trying to think how Travieso would handle this situation.

Vince looked me in the eyes and said, "OK Guero, we try it your way, but if those mayates want some drama I got mad drama for them, me entiendes?"

Snake nodded also and asked me if I had a shank stashed in the cell. I told him no and hoped that I could dead this bullshit that Snake's stupid-ass homie had created.

I looked out the cell window again and noticed this Jamaican Checkly that I played soccer with talking to the group of five Jamaicans, including the dread. They had advanced to the staircase that led up to the tier my cell was on.

"Alright, watch my back," I told them and checked my sock for the two $25 pieces I knew I had there. I saw Snake attaching my lock to his belt in case something went down as I cupped the two packets of weed in my hand and went out to talk with the Jamaicans.

"Fuckin' bumberclots, mon, sucker punch me in me nose, for what? For what? Cuz me want some ganja, mon?" The dread said to Checkly. "That one of dem right there, mon. Fucking amigos. Sock me in me fuckin' nose. Bumberclot."

I saw the five black faces glare in my direction and I motioned to Checkly that I wanted to talk. I looked back to see my carnals checking out the scene from the inside of the cell, then turned back to see the group of Jamaicans at the top of the staircase. I knew if I didn't handle it right shit was about to jump off. When Checkly came up I told him what's up.

"What's up, mon? It seem we be having a little problem here, Guero," he said.

"Yeah, I know," I said. "But check it out, I wanna make it right. Vince was wrong for punching your homeboy, alright? But your homeboy was also in bad form coming up on us like that in the common area asking for some weed, you know?" Checkly nodded as he heard my side of things. I didn't know him well but I respected him and he me and I had never heard anything bad about him. He waited for me to go on. "I want to dead this," I continued. "We ain't looking for no beef. It was a mistake, you know?"

"A mistake, mon? Your man punched my homeboy in the face," Checkly said. "How was that a mistake, mon?"

"Look, Checkly, I said Vince was wrong. But check it. You straighten this out. Make it right, OK? No repercussions. Dead it," I said as I handed him the two $25 pieces. "That's the chronic shit that's been going 'round. Take one for yourself and one for the dread. Look, I'm sorry for what Vince did but you know he will never apologize. So just take that and dead this issue for me, OK? We don't want no beef anyway, you know?"

Checkly looked at me and then looked back at his homeboys. "Me see, OK, mon?" He walked back to his homies. There was some gesticulating and some "bomberclots" but it seemed like Checkly had deaded the issue. The group of Jamaicans bounced and Checkly nodded to me. The dread waited a second and then walked over to me. I could see his nose swelling up and hoped it wasn't broken.

"Me no want no problems, mon," he said to me as he looked toward my cell where Vince and Snake were waiting. "No problem, mon," he repeated in their direction while holding up his hands as if surrendering. I nodded to Dread and he walked down the staircase.

I went back to the cell and found Brian rolling up a fat joint. Just what I needed, I thought. "That shit is dead," I told them and waited for Brian to spark the joint up.

Vince smiled and said, "Good for them, esse, because I was ready to bust some bomberclot ass."

Snake laughed and we all joined in. Sometimes it was better to make light of a serious situation, especially when violence was concerned. Because in prison you never knew when it could overtake you or for what reason. Dudes were killed for trifling shit. And a lot of beefs were over small things.

A week later the kid Brian went back to court on a writ. He said he didn't know why but a lot of times dudes are going back to tell and they just don't want to say. No one was gonna admit straight-up to being a snitch. But with the War on Drugs and the influx of federal prisoners it seemed like there were more and more snitches coming in or going out to court all the time. And it was also a given that a dude was going to snitch when he went back to court within his first year. Dudes would get that 20-year bid and decide they couldn't handle it so they went back to court telling on people and trying to get a sentence reduction. Others already had their deals worked out beforehand and were just waiting to go testify and make someone's family cry. In the feds that type of shit was happening all the time.

The concept of honor and integrity were quietly eroding. The code of the streets was getting twisted as dudes snitched on their mans, their homies, whatever. That was why when dudes came back after going to court the convicts on the pound wanted to see some paperwork so they could know why you were in court. Because if you couldn't produce any paperwork showing an indictment, court date, new charge, evidentiary hearing, or whatever, then the odds were that you were snitching. And dudes would get labeled. And being labeled a snitch was the worst jacket to hang on someone in prison.

I didn't really know about Brian, but the whole thing sounded rather dubious. Plus I was sweating the whole Carley thing. What happens if it was all just a set-up, I thought? I could catch a new case and all. I guessed I would just have to wait and see. But as far as I was concerned that whole Carley weed deal was dead. I stopped writing her and took her off my visiting list so I wouldn't get any temptations. I loved the weed but I wasn't trying to get cased up.

I didn't really talk to Snake after that. I think the whole thing with Brian going back to court fucked him up. I knew he wasn't trying to catch a case either and with these conspiracy joints the prosecutors were vicious. The only one who seemed unaffected by the whole affair was Vince. But he was bad on the hooch. I guessed he was chasing away those demons.

Snake bounced to the halfway house a couple of weeks later and I knew Vince's turn was next. In fact, Vince told me that same day that he was leaving on the following Monday. Damn, I thought. All my carnalitos gone. La Raza were still present on the pound, but a lot of the vatos were new and I didn't really fuck with them.

That weekend I was hanging tight with Vince, who was drunk on hooch. We were in my cell bullshitting. Or rather Vince was with his drunk ass. I didn't drink hooch. For real, I couldn't stand it. It tasted like some flat-ass beer to me and had all kinds of pulpy fruit in it. I tried it once but threw the fuck up and never drank it again. Vince went hard on the hooch though. He was big on making it too. He always had some cooking. Hidden back behind the toilet in the wall of the cell.

Vince was jabbering away in spanglish, telling me all the stuff he was gonna do. How he was gonna be with his kids and family and the like. He was drunk like a motherfucker and prone to fits of laughter. Then all of a sudden he got very serious. "Guero," he said. "Mira, buey. You gotta do something for me, OK, buey?"

I looked at him wondering what he would ask me in his drunken stupor. "I'm serious, Guero," he continued. "I'm not playing, me entiendes?" He looked at me all gravely and told me, "If you ever see that pinche cubano, Roberto, kill him for me, entiendes Guero?" The vato was staring hard right into my eyes as he said this. "Me entiendes, buey?" He asked again. "Kill that motherfucker."

"Simon, carnal," I said, regretting the words as they came out. Because for real, you never knew. And in prison, word is bond.

INTERLUDES 5

"In prison more than elsewhere one cannot afford to be casual."

—Jean Genet

INTERLUDES XVII: KGB

Kensington Gang Bangers. A white boy set out of the Kensington area of North Philly. A gritty and rough section of town with a multi-cultural population. Spider and Vinny were hardcore KGB and these two were schemers. Always up to something. They had their hands into everything on the pound. Whatever hustles they could manage or imagine.

Vegetables, stuff from the laundry, radios, sneakers, boots, stamps—whatever they could buy, steal or trade for a profit. For real, these dudes weren't happy unless they were in the mix or into something. Fights, tattoos, drugs, checking people in, loan sharking—it didn't matter. The Kensington Boys went hard.

Spider was the leader. He was a straight convict. All sleeved-out, tattoos galore, with a reputation as a nutter. He was that type of unpredictable dude. One where you never knew what his next move would be. And with this unpredictability he kept dudes off balance. They tread carefully when they walked his way.

His partner Vinny was the wildcard. A straight I-don't-give-a-fuck motherfucker. This dude had a mouth. He would say whatever came to mind, consequences be damned. I remember this one time he told this white supremist Nazi dude right to his face—"You're a clown, man. A fucking clown. You don't like it? Strap the fuck up. I'm right here, you fucking clown." And the Nazi dude didn't do shit. He just slinked away, hoping no one heard. But dudes took notice.

There were other KGB dudes on the pound but they took a backseat to Spider and Vinny. If called on, KGB could go 10 or 15 deep but that was only if some major drama jumped off. They were a collection of white boys, Puerto Ricans, and blacks. All banded together by the area they were from. They were nothing major on the pound. But they represented.

Spider and Vinny were some serious knuckleheads, though. They were always in the mix. I don't know if they were thick or if they just really didn't give a fuck. Probably the latter because they were always in and out of the hole on various shots and investigations. Just petty shit.

The LT's could never bust them for nothing major, although they were trying all the time. But these dudes were like the Teflon Don. Nothing stuck. They would be under SIS investigations and all but the LT's could never corroborate anything or catch them red-handed. But they were sure trying. There was this one, LT Kerry, who had it out for them. He was always singling them out on the compounds for shakedowns and calling down to the unit and telling the cop to tear apart their cells. It didn't matter if they were up to something or not. LT Kerry always figured they were doing something at all times. He just knew they had their hands in the cookie jar, so to speak.

One time Spider and Vinny took over the eight-man room in the unit and moved all their homeboys in. They were holding card games, making hooch, doing tattoos, and running a store. They had a nice little run. Came up, you know, but as soon as LT Kerry, their nemesis, found out about it he broke the room up. Splitting the crew up and putting them all in different units. He told Spider dudes were dropping notes like crazy. That's how it goes when cowards get jealous. They can't step to you like a man. They can only run to the cops.

For real, the KGB had dudes shook. They weren't on the level of the Bloods or Latin Kings on the pound or even the Muslims, who were the deepest, but they were putting in work. Especially for a mostly white boy set. And they were all homeboys too. Loyal to each other from the street.

When one of Spider's boys got beat up, Spider took it upon himself to right the wrong and rolled up on the offending party. Spider cracked the dude's dome and that was that. He did a little hole time over it but dudes recognized. It wasn't no open season on KGB members.

And in the hole Spider and Vinny raised hell. They would be in there for some bullshit investigation and would fuck with the hole cops for pure amusement. They would flood their cell by clogging up the toilet and repeatedly flushing it until the whole tier was covered in water. Then they would laugh at the cops as they had to walk through it when they counted, soaking their pants and shoes. Spider and Vinny just did not give a fuck. Also, they would shit in a card and put it in an envelope and slide it under the door so that when the cop picked it up for the outgoing mail and inspected it he would get shit all over his hands. These dudes were buck wild and not above anything for some amusement.

And Vinny would get busy, too. He had a habit of exposing rats and bullshitters. He would call them out. One on one, you know, if they wanted it. Fists, shanks, lock in a sock—whatever. Vinny didn't give a fuck. I remember Vinny had this crazy laugh, too. It sounded like something from an insane asylum. And the motherfucker had a big-ass head. Dudes would call him jughead and shit. But not to his face.

The KGB boys had it going on. A lot of them worked on the PM compound shift. They would move about the compound with their Cadillacs (cleaning stuff) bullshitting, hanging out, and making moves. They always knew what was up because at night they had the compound on lock. Scoping out what was going on.

They were making moves, too. They had two cops who would take them into the kitchen, the laundry or whatever and let them fill up net bags with vegetables, kitchen food, laundry items, clothes, boots, thermals, or whatever. Back on the block they would sell these items off, and for cheap, too. They weren't trying to get rich. Just make a hustle. Live a little, you know.

A lot of dudes didn't like Spider and Vinny. They talked shit behind their backs, but never to their faces. And don't let them find out because they would bring it. They weren't no fake-ass clown motherfuckers. They got their respect.

They would steal anything, too. Vinny was the bold one. Creeping up to the cop's window on the outside on the unit and sticking his hands in and stealing whatever he could reach.

Be it a pen, a sandwich, a soda. He didn't care. He was a kleptomaniac for real.

He would talk mad shit to the cops, too. Dare then to do something. But most of the police knew that Spider and Vinny didn't give a fuck. On the pound or in the hole, it didn't matter to them. They were just biding their time trying to get their hustle on.

Waiting for that big score so that they could come up. No different then a lot of dudes on the inside. They were just a little more aggressive. I figured for every one thing they got busted for they got away with nine. Not a bad success rate by any means. Now if they could just stay outta the hole.

INTERLUDES XVIII: SNEAK THIEVES

Mo-Mo was a sneak thief. He didn't give a fuck. He would creep up in a mothefucker's cell and clean it out. That was how he did his bid. He wasn't getting no yellow slips in the mail and he had plenty of nerve, so why not, he thought. He only stole from suckers anyhow. And he covered his bets. Because Mo-Mo was a gambling man. And he decided long ago that he wasn't taking no fall for stealing or being branded as a thief. Because once branded the label stuck and Mo-Mo had some years to do. He couldn't afford no shank in the back or sneak thief jacket, so he created contingency plans.

He went in with the thought that every potential theft would be found out. Because a prison compound is like a fishbowl. One way in, one way out and somebody will always see something. So Mo-Mo always recruited a not so bright partner to do the actual heisting and holding of stolen objects. Then he would always be in the clear. And if something did go down, Mo-Mo could always point the finger at his fall guy.

Like I said, Mo-Mo wasn't going down for no bullshit and prison was a violent world. He didn't want to have to face any repercussions. So he schemed, plotted, and betrayed as necessary. He wasn't greedy. He just needed a little something so he could live. He wasn't trying to be no broke-ass cat, but he could share the wealth. Share the danger, share the wealth, he thought. Especially if it entitled him to less risk of getting his dome cracked.

Mo-Mo had been on the block a couple of years and he had pulled off a bunch of heists. He had manipulated events so that often his partners in crime or other dudes altogether took the blame when shit jumped off. Mo-Mo played the dumb country boy from Tennessee but he was a cutthroat for real. Some dudes on the block knew the score but they didn't fuck around with Mo-Mo and Mo-Mo didn't fuck around with them or their stuff. It's called respecting a man's hustle.

Mo-Mo had perfected his act over the years and he was a combination of both slick and vicious. He preyed on new dudes. The unaffiliated, the new commitments, the rats, and the suckers. They were Mo-Mo's hustle.

A lot of new cats had transferred in recently and been assigned to the block. And anyone in prison knows new dudes are fair game. Mo-Mo scoped them out and figured he found his next vic. The dude was a high roller and big gambler out of Virginia. Just came down from the pen and word was he had money. A big willie type. But for real he wasn't no killer and Mo-Mo figured that dude wasn't built for no action. He had also heard that dude got robbed at the pen. So Mo-Mo started planning his heist.

Mo-Mo liked to work with partners so he recruited this young kid from New York who thought he was gangsta. This cat was a perfect fall guy, Mo-Mo thought. He worked as an orderly in the unit, like Mo-Mo, didn't have any money coming in, and had the run of the unit during the day when most other prisoners were at work or in the yard. The dude from Virginia went by VA and he was assigned a job in the yard so every morning at work call he was off to the yard and didn't return until after lunch.

A couple of weeks passed while Mo-Mo checked and studied VA's routine and gave him a chance to stock up from the store. Then one Monday Mo-Mo heard that VA hit the parlay ticket big and got paid off in stamps. Sixty books or something was the rumor. Mo-Mo knew it was time to strike so the next morning after he laid out the plan to the NY kid, Sean, they struck. Those 60 books would be his, Mo-Mo thought.

When VA went to the yard at work call Mo-Mo and Sean put their plan into action. They had some mop buckets and garbage cans up on the tier by VA's cell and Mo-Mo was mopping the section right by VA's cell, effectively cutting off that end of the tier to traffic. Not like there was that many people there anyway. While Mo-Mo stood lookout Sean went into VA's cell, smashed the lock, and robbed his locker. He took commissary, shoes, sweats, a radio, Koss headphones, and the 60 books of stamps that were stashed in a pair of Air Jordans.

Sean loaded the stuff in a mop bucket, wheeled it out and then he and Mo-Mo pushed it down the range transferring the stuff to a garbage can in the mop closet. They would get the stuff later when the coast was clear and move it into Sean's locker. At least that was the plan.

When VA got back to his cell at lunch he was pissed. Sneak thief motherfucker, he thought. He didn't raise no fuss, though. He played it cool. He had learned from that time at the pen when those Detroit cats robbed his locker. He learned to play it cool and wait. If you got all blustery and made a big scene like most dudes did all that did was make you out to be a chump trying to draw the cops attention. Especially if you didn't bust nobody's head. Then dudes would be saying you were fronting for the cop. VA would play this one cool, scope out what really went down and then bust some ass. It was time to play the waiting game, he thought. And then I'll get mines and punish the motherfucker that did this, he promised himself.

Mo-Mo watched VA walk in and back out of his cell like nothing had happened as he mopped the opposite end of the tier. This puzzled Mo-Mo because usually when dudes got robbed they came out all mad, talking about how they were gonna fuck somebody up, and asking prisoners if they saw anybody by their cell. But this dude VA played it real cool like. Just walked back out the unit like he was on his lunch break and shit. Damn nigga, Mo-Mo thought. What the fuck is up with that? Like you ain't all concerned and shit that your stuff got robbed.

Mo-Mo figured he was right on when he pegged the cat as soft. Nigga ain't gonna do nothing, he thought. Good—him and Sean would divide the shit up later. After I pick out any good stuff and pocket all the 60 books for myself. Mo-Mo smiled to himself for a job well done. That shit was easy, he thought.

But later on he wasn't too sure. A bunch of Virginia dudes had been down on the block. Asking questions and shit. Dude called in the calvary. One even stepped to Mo-Mo and asked him if he knew anything about some shit getting stolen on the block. Bitch-ass nigga ran to his homeboys, Mo-Mo thought. Well ain't nothing gonna come of it. Nobody seen shit, at least that was what Mo-Mo thought.

It seems somebody did scope out the move and he was a Virginia boy, too. A white boy, though. Straight country dude who went by Hillbilly. Now Hillbilly was an old coot and racist, too. He didn't fuck with no blacks but he knew the score. He'd been on the block awhile and he knew how Mo-Mo operated. He was medically unassigned so he stayed up on the block in his corner cell, which gave him a view of the whole triangular-shaped unit. And Hilbilly hated Mo-Mo's black ass. Thought the brother was a parasite, feeding off the life blood of other prisoners. But Hillbilly was old school also. He wouldn't snitch on his worst enemy. He didn't fuck with VA either. Didn't even know they were homeboys. Not like he would claim a black for a homeboy, anyway. But he knew some of the Virginia dudes that came down on the unit asking shit on VA's behalf. And nigger or no nigger, Hillbilly thought, some of them dudes were straight. So a couple of weeks after VA had been hit he got a little jewel.

VA's homey Big Mike gave him the 411. Told him he should step to that orderly cat Mo-Mo. Told him Mo-Mo knew what the fuck was up. You see, Hillbilly didn't finger nobody, he just pointed them in the right direction. What would be, would be, he thought. It's them niggers' business anyhow, he told himself. But for real, Hillbilly hoped Mo-Mo got what he deserved. Hillbilly just couldn't let himself tell outright though because then he would be a snitch and he couldn't live with that. He was an old-school convict. Had morals and shit. Not no new jack like all the prisoners who populated the feds nowadays.

VA stepped to Mo-Mo on the low. "Yo, my brother," he told Mo-Mo. "I ain't saying nothing but someone told me you might know something about that locker break in a couple of weeks ago."

Mo-Mo did a double take because he had to figure out if dude suspected him or if he was just fishing. Mo-Mo figured the latter and played along with the dude. "I don't be knowing for sure, boss," Mo-Mo drawled in his Tennessee accent. "But I be seeing things. You know I be working on the tier and shit. I let you know, alright, boss."

VA looked Mo-Mo in the eye and said, "Alright, get back at me."

As he walked away, Mo-Mo figured he had played the dude with that slow country routine. But now, thought Mo-Mo, I am in a jam. And he wasn't taking no heat for the job. Especially since dude had all his homeboys in on it. Investigating and shit. But Mo-Mo had taken precautions. He had Sean, the NY kid, as his fall guy. And it seemed that Sean might have to play his part. It was the part he was meant to play in Mo-Mo's master plan. But Sean didn't know this. Sean was fucked up over the whole deal anyway. He figured Mo-Mo played him. Took the whole 60 books of stamps and didn't give Sean shit. Plus Mo-Mo took the Air Jordans and they were sweet. Not that Sean could have worn them but he could have sold them. I ain't fucking with that nigga no more, Sean thought. With all that slow country shit. He a crafty nigga. But Sean didn't know how truly crafty Mo-Mo was.

As soon as Mo-Mo decided what to do it was only a matter of putting his plan into action and letting it play out. As long as he was home free he didn't give a fuck for real. Fuck that nigga Sean, he thought, he knew the risks. You play, you pay. So Mo-Mo took the Air Jordans, gave them to his man in D-block and told him to sell them cheap to some New York dudes. At the same time Mo-Mo hollered back at VA.

"Yo, bossman, check it out," Mo-Mo said conspiratorially. VA came over.

"What's up, my brother."

"Look, I ain't no snitch but I saw this kid walk out your cell with some Air Jordans," Mo-Mo said, setting the bait.

"Oh yeah," replied VA with interest.

"Yeah, that kid from cell 26. I heard he sold the Air Jordans to some of his New York homeboys in D-block."

"Alright, thanks, my brother, good looking," said VA as his mind started spinning. He wanted to punish the dude but he had to do this right, he thought. He had to check up on Mo-Mo's information so he bounced on the move to holla at his homies.

Mo-Mo watched him go, knowing he had set the plan in motion. Now he would watch it play out.

VA's homeboys confirmed that some New York dude in D-block was sporting the Air Jordans that matched the ones stolen from VA the next day. That was all the proof that VA needed. That kid Sean from New York was the one. VA didn't worry about getting his shit back because that would create more problems, but he would get his respect. That was for sure.

VA waited another week. He didn't want to rush nothing. He played it like that shit was dead. Like he didn't even know. He watched that cat Sean. Checked his routines. He noticed that Sean stayed up late night watching videos in the BET room on the weekends and slept late until the 10AM count. The weekends were his only days off from mopping the tier so Sean relaxed. VA made up his mind that next Saturday would be the day.

Mo-Mo was watching, too. He expected some shit to jump off by now. He figured it would be a big Virginia-New York beef on the pound and they all would get locked up and shipped. Mo-Mo couldn't stand the waiting. He didn't know what that cat VA was up to and that worried Mo-Mo, but he played it cool and waited as well. That next Saturday morning he was woken about 8:30 AM by some prisoner screaming bloody murder.

Again, Hillbilly saw the whole thing go down. He was sitting in his cell like normal, drinking coffee with the door propped open. He watched VA go down to the microwave with a coffee cup, take a bottle of baby oil out of his pocket, look around, and squirt the baby oil into the coffee cup which he then put into the microwave.

It's going down, thought Hillbilly, and about time. He only hoped that Mo-Mo got his. But Hillbilly was disappointed when VA went into cell 26 instead of Mo-Mo's cell. That was the cell of Mo-Mo's partner in the heist, Hillbilly knew, but he was hoping Mo-Mo would get it, too. It wasn't a second later that the screaming started.

VA had gone into Sean's cell and found him sleeping. "Yo, nigga, wake up."

Sean looked up from under his covers, just waking up and wondering why that dude VA was in his cell. The next moment Sean was screaming in pain. His face and hands were burning. Melting, even. It was unlike anything Sean had ever felt before. That dude VA had thrown something on him, Sean thought somewhere deep inside his mind. But the pain and screams drowned out all further thoughts. VA looked at Sean on his bed in shock and screaming. He was sitting up in his bed with his hands in front of his face. His arms, hands, chest, and the whole front of his face were burnt bad, almost melted like, from the baby oil. The dude looked horrific, thought VA. Like a wax statue melting. But fuck it, he had it coming, the sneak thief motherfucker, VA told himself.

VA kicked the screaming burnt dude in the face with his prison-issue steel-toe boots. "Fucking sneak thief punk," VA spit as he kicked Sean again, smashing his nose in the process. "Was it worth it? Was it worth it?"

But Sean didn't answer. He was still screaming in pain and hadn't even felt his nose shatter as the boot impacted on his face. Blood started gushing on the white cotton blanket, which was partially burnt and drenched in baby oil.

VA turned around and left. At least I got my respect, he thought. Motherfucker will think twice before stealing from me again.

The cop eventually came and found the mess that was Sean. They took him to the PA and then to an outside hospital. They said he scarred something awful and that he was pressing charges against VA.

I never saw VA again. They locked him up in the hole later that day. But Mo-Mo is still up on the tier, mopping and planning his next heist.

INTERLUDES XIX: MISCONCEPTIONS

Matty Ward was a young street tough from Charlestown, a rough-and-tumble area of Boston notorious for bank robbers. Throughout the Bureau of Prisons, Boston dudes, especially those from Charlestown, were renowned as go-hard motherfuckers. These inner city hoodlums were of Irish stock and bred in the Irish tradition of booze and brawling. It was just how they carried it. How they were brought up, you know.

But anyway, Matty was a young kid, coming up in the world. Early 20's and in the feds on an ecstasy possession charge. He was only doing a couple of years but he still went hard. He had earned a reputation on the streets of Charlestown as a hothead and a dude not to be trifled with. And for real,

Matty reveled in his notoriety. He perpetrated his infamy whenever and wherever he could. And his legend grew.

The thing was, Matty was a little tiny dude. About 5'4" tall and a buck fifty. But he had this reputation as a monster. As an ass kicker of gigantic proportions. A real bootstomper, you know. He had developed this reputation through random outbursts and actions designed for the grandest effect in prison and on the streets. How much was true and how much wasn't was open to debate, but as they say, Matty was a legend in Charlestown and a hero to many dudes his age.

Matty had been on the pound for a couple of years. It was only a low-security prison but it was still prison. Matty spent his time making connections and enhancing his legend at every opportunity. He hung out with Mexican gangbangers. Hobnobbed with mafia guys. He even had his own little crew of roughnecks who extorted, robbed, and terrorized other prisoners. One of the capos from John Gotti's Gambino crime family was a personal friend of little Matty Ward. Matty was running with men twice his age and his name alone conjured fear and respect in the prison and back home in the streets of Charlestown as his exploits touched Boston.

One day another Charlestown tough and legend arrived at the prison Matty was at. All the Boston dudes came running to Matty. "Matty," they said. "Ronny Doe is here. Ronny Doe is on the compound."

Ronny Doe, Matty thought. Now there was a real Charlestown legend. Matty had been hearing about Ronny Doe since he was nine years old. Ronny was a tough guy who had done a stretch of state time at the most violent of Massachusetts's prisons. Now he was in the feds, too. Matty knew he just had to meet Ronny Doe. In fact Matty had always wanted to meet him since he was a kid. Everybody in Boston had heard of Ronny Doe. He was infamous. He was everything Matty Ward wanted to be.

"Set it up," Matty told his boys. "I gotta meet Ronny Doe." His boys ran off to set up the meeting between two of

Charlestown's most notorious thugs. Matty looked up to and admired Ronny Doe, but still, he was Matty Ward, he wanted to meet Ronny as an equal. He wasn't a kid anymore and from everything he had heard about Ronny Doe he knew the guy was about all of it—a straight killer, you know. Matty could only wonder what the infamous Ronny Doe looked like. He must be a monster, he thought.

Matty's boys relayed the message to Ronny Doe. Damn, Matty Ward, Ronny thought. Who would have thought that I'd run into that crazy motherfucker. Ronny Doe had heard the stories that said Matty Ward was certifiable. A verifiable lunatic. Do I really want to meet this young lunatic, Ronny wondered. He was getting older and was finding it harder to live up to the notoriety of his youth. And here was this up-and-coming tough who might use Ronny to further his own legend. But these thoughts quickly subsided as Ronny thought, fuck that, I'm Ronny Doe. A fucking legend. Am I not?

The meeting was set for after dinner on the yard. All the Boston dudes were gathered. Two of Charlestown's legends were going to meet for the first time. Dudes didn't know what to expect. Would they meet peacefully or would there be some drama? A lot of dudes thought Matty would try to knock Ronny off so that he could claim the title of big dog on the pound. As it was, Matty was already calling the shots for the Boston dudes but Ronny's presence could threaten Matty's position with their homeboys on the pound. And everybody agreed Matty didn't want that and wouldn't tolerate it. But then again, Ronny Doe was Ronny Doe. Everybody had heard of him. He was an original gangster. Notorious, and a true legend from the streets. Expectations were running high and you could cut the tension with a knife.

Matty walked onto the yard with his entourage not knowing what to expect. He was looking all over, scanning the faces, checking for Ronny Doe. He must be a monster, Matty thought. But he didn't see anyone who fit the profile he had imagined.

One of the Boston dudes hit Ronny's arm. "Here comes Matty Ward," he said. Ronny scanned the group of youths coming toward them trying to figure out which one was Matty. He imagined that Matty was a big dude from all the stories he'd heard but, like Matty, Ronny couldn't see anyone that fit the profile.

The two groups came together and everyone held their breath in expectation. Matty was looking all around trying to figure out who Ronny Doe was. He didn't see anyone who he imagined could be the infamous Ronny Doe.

Ronny looked back to one of his homeboys with a questioning glance. At the same time, Matty was questioning one of his boys and as the dude pointed Matty looked up to see a goofy-looking, kinda fat dude with glasses staring right at him.

Ronny's homeboy pointed at this little pipsqueak dude that Ronny had hardly noticed. The little dude was staring right at him. Almost simultaneously Matty and Ronny said:

"You're Ronny Doe?"

"You're Matty Ward?"

Both in disbelief, they each nodded their heads. All the Boston dudes looked on not knowing what to expect. Damn, Ronny thought, he looks like's somebody's kid brother. This is the big, bad Matty Ward I've heard so much about?

God damn, Matty thought. This is the notorious Ronny Doe? He looks like someone's nerdy, broken down computer geek uncle. But all at once the tension of great expectations fell off of both Matty's and Ronny's shoulders. They smiled at each other. A kind of secret, knowing smile that those in the limelight share.

"Matty Ward," Ronny Doe said, nodding in acknowledgement.

"Ronny Doe," Matty nodded back. They both stepped forward, shook hands, and patted each other on the back. The crowd of Boston dudes erupted in a cheer as their two heroes met.

"Damn, Matty," Ronny said in his ear. "I expected some kind of lunatic."

Matty stepped back, astonished for a minute. "Yeah," he said. "I thought you were a fucking monster or something. All the stories, you know?"

"Well, you know how that goes," Ronny said good-naturedly. "I'm glad to know you're just a regular guy like me." He winked at Matty and they both laughed.

"But come on, kid, we're Ronny Doe and Matty Ward. We gotta give these guys a wicked good show, you know?" And with that Ronny started screaming. "It's fucking Matty Ward." He said pointing at Matty. "Unfucking believable. Matty motherfucking Ward." The crowd of Boston dudes cheered louder again.

"Yeah, motherfuck. It's goddamn Ronny Doe. Can you fucking believe it?" Matty yelled. "Ronny Doe." The crowd cheered again even louder.

Everybody started patting Matty and Ronny on the back and shaking their hands. As they both reveled in their notoriety Ronny winked at Matty again as if to say, good act, kid. And Matty knew exactly what he meant.

INTERLUDE XX: CELL REMOVAL

Dean Valley went hard. He was a marine in Leavenworth, the military prison, for a rape charge. Supposedly the rape charge was bogus but Dean took it anyway. Like he had a choice.

He was on shore leave in Italy with two of his semper fi buddies, shit-faced drunk, and in their drunken stupor they decided to hire an Italian prostitute. All three of them fucked her one after the other but due to the language barrier there were some discrepancies about the cost of the services. The price the prostitute first told them was quickly multiplied by three after Dean and his buddies finished with her. The drunk marines figured she was trying to scam them and they weren't going for it. So they beat the shit out of the prostitute after she attacked them demanding more money.

They didn't know it at the time, but they had seriously fucked up. The prostitute went to the Italian authorities claiming rape by three American marines and they were quickly snatched up. But just as quickly, the American military stepped in and snatched them back. They weren't leaving three of their boys to face Italian mob justice.

Dean thought it was all bullshit anyhow. How the fuck do you rape a prostitute? he thought. And anyway he didn't rape nothing. He punched her around a bit but the fucking whore deserved it, he thought. All up in his face demanding more money when they had already paid her. Gold-digging bitch, Dean thought. But now he was in some shit.

To appease the Italian authorities the American military quickly held a military tribunal for the three marines. What really fucked Dean up though was that one of his marine buddies turned state and testified against the other two. He was a little rich boy from a family with a long military lineage and couldn't afford the strain the trial might put on his family. So he copped out to a lesser battery charge and offered up the other two, Dean being the main one as dude old it.

So Dean was convicted by the military for a rape he didn't commit. He was sent to Leavenworth the military prison with a sentence of 3 years and was dishonorably discharged from the marines. To say the least, Dean was mad. Infuriated even. He was a determined, strapping young man who had wanted to make his fortune in the marines. He was ready for battle and the glories of war. He was ready to kill for his country and now there was nothing. It was all over. He was kicked out of the marines and sentenced to three years in the military prison for a crime he didn't commit. He couldn't believe it.

And in fact, he really didn't give a fuck anymore. Everything he had wanted, everything he had aspired to be, was gone. In his anger, Dean started lashing out immediately. At other prisoners at Leavenworth, the military police who acted as guards, whoever. It didn't matter. In his mind, Dean was fighting the whole world. The military establishment. Everybody. Wrongly convicted and with his life taken from him he figured he had nothing to lose. Like I said, Dean Valley went hard.

He first got in trouble at Leavenworth when he jumped on an older ex-Navy guy who sex played him. Dean beat the shit out of the guy and when the old head came back later with a shank Dean took it from him and beat the shit out of the old head again. But Dean didn't kill him or even cut him up with the shank. He let his fists do the talking and the old queer got the message. Dean gained a lot of respect on the yard after that and dudes gave him a wide berth.

But it didn't take much to set Dean off. He had a couple of other beefs with prisoners. Went to the hole a couple of times and was generally just disorderly but then he seriously fucked up for the second time in his life. He had always been lippy with the guards. Flippant, even, and the guards knew he was one to watch. But some of them were young men, too, and they really tried Dean. Again and again they would try to humiliate and disgrace him. Using and abusing their authority over him. Power tripping on this prisoner who was in on a rape charge and who was considered to be a tough guy at the prison.

"You're not so tough," they told him. "Did it make you feel tough to rape that woman?" they asked. The guards went on and on, fucking with Dean in every way imaginable. Shaking down his cell. Ripping it apart. Confiscating his property. Singling him out for strip searches. Whichever and whatever way they could. They fucked with him.

It was psychological warfare. They were conducting an intimidation and harassment campaign. They were trying to break Dean. But Dean wasn't having it. Some of the older prisoners told him to chill. To just take it all in stride. That the MP's were just trying him and that they would back off eventually and tire of fucking with him. Dean followed their advice for a while but eventually he couldn't take it anymore and he snapped. He attacked a guard and beat the shit out of him. Breaking the guard's nose and eye socket. And when the inner and repressed rage was released there was no turning back.

Dean was locked up in the hole and was cased up again for his assault on the guard. He received three more years for assaulting the MP. But that wasn't the only repercussion he faced. Late one night a group of guards came to his cell, asked him to cuff up, and took him to the recreation area where some more MP's waited and beat the living shit out of him while he was handcuffed and had no ability to defend himself.

Then they returned him to his cell and left him there to heal. This became like a regular game for the guards. They would cuff Dean up in the middle of the night, take him to the rec cage, and beat the shit out of him. Again and again this happened. For Dean it was a never-ending cycle and sometimes it would take him months to heal. At first he went along with these beatings figuring he had it coming and that the guards would tire of their sport. But as it seemed to go on and on with no end in sight Dean decided to make a stand.

The next time when he healed up and the guards came to his cell he refused to cuff up. This seemed to deter the guards but in effect it started a new chapter in Dean's never ending tragedy. The cell removal. When a prisoner refuses to cuff up and leave a cell in the hole the guards call in the goon squad who come in battle-ready gear with body armor, shields, helmets, batons, stun guns, and mace. Their job is to remove the prisoner from the cell by any means necessary. These events are supposed to be videotaped to ensure that proper procedure is adhered to, but such atrocities occur in cell removals that they are barely ever recorded in full.

Dean was a tough guy and he went hard but he had no idea what was about to happen to him. The cell removal team treated their targets no better then animals being led to the slaughter and they used maximum force in their cell extractions. When Dean refused to cuff up and get beat the fuck up he figured he had won finally. But never in his worst nightmares could he have figured how badly he had really lost.

The cell removal team arrived in the hole looking like some mother-fucking teenage-mutant-ninja turtles and ordered him to cuff up. When Dean refused, they went into action. They came into Dean's cell with shields up and batons flying. Striking him in the legs, arms, and torso as he tried to defend himself. Dean's only advantage was the confined space. Only two of the cell removal team members could effectively maneuver in the cell at a time. Dean fought but it was in vain. They pinned him against the wall with their shields then zapped him with the stun gun.

As Dean lay dazed they restrained him by choking him with the baton and putting two feet into his back as he was pinned on the floor. They didn't care that they were choking the life out of him. After they restrained him they stripped his cell of all amenities—books, toiletries, soap, mattress, sheets, blankets, whatever—and four-pointed him to the cold metal bed frame in his underwear. Being "four-pointed" is when they handcuff each of the prisoner's limbs to a corner of the bed so that in effect the prisoner is lying spread eagle on the bed, completely restrained. They kept Dean like this for three days, turning him over every now and then. They didn't even care if he had to piss or shit or anything. And they threw his chow in front of his face for him to nibble on like a dog.

The beatings had been bad but this was the worst humiliation Dean had ever borne. But still he would not break or give his keepers the satisfaction of hearing him complain or whine. He vowed revenge and started making plans. Other prisoners in the hole noticed his plight and when he was un four pointed and led to another cell they cheered for him. Banging against the doors in a frenzy of noise. But Dean heard nothing. He just knew that the next time it would be different. When they placed him in his new cell in the hole and gave him his property back he would be ready.

During this time he was accumulating an obscene amount of incident reports. Refusal to stand for count, insolence, refusal to obey an order, attempt to start a riot, refusal to obey cell assignment, minor assault on an officer...the list went on and on. But Dean didn't give a fuck. He was too far gone. It was him against them. Dean Valley versus the world.

Every time they came to his cell to give him a shot or attempted to take him to a disciplinary hearing he refused. He would not leave the cell. And he knew the cell removal team was coming. They gave him a break for about a week to see if he would come around and conform but after the umpteenth refusal to cuff up they sent the cell removal crew in. But Dean was ready. Dean shaved all the hair off his body with a razor. Even his eyebrows. He didn't want anything the guards could grab onto. His underarm hair and everything. Next he stripped down to nothing, buck naked, and squirted baby oil all over himself. He covered his body in baby oil and Vaseline so that he would be all slippery when they tried to grab him. Finally he squirted shampoo all over the floor to make it slippery for the goon squad in their boots and teenage-mutant-ninja turtle getups. Naked and glistening he stood there ready.

The cell removal team stood ready at Dean's cell door and ordered him to cuff up. When he refused they entered and tried to grab him but Dean was too slippery because of the baby oil and Vaseline and he fought them. Slipping out of their grasp. Also the guards kept slipping as the shampoo underfoot mixed with water made getting proper footing impossible. As they slipped and fell Dean wiggled and squirted away from them, punching and kicking as best he could. He managed to grab a hold of a stun gun and started zapping the guards. Dean had taken the extra precaution of taping up his genitals also so the guards wouldn't try to grab hold of his dick to restrain him.

As Dean zapped the guards more goon squad members entered the cell, as the first two were laid out on the floor stunned. They slipped and fell too, and as this Keystone Cops routine played out Dean had seven of the cell removal team members in his tiny cell either on the floor or on top of each other. It was a mass of bodies all trying to restrain Dean.

The sounds of all this were heard by the other prisoners in the hole and they started banging on their doors, yelling, screaming and cheering for Dean. Eventually the guards restrained Dean as he tired but it had taken them a full 15 minutes to do so. This was an unheard of amount of time for a cell removal as most were usually completed in about 2 or 3 minutes.

When the Lieutenant came in the cell he was livid. Never had he been so embarrassed. As Dean was pinned face first on the ground with a baton pinioned under his chin choking him, the Lieutenant kicked Dean in the side and cursed him. He grabbed a baton and told the guards to spread Dean's legs so he could shove the baton up Dean's ass. But Dean figured out what he was attempting to do and fought for all he was worth, tired as he was. Dean would not allow himself to be violated like that.

After 10 minutes of struggling the Lieutenant gave up and instead zapped Dean repeatedly with the stun gun and sprayed mace in Dean's eyes. Luckily for Dean more staff showed up by this time, including the medical officer, after the unheard of 25-minute cell removal struggle. With the presence of other staff the sadistic Lieutenant couldn't re-attempt his earlier efforts. Dean relented as he fell into unconsciousness.

He woke up four-pointed to the bed again. They left him like this for three more days, then took him to a new cell, and gave him his property back. But Dean wasn't through. This was a battle. His own little personal battle of will versus the institution, the administration, and the whole system. Dean wouldn't give in, ever.

So the cell removals continued. Fifteen in all over the next year. And all as violent and time consuming as the first one. It got so that the goon squad dreaded performing the cell removal procedure when they knew it was Dean. "Not Valley again," they would say. And on the compound Dean was slowly becoming a hero, a legend, as word of his battles seeped out of the hole. It got so bad that prisoners on the compound started demonstrating to get Dean released from the hole.

But the administration would never do that. That would be admitting defeat. Instead, they shipped Dean out into the federal system. The military did that a lot. When they couldn't handle a prisoner they shipped him into the Bureau of Prisons. It was as much as admitting defeat as it was anything else. So at Leavenworth Dean Valley lived on in infamy. The cell removal king. And in the feds Dean cleaned up his act, at least a little. I mean, he had won, right? And he was gracious in victory.

DRUG DEALER

BOOK SIX

"When you're a houseguest in hell, you learn the devil has many mansions, and you keep shuttling between them for no known reason."

—Leonard Peltier

PART 24: UNICOR

The next Monday Vince gave me a pound and he was out. Back to Cali, you know. He had a wife and kids so I hoped he'd make it but you never knew. The way the system was set up things were defintely stacked against an ex-con staying free, like betting against the house in Vegas. Plus, Vince was a knucklehead. I just had visions of him catching a murder beef for some stupid reason like a dude looking at his baby mama's booty or something.

As I walked back to the unit from R and D I was thinking how all my road dogs had left. All my carnalitos, you know. Travieso, Vince, my homeboy Mike the inkslinger, they were all gone. Even the others like Snake, Leonardo the Latin king, Black Steve from Mo-town, and Dave the Boriqua, who was still in the hole. It seemed everyone with whom I started my bid, everybody who taught me how to bid was gone, you know, for one reason or another. Only Larry the country boy, Fox the NY hustler, and Duncan the skinhead were still on the pound.

And Larry was going square, dude was scared for real. He was totally getting back into the hobby craft thing. Up in rec 24/7, you know. Well not really, but you get my point. I guess that six months in the hole spooked him. He wasn't trying to get in the mix or into any drama or nothing. Dude was turning into a model inmate for real. Sometimes I figured maybe he was getting it right. But you know, water under the bridge. Blah, blah, blah and the whole nine.

Fox the NY hustler was still game but he was getting short, too. He almost had a 10 piece in and he was on point putting down his workout game. Dude was going hard for real and getting sheathed up. The kid had super hero cuts and a serious workout jones. Morning or night it was like, what's up? I'm going to get my money. He was trying to get right and had one eye on the street.

So basically, there wasn't shit happening. Nobody or nothing was jumping off and I started to get bored as fuck. I needed to be in the mix for real. I started hanging out with Duncan the skinhead more. Just for the drama, you know. I guess I was an adrenaline junkie and Duncan and his crew of go-hard white boys were always checking dudes in and having PSI parties. That was what we called a paperwork check.

All the white cons on the pound called Duncan and his crew the Regulators. Because basically they were regulating the white dudes on the pound. But another plus to hanging out with Duncan and his crew was the weed. They were fiends. They would buy the pot, rough it off, or steal it. They didn't give a fuck. And I was down with the weed by any means possible, you know. I spent a lot of time with Duncan and the Regulators just chasing that monkey. Trying to get some buds and the like. Duncan was straight, plus he was my homeboy as a lot of the Regulators were. I was down with them because they loved to get high, you know. They would preach all that white pride stuff but for real, I was not into that racist shit. But they were so I didn't knock it.

I had grown up in Cali and had had all types of girlfriends: white, Filipino, Mexican, black. It didn't matter to me. A pretty girl was a pretty girl. But Duncan and a lot of the other white cons in prison were hung up on preserving the white race. They'd be like, "How could you fuck a nigger chick?" But I didn't sweat it. A lot of dudes were full of shit anyhow, you know. I didn't knock their beliefs but I wasn't trying to be converted either. To me all that shit was wack. Plus, I was down with La Raza. I always wondered what would happen if there was a riot; what race would I be down with? Probably I'd be down with my people if need be but I did wonder about it. That was just how it was in prison. Your skin was your flag color. But for real, I could relate multi-culturally and sometimes the Latinos and blacks just kept it real, you know.

Anyway, Duncan kept pressing me to get a job in UNICOR and eventually I did. I don't know what I was thinking; maybe it was because I was bored. I remember how I'd said at the beginning of my bid that I would never work in UNICOR. A lot of the cons equated it to working in a slave factory and I definitely wasn't a slave, but I did end up working there.

For real though, it wasn't bad. I mean, besides having to get up and actually go to work. From being a drug dealer since the age of 16 until the time I was incarcerated at age 22 I had never had a real job. So I guess you could say Uncior was my first job. Most of the dudes who worked there were the older cons who had been down a minute and had come down from the USP's like Atlanta, Leavenworth, and Terre Haute. On my first days in the factory they would tell me about the massive, three-shift UNICOR factories at those pens that made everything from paper and envelopes to bunk beds and office chairs.

It seemed like some 1984 Orwellian-type shit and here I was stuck in it. And the more I looked around the more it seemed like all the junkies on the pound worked in the factory. Like the cons said, UNICOR was "free money." Nobody really did any work. Dudes were hanging out, talking sports, betting, drinking coffee, smoking cigarettes, and trying to find out who had drugs for sale. It seemed like most of the cons worked UNICOR to support their drug habits.

The factory made army fatigue jackets. For real, it was like a sweatshop, full of prisoners on sewing machines making a dollar an hour. If the ballers on the street could see this, I thought. All these drug dealers, bikers, gangsters, bank robbers and thugs working for peanuts on mother-fucking sewing machines like a bunch of grandmas or sweatshop immigrants. And for real, a lot of them were immigrants.

Illegal entry was a big federal crime it seemed. And some of these dudes could sew their asses off, too. They were regular seamstresses. Only in the feds, I thought. Dudes were working 40-hour weeks for $200 a month just so they could make commissary. And in prison if you didn't have any money coming in that two bills was good living. Big Willie status and all that. If a dude worked in UNICOR you knew his money was good cuz he'd be getting that check every pay week.

The "factory" was just a big aluminum-foil-like rectangle building built up over a slab of concrete. There weren't any walls or offices or anything. Everything was out in the open and cordoned off by painted lines. Duncan's boss was this redneck who pretty much gave Duncan the run of the section if everything ran smoothly.

Duncan was the supergrade expeditor, meaning he was like the floor manager for that section of the factory. I started in a grade two expeditor position even though it would take me a couple of months to work up to that pay grade. I didn't really do shit though. Just pushed carts of material around for the dudes who sewed the pockets on the jackets or whatever. And most of them were on piecework so they were trying to work, you know?

"Damn, Guero," said one con seamstress, "bring me some more bundles. Keep 'em coming, you know."

That was what I got all day. And don't get it fucked up, you know I was stoned every minute. On the smoke breaks me and Duncan would be firing joints up. We had this little cut where we took our breaks. I wasn't selling weed but I was chasing dimes and quarters across the pound with Duncan. We were some fiends and UNICOR paid for it all. Free money, you know.

I could chill whenever I wanted to because Duncan was pretty much my boss. And the dude was a maniac. He liked to stay busy all day. Like a speed freak or something. Sometimes I would swear he was on some crystal meth or something. But dude was just hyper. If there was something that needed to be done, he usually did it. He would be running around all day gossiping and the like, talking about who was a rat or who was no good or who's paperwork was out of order. Duncan loved to expose people. And he backed his shit up. With a shank if necessary. That was just how he bidded.

A couple of weeks later Duncan got me moved up to Whitley-B, which had just been turned into the UNICOR unit. It was pretty cool. Everybody on the block worked in UNICOR so there was a lot of respect on the block. Dudes weren't trying to catch no drama, plus, after 10 at night it was quiet like a motherfucker because all the cons would go to sleep early in preparation for the next day's work. There were about 15 unit orderlies who stayed on the block and cleaned during the day so the unit stayed in first place in the weekly sanitation expectations. That meant we got to eat chow first, stay up late and watch TV, and go to the yard first. The fringe benefits of being a government worker, I guess.

Also at this time there was this big controversy going on at the factory about the INS detainees who worked in UNICOR, most of whom were illegal immigrants, primarily Mexicans. It seemed the American prisoners didn't appreciate the INS detainees taking their American jobs, so to speak, so there was a massive beef going on about who got what pay grade in the factory. If it ain't one thing, it's another, I thought. It was scary how much prison life mirrored the outside world in some ways.

Dudes were twisted because the amigos from Mexico were making more dinero than they were on the regular. But for real, a lot of the amigos worked hard like a motherfucker. But dudes were always hating on something. Jealousy and envy ruled on the inside. This little fracas mounted and when some Mexican got the supergrade position in a section of the factory over a black dude, shit jumped off.

There was some serious drama in the UNICOR factory that day. Dudes getting shanked all around. It was like mass chaos. Mainly it was between the blacks and the amigos. There weren't really any Chicanos involved because they were Americans but they still sympathized with the immigrants. La

Raza was about all the people, even the immigrants most of the Chicanos called wetbacks or muhalos.

After a couple of dudes got stabbed and started leaking all over the factory the SIS LT's came in and closed the factory down while they investigated. The factory managers and prison administrators were hating this because UNICOR was their moneymaker. They had us locked down in the UNICOR unit as SIS did their little Sherlock Holmes impersonation. And due to my Chicano affiliation I got locked up in the hole for the duration of the investigation.

The summer had been passing quickly until I got thrown in the hole. But I knew it wasn't nothing. I didn't fuck with any of the people involved. Hardly even knew them so I knew I would be cut loose after SIS interviewed me and tried to squeeze me for information I didn't have. As soon as they figured that out I would be back on the pound. So I settled in to get some down time when I heard a tapping on my cell window.

"Guero," somebody said. As I looked up I saw a face from the past. Not far from the past, but somebody I wasn't really trying to see. It was Dave the boriqua. He tapped the cell window again, wearing a big smile on his face. "What's up cabrone?"

I stood up to holler at him. "What's up, Dave?" I quickly thought of all the foul shit I had heard about him since he'd been in the hole.

"I'm alright," he replied. "Whatcha doing in here?"

"That UNICOR bullshit," I told him. "I should be out soon though cuz I don't even fuck with any of those dudes involved."

"I heard that," Dave said, still wearing a smile. "You know the cop took a plea?"

That was news to me but I guessed if somebody knew the scoop, Dave would.

"He got fired from the BOP though," Dave continued. "And they gave him probation. Leonardo is lucky he transferred because the cop rolled."

I was wondering what Dave was on about. Just trying to bullshit, I guess. Maybe he thought I was stupid or he was just trying to convince himself of something. I was also thinking that I shouldn't even be kicking it with him but I stayed at the window.

"I didn't get charged with nada," Dave said. "I got a 100 series shot, though and lost good time for the coke. That fucking Roberto. Fuck that Cuban. Carlitos, my bunkie got a shot for the coke tambien."

Oh yeah, I thought, the other cuban.

"I've been an orderly here for almost six months now. I painted every fucking cell in here twice" Dave laughed. "So what's up with Larry?"

"He's chillin," I told him. "Back in hobbycraft, staying busy. I don't think he liked doing that hole time."

"Yeah," he agreed. "The hole sucks. But at least I can move around. They might transfer me soon."

"Oh yeah," I said. "Where to?"

"I don't know yet," Dave said. "What's up with that puto Vince?"

"He went home," I told him.

"Did he? Tu sabes, if I see that puto I'm gonna fuck him up," Dave said. "You know he got over on some of my money don't you?"

I shook my head no thinking that Dave was full of shit but I didn't say anything.

"Yeah, Vince," Dave said as he pounded his fist into the door and kept smiling. "I'm gonna fuck that puto up for real. He's a piece of shit."

It sounds good, I thought, knowing that Vince would fuck this wanna-be, fake-ass Scarface up. "Alright, boriqua," I told him, nodding my head and thinking how much Dave had fallen off. And to think that at one time I actually looked up to this guy. We all live and learn I guess. As Dave bounced I thought to myself, what a snitch-ass motherfucker.

PART 25: THE TRANSFER

I was back on the pound the next week. "Teflon don, Guero," joked Duncan, but he knew I wasn't involved in that bullshit. While I was in the hole they opened UNICOR back up and the day after I got out I was reassigned to my job detail there. Everything was chill in the factory, as everyone was just happy to get back to work and just resume the routine after the week off.

A lot of convicts cried about UNICOR saying they were "working like Hebrew slaves" or that they were "slaving for the man," but for real, most dudes liked it. And with overtime some prisoners were making that $300 or $400 dollar check. Free money, indeed.

I told Duncan about my run-in with Dave the boriqua but Duncan wasn't hearing it.

"Fuck that snitch-ass motherfucker, Guero. You should've spit in his face and not even given him the time of day. Cell gangsta motherfucker."

I knew Duncan was right but I was still accepting the fact that Dave was a snitch because it wasn't so long ago that he was the so-called "man" on the pound. And old loyalties died hard. But I guess that was how shit went in this game we played. Be it on the streets or behind the fences. Because for real, it was all the same. Dog eat dog and vicious for sure. The old clichés of "honor among thieves," "the code of silence," and "death before dishonor" were slowly eroding under the feds' two-pronged assault of the war on drugs and mandatory-minimum sentencing guidelines. Not like I was O.G. or anything. I was just a kid from the suburbs trying to make my way and discover my identity, be it vato loco or whatever.

I wasn't even back in UNICOR for a week when I was called back to my unit to see my team. "Mr. Johnson," the unattractive and beat-up looking country girl asked me.

"Yeah," I said feeling uneasy being called by my given name.

"You need to sign this progress report," she directed.

"What for?" I replied.

"You're being transferred."

Transferred, I thought, what the fuck was up with that? I hadn't even been to team or anything. "I'm not trying to go anywhere," I told her, as if I had some control.

"That doesn't matter, Mr. Johnson," she said curtly. "The BOP has to fill up its new prison in West Virginia and you fit the profile of inmates we're sending up there."

Damn, I thought. Ain't that a motherfucker. But being the convict that I was portraying to be I refused to sign the progress report. Like my defiance would stop the transfer. Logically I knew it wouldn't but I was in my feelings and when I refused to sign the paperwork the ugly case manager got in her feelings too. Like I was hindering her job productivity or something. Fuck that bitch, I thought.

"Well, Mr. Johnson, you don't have to sign it but you will still be transferred. You can bet on that. That's all. You can leave," she said rudely.

I was thinking, it's like that, right? I wanted to smack the smart-ass bitch in her face but I didn't. I held my tongue; no need to argue when I was in my feelings and the case manager was put out. Anyway I was wise enough to know that I could never win an argument with staff. It was impossible, even if I was in the right.

I went back to UNICOR and told Duncan what was up. "Fuck, dog," he said. "That shit sucks. At least you can hook up with Mike though."

That was right, I thought, my homeboy Mike the inkslinger was already there. He'd been on the first bus up there. I knew he would be holding it down. At least I wouldn't be walking onto a new compound without knowing anyone.

I found out later a bunch of dudes from the UNICOR unit had been selected to be transferred to the new joint. A lot of the dudes were salty but what can you do. We were committed to the custody of the attorney general, you know.

The BOP would be transporting a whole busload of us up there. That was good, I thought. At least we wouldn't be on no diesel therapy shit. That was what the cons called transit, which could take weeks or even months. But it seemed we would be going on a straight shot.

I packed out later that week and me and Duncan canvassed the whole pound to get some weed for my last weekend. On Saturday when we were chilling on the yard, stoned in the late summer sun, some vatos who were down with La Raza stepped to me. I didn't really know these vatos that well but I knew they were out of Cali and that they were cool with Travieso and Vince. I hit rocks with them and asked what was up.

"Oye, vato," the one esse said to me. "Que pasa?"

"Tranquilo, buey, tu sabes," I told him wondering what was up. "Que onda?"

"Mira, homes, I got word from la calle about Travieso," the esse said.

"Oh, yeah," I replied, my interest piqued. "What's up with that vato?"

"Shit is fucked up for him, homes," the esse said, and I could tell it was bad news.

"Travieso got cased up," he continued. "Mi hermana told me he's locked up in LA county on an armed robbery beef."

Damn, I thought, my motherfucking carnalito, that shit was fucked up. Cali had that 3-strikes law and Travieso was definitely a 3-time loser. Plus he was gang affiliated. He'd be up in Pelican Bay on 24-hour lockdown, I thought.

"The vato was robbing Western Unions, tu sabes," the esse continued. "Mi hermana told me he was strung out on chiva and was trying to get la feria together to pay his dealer, me entiendes?"

I nodded my head as everything he said hit me. I knew Travieso was probably looking at life because Cali did not play when it came to ex-cons. There were no second or third chances. Travieso was hit. Motherfucking hell. That shit sucked, I thought. I thanked the vato for giving me the 411 and gave him and the other esse a pound. "Good looking out, vatos," I told them, thankful that they'd let me know what was up.

"Es nada, homes," the one esse said. "I knew you was down with my homey, tu sabes. He always let us know you were straight. Alright, homes."

The vatos nodded and left. I was sitting there stoned and contemplating. I was mad for real. Mad at Travieso for fucking up. We had spent so much time talking about him going straight and making a life for himself outside, but I guess the esse just couldn't maintain. The streets sucked him back in, chewed him up, and spit him back into a jail cell. Just the place he wasn't trying to be. But I guess it's hard to adjust to the street when you've spent so many years in prison.

Because for real, my carnalito was a convict, through and through, so I knew he would be straight. I had heard the California system was one of the roughest but Travieso was a soldier. Vato loco, tu sabes. I just hoped he'd make it out of Pelican Bay because word was that place was vicious and could sap the life out a motherfucker. He definitely wouldn't be back in the feds, though. Just another wasted life filling space in the corrupt machine that Americans call the judicial system.

Wasn't anything judicious about it, though. How could a vato like Travieso, who was basically just a junkie, come to jail for feeding his habit, spend eight years incarcerated— during which time he still fed his habit— and never get the help that he needed to overcome his addiction?

The BOP just put him back out there knowing he couldn't survive. They didn't give him any hope, any tools to work with. They just spit him out. They called it the war on drugs but they couldn't even keep the drugs out of there own prisons, so what kind of joke was that? Once a criminal, always a criminal must have been their logic, but it was fucked up. Drug addict in, drug addict out, and drug addict back in again. The whole time trying to feed that monster. You would have thought that in a civilized society someone would have figured out that the monster, heroin, was the problem—not the person—but the feds didn't give a fuck. They were too busy building a prison empire.

As I walked back to the unit with Duncan at recall I was hit with the overwhelming feeling that the pound just wasn't the same. I had learned a lot in my first two years of incarceration but I still had a long way to go to become a man. I realized I had to re-prioritize my values. I thought of all the jewels Travieso had dropped on me and wondered why he never took his own advice.

I wondered if I would be like him. Stuck in the life. Stuck in criminal mode. Unable to correct myself and return as a functioning individual to society. I knew I had a lot of growing and learning to do. Being a vato loco in prison brought me respect but what would it bring in the real world? A life sentence like Travieso? Was that what I wanted? Or was it time to strip away the facade of prison life that I was living. All I knew in my stoned mind was that I wanted to survive and to be respected. Because in prison, in the eyes of your peers, that is what it is all about. And for real, we lived in the moment. And I would get that respect by the dull edge of a nine-inch shank if necessary. Fuck all the bullshit. I was bidding.

The next morning I made my rounds. Hitting rocks with dudes and saying my goodbyes. Like I said, the pound wasn't the same, but I still had peoples that deserved props. I couldn't just cut out on them. That would be grimy. And I wasn't no grimy dude.

I said 'later' to my dogs, Larry the country boy, Fox the NY hustler, and Duncan the skinhead. I exchanged addresses and told them I'd holla. And you never knew in the feds—I might see them all again. Duncan gave me a kite for our homeboy Mike the inkslinger. It was just homeboy shit and Duncan exposing dudes as rats but nothing he could've sent through the regular mail. Even though I wasn't trying to go at first I kinda looked forward to hitting the new pound now. Like a fresh start, you know.

I would miss my dogs, for sure. But I was thinking maybe I would stand on my own two feet and not be so dependent on other people. I was sick of being down with the clickas, you know. I mean, I was glad vatos like Travieso and Vince and even go-hard whiteboys like Duncan broke me in, but I was ready to be my own man and not be up under anybody's wing. It seemed like all the cons wanted me to be down with them but for real, I was through with the cliques. Too much drama, you know. I wasn't trying to catch no life bid. I didn't need that kind of drama. I was starting to think about the future and what I would do when I eventually got out but even though I set out with the right mind set my problems were really just about to begin.

On Monday morning at 4 AM I was taken to R and D and after four hours in the small bullpen, crushed in with 30 other convicts who hadn't drank their morning coffee or smoked a cigarette, I was stripped out, chained up, and put on the bus. West Virginia, here I come, I thought as the double hurricane, barbed-wire fences of the first prison I had ever been in faded away against the backdrop of the rising sun as the bus drove away.

PART 26: NEW COMPOUND

It was dinnertime when I strolled out on the new pound where I would be residing. I staggered under my two duffle bags of property as the 30 or so prisoners who journeyed with me followed me out of R and D. It had been an all-day affair and the sun was setting and glaring right into my eyes as I saw prisoners exiting the mess hall straight ahead. All I knew was that I was on top of a motherfucklng mountain in motherfucking WVA in a brand new, medium-to-high security prison.

"Homeboy, what's up, dog?" I heard as I squinted my eyes into the glaring sun, trying to figure out who was calling me. "Motherfucking Guero," the voice said again as my homeboy Mike the inkslinger came into my view and grasped my hand.

It was nice to see a familiar face. "What's up, dog?" I said, happy as shit to see my homey.

"Damn, Guero, you made it, yeah?" Mike said. "I was hoping you'd make it up this way. What unit they put you in?"

"Popular B-Upper," I told him.

"Damn, homey. That ain't my unit, but you'll be straight. I think we got some homeboys up in there." Mike looked at me and smiled. I could tell he was happy to see me too. It was always nice to hook up with a dude you did time with before at a new joint so he could give you the lowdown and the like. Because in prison dudes were always preying on the unaffiliated or trying to expose suckers. So it was good to show dudes on the pound that you had back up.

I came to view prison as a fishbowl with a bunch of sharks swimming around in it. Wasn't any hiding and you couldn't avoid nothing or nobody so you got to just deal with it. Drama or not. And little did I know that I was about to have some serious shit to deal with.

"Let me take that bag, dog," my homeboy said, so I eased one of the bags off my shoulder and gave it to him as he showed me the way to my unit and pointed shit out so I could get a layout of the pound. He made sure I was settled into my cell and told me to hit the yard on the next move so he could give me the 411 on the pound.

I was put in a cell with this kid from West Virginia who was in on a bank robbery charge. They called him the blue-eyed bandit. We kicked it for a minute as I put my stuff up in my locker. "You been in long?" he asked with a drawl.

"For a minute," I answered.

"Oh yeah? This is my first federal bid but I did state time before," he said.

"What's up with this unit?" I said.

"Well," he told me. "There's some white boys in here but it's mostly niggers. Them North Carolina crips, you know."

"Oh yeah," I said. "They cool or what?"

"Yeah," he answered. "They don't really fuck with no white boys but they be punishing other niggers."

This dude was straight country, I thought. Probably raised in these same mountains they built the prison in. I asked him, "Ain't no Virginia boys in here?"

"I reckon so, but I'm not sure. I'm pretty new myself. In fact, everyone is. They just opened the joint in April," West Virginia said.

When they called the move at 7:30 PM I bounced. "Alright WV," I said as I left.

Mike had pointed out the gates to the yard when I came out of R and D. It seemed this new joint had the same layout as the other prison I just came from. Since the feds were opening up so many prisons I guess they had a blueprint. Mass producing prisons, you know. I made a straight shot up the sidewalk to the yard. As I was taking in my new surroundings and checking out all the other prisoners on the move I kept seeing familiar faces but none that I was down with. Just dudes I had done time with. A few nodded and others who I recognized as known snitches or check-ins put their heads down as they walked by, not willing to look me in the eye.

It's kind of funny how shame can turn a grown man into a bitch, but I wasn't sweating those dudes because the feds were chock full of their types. And with the rapid growth of the BOP due to the war on drugs, known snitches walking around in the open was becoming more common. As a solid prisoner I just tried to avoid them because convicts judge you by the company you keep. So it wasn't smart to be down with a snitch because next thing you knew dudes would be saying you're a snitch too. And that was a jacket nobody was trying to wear.

The prison resembled a college campus, really. Maybe a bland-looking campus, but still. Everything was new and clean and the landscaping was perfect.

As I shuffled through the prisoners on my way to rec I caught a familiar face walking down the sidewalk to another unit. But for real, it was the last person I wanted to see. It was Roberto, the Cuban snitch.

My blood started flowing as I thought, motherfucking hell. Roberto?! I could not fucking believe it. The dude who set Dave up. The motherfucker who blew up the whole sweet hustle we had going down. The snitch-ass motherfucker that Vince personally asked me to stab. He was right motherfucking here. I started walking faster as my body started tingling. From excitement, from rage, from anger and anxiety. I didn't know what the fuck was happening inside me—it felt like some sort of chemical reaction—but I needed to keep my head and not give in to my anger. I made for the yard and my homeboy Mike.

"I need a shank," was the first thing I said to my homeboy when I hit the yard. He seemed a little taken aback and surprised.

"Damn, Guero, already?" Mike laughed, but when he saw that I was serious he cut his laughter short.

"Yeah, homeboy, I can get you a shank," he told me. "But what's up? You need some back up or something?"

"Let's walk the track," I said. "I need to release some tension."

"That's cool, dog, I got just the thing for that," And with that, my homeboy whipped out a joint. It was a pinner but I was jonesing for real.

"Damn, that'll take the edge off," I said as we began to walk and he sparked it up.

After we puffed up the joint I was feeling mellowed and my homeboy asked me, "Now what's all this bullshit about a shank, Guero. Run it down to me."

I told him how I saw Roberto and how I had given my word to Vince that I would stab him if I saw him. Mike looked at me seriously as he saw where I was coming from.

"Where is Vince at, dog?" Mike said.

"He went home," I answered. "But he was my carnalito. I gave my word, you know, and word is bond, right?"

"That's right, homeboy, but you just can't rush into nothing. Does this dude Roberto got beef with you?" Mike said.

"No way, dog. But he snitched on my carnalitos," I told him. Mike kind of took it all in. I knew he would get me a shank though because he was a convict. He wouldn't try to convince me of what to do. A man's business was a man's business. But I had jumped right out there. Would I be able to convince myself?

As we kept walking around the track I was thinking, what is up with this fucking joint? It seemed all the snitches and check-in artists from the previous spot were now all back out on the pound like they were free and clear or something. That's how the feds do it, I thought. Move 'em around. Like Fed Ex, you know. Dudes would snitch, ruin their reputation and move on to another compound in the hopes that the bad news wouldn't follow them. But in Roberto's case he wasn't going to escape the reaper. Because I was gonna be that reaper and like they say you gotta reap what you sow.

It wasn't two days later when that joker stepped to me. I was going down to my homeboy's unit to holla about the shank when this fool sees me walking up the walk. His eyes bugged out in surprise and then he walked right for me with his hand stretched out. He caught me off guard as I was thinking about my decision to stab his snitch-ass, so I played it off and shook his hand with disgust in my mouth.

"Que bola, Guero," he said, looking me in the eye and trying to feel me out. This dude is a smooth one, I thought.

"Que pasa," I said, not really wanting to converse with the dude but he got right to the point.

"Tu sabes, all that bullshit, that was Dave's fault. He's a snitch," Roberto began.

"Mira, Roberto," I said. "No me importa. I ain't interested in that shit."

He looked down toward the ground and then slapped my shoulder and smiled. "Alright then, Guero. Nice to see you again. You know I'm going home soon."

"Oh yeah," I said through gritted teeth. "Buen suerte." The whole time I was thinking about how I could not believe this snitch-ass motherfucker slapped me on my shoulder like we were homeboys or something. But I knew if I was gonna cut the motherfucker I had to keep up the façade to make him think we were OK. That motherfucker probably thought he played me but he had no idea what was in store for him. All I needed was that shank.

PART 27: THE DECISION

Roberto walked down the sidewalk, probably going to rec or something. It seemed he was still a big pool player. The outlines of a plan started formulating in my mind as I stared after his punk-ass. I must have been gritting something fierce because my homeboy Mike walked up and looked at me perplexed for a minute.

"You all right, dog?" he asked.

I motioned down the compound toward the snitch.

"So that's the dude? I knew I recognized him from somewhere. What was that all about?"

"Fuckin' rat was trying to cop a plea, you know. But I ain't co-signing that bullshit," I said as I felt my anger rising. I quickly throttled my rage to keep my head clear and asked Mike what was up with the shank.

"I got it right here, homeboy," he said, motioning to the net bag he was holding. "Dude in facilities sharpened it up for me this morning and I just finished taping up the handle."

I nodded and put my hand on my homeboy's shoulder as I took the net bag. "Thanks homeboy," I said and as I turned to leave my homie stopped me.

"Look, Guero," he said. "A man's gotta do what a man's gotta do, so I ain't telling you one way or the other. But don't go into no shit half-cocked, you know. Think it all out and consider all the angles. And trust your instincts, you know what I mean."

"Yeah, man, I know," I told him. "And thanks, homeboy." I gave him a pound and bounced back to my unit with the shank wound up in a t-shirt inside of the net bag. It was time to do some planning.

I decided that I would do the deed the next day. The anticipation was a motherfucker. I was hyped for real. In my cell I put up the shit sign and got the shank out and just held it. Feeling its weight in my hand as I imagined the point slicing into Roberto's back.

For real I had never done anything like that before except the one time with that other cuban, Chato. But I froze then and Vince had to handle it so I kept telling myself it was time to get mine. Wasn't any Vince to back me up this time. Only me, myself, and I. And this shit was for real. Because this was for my carnalito, Vince. Because he had asked me and I gave my word.

But for real it was for so much more. It was for Travieso and Larry and Fox and Duncan and Carlitos and Leonardo and the Puerto Rican cop and even for Dave, who had broken weak and snitched himself. But most of all it was gonna be for me. To prove to myself that I was a man. A convict. Vato loco, tu sabes. All these convicts gave me my props but somehow I didn't feel as if I deserved them. I felt like I was fronting and faking. I had to validate myself. To prove it to myself. Not that I was a killer but that I was a man. A man's gotta do what a man's gotta do. Consequences be damned to hell and back again. And stabbing Roberto's punk-ass was legit. That was my come-up. I had a lot of time and I wanted motherfuckers to be in the know. And the dude was a snitch. The worst kind of prisoner in the system.

And he disrespected me by even trying to talk to me or play me. Like I was some sucker-ass motherfucker. He disrespected my carnalito's also by running that game on real men and getting away with it. The fucker disrespected the whole concept of honor and integrity with that bullshit for real and it was time for him to pay. And I was gonna be the one to collect.

Wasn't no faking it. It was time to pay the repo man. I was gonna punish Roberto to show all the motherfuckers on the pound what happened to snitches. I was gonna make a statement to the whole federal system because shit was fucked up for real. Snitches walking around in the open like they ran shit or something.

It was time to pay the piper. As all this was running through my head I looked down to my hand, which was turning white because I was squeezing the shank's handle so hard. Chill out, dude, I told myself as I wrapped the shank back up in an old T-shirt and placed it back into the net bag, which I placed under some dirty clothes in another net bag hanging from the wall.

I figured I would wait on the walk by Roberto's unit at the 8:30 PM move when they closed the pool room for cleaning. It would be getting dark and I would be able to hit Roberto as he walked back to his unit.

I started to think what would I do then but I pushed those thoughts out of my head. What happened would happen, I told myself. I took the shit sign down and went to get some ice from the ice machine that was in the laundry room. I looked around, thinking that tomorrow night I would probably be in the hole. Because if I stabbed him on the compound in the open somebody would see and snitch. But if it had to be done that way then that's the way it would be.

I was determined and as I walked back to my cell I nodded to a couple of the white dudes as I passed. My bunkie, West Virginia, came back to the cell for count and tried to engage me in conversation but I wasn't pressed for conversation. I was so focused on what I was planning to do that I brushed him off, telling him I was tired. But for real, I couldn't sleep. I was all geeked up and ready to bounce off the walls like a tweaker on meth. I closed my eyes and tried to rest but my brain was moving a thousand miles an hour.

All these thoughts and images kept floating across my head. I had visions of Roberto bleeding, laying on the concrete sidewalk, looking up at me and holding his side where I punctured him. I saw the compound cops running for me as I threw the bloody shank into the grass and just stood there accepting the inevitable.

I saw the looks of all the passing prisoners as they moved along the sidewalks like cattle to their units. They looked at me and then they looked down at Roberto who laid there leaking his life's blood onto the concrete. The red blood formed a puddle that kept growing larger by the moment as the blood seeped out of Roberto's side.

Nobody clapped or told me good job or said, "Snitches deserve that." Nobody said anything. They acted like they didn't even know Roberto was a snitch. They acted like they didn't even care. They just looked at me like I was crazy or stupid or something as the cops tackled me down in the grass and handcuffed me behind my back.

I started to doze off a little as these images consumed me. But from one part of my brain I heard myself say, *"Don't do it, dude. It's not worth it."*

This statement echoed as I confronted myself.

"Fuck that, man, you're a vato loco. Shank that rat."

"You gotta think about your future, dude."

"Fuck that shit, vato. Stab him for your carnal."

"Now wait a second, dude. What did that snitch ever do to you?"

"It's not that, vato. It's the fact that he is a snitch."

"That's bullshit, dude. It ain't your problem."

"The fuck it is my problem. That snitch disrespected me."

"He never disrespected you. You're making shit up."

"The fuck I am. That motherfucker deserves to die."

"Kill him."

"Don't do it."

"Kill him."

"Don't do it."

"Word is bond, vato."

"Word is bond, me entiendes?"

I woke up in the dark, sweating. It must be past lockdown, I thought. I looked down to see my bunkie quietly snoring away. I started to toss and turn, thinking about who I was and who I wanted to be and what was important and all that. I started having doubts about stabbing Roberto but as soon as those doubts popped into my head I grabbed them with a vice grip and crushed them.

What am I, a pussy? Am I scared? Is that it? Am I a soft-ass cracker? A bitch-ass clown? Fuck that, I'm not no sucker-ass motherfucker. I ain't no buster. I'm a vato loco. I'm the real. Death before dishonor. Go hard white boy. Ain't no faking it. I had to keep it real. I had to go hard.

I finally fell asleep deep into the night, telling myself that I wasn't no joke. Dudes would know, I promised myself. Roberto would know. All the snitches would know. Shit was going down. It was time to strap up. I smiled as I envisioned the shank in my hand plunging into Roberto's midsection.

I woke up tired after a fitful sleep. My bunkie was gone. Probably to his job in facilities or something. I started to collect myself. It was just lunch and then dinner then it would be on. I was glad there weren't any metal detectors on the pound. You only had to pass through one when you went to rec or facilities. So I would be cool. I just had to walk down the sidewalk on the 8:30 PM move and wait for Roberto who would be coming back from rec. I hoped he enjoyed his last games of pool, I thought. Today was the day, I told myself. Time for Roberto to bleed.

I watched some videos and read a book to keep my mind occupied as the hours ticked away. I thought it would never be 8:30 PM but lunch came and went. Then it was count time and then dinner. The waiting was the worst part. I just wanted to get it over and done with. The anticipation was killing me.

Finally it was almost 8:30 PM. I put on my khakis and institutional boots and got the shank out and taped it to my stomach under my t-shirt. It would be easy enough to grab from underneath my 3X khaki shirt when need be. As the PA announced the move I felt real calm and lucid. Everything started moving really slowly as I made my way down the walk and looked up towards rec, waiting for Roberto.

The sun was setting to my right as darkness descended on the compound. I spotted Roberto up the walk a little. He was strolling briskly toward the intersection where I was waiting. Everything moved in slow motion as he got to within 10 feet of me and looked up. His eyes met mine and I could tell he knew something was going down. He stared at me and walked closer as I ripped the shank off my stomach while still keeping it concealed underneath my shirt.

I felt a strange sensation of satisfaction when I registered the fear in Roberto's eyes. He knew what was going to happen but he kept walking anyhow. Forward to meet his fate. To meet his destiny at the dull edge of a shank.

It seemed the whole time leading up to this event that I was scared of something. It was like a nervousness in the pit of my stomach or the back of my throat that just wouldn't go away. The doubt in my mind or in my heart that consumed me. But as Roberto moved within a few feet of me I noticed that I wasn't scared anymore. I had my hand gripping the taped end of the shank and my mark was too scared to react. Like a deer in the line of fire he was waiting for the shank to bite into his skin.

He accepted it. Maybe even thought he deserved it. It was inevitable, I guess. What comes around, goes around, you know. The law of averages. As Roberto closed within a foot of me I knew it was time to act and the funny thing was he didn't even flinch or say anything. He just looked at me with those wide, scared eyes. Not doing nothing. Accepting the fact that he was about to be stuck.

As I gripped the shank tighter I felt a great relief. Like a burden had been lifted from my shoulders. Like I was about to pass some kind of test. I gritted my teeth as I anticipated the impact of steel sliding into flesh.

PART 28: THE END

Roberto went home the next week. At the last minute, the crucial moment, I just decided that I wasn't going through with it. It wasn't that I was scared or shook or froze or anything like that because for real, I could easily have stuck the motherfucker. He was mine. I saw the fear in his eyes. I just decided at the last minute, as I was about to plunge the shank into Roberto's flesh, that it wasn't worth it. I mean, he wasn't worth it. The piece of shit that he was. But also that all the bullshit, go-hard, vato loco, ra-ra rhetoric that I had been force fed during my first two years of prison wasn't worth it. Travieso had kicked me some jewels and I was standing there ready to stab this cat and one of them popped into my head. I clearly remembered Travieso telling me. It was like a vision or something.

"If you don't feel comfortable doing something, then fuck it, vato. Don't do it," Travieso had told me. "If it doesn't feel right, you gotta be true to yourself and not to some other man, me entiendes?"

I don't know why that shit popped into my head right then but it did. And that shit had saved Roberto. For real, I felt enlightened and relieved at the same time as I realized I only had to live up to my expectations and not somebody else's. Word is bond and all that shit but only if you are remaining true to yourself. Because for real, you can't go crossing yourself because if you do then you are the person who has to look in the mirror everyday. I decided that taking on another man's beef or vendetta or whatever was stupid. Was I that easily manipulated? Was I that weak of a man? That I had to take on another man's ideals. A real man lived by his own rules in righteousness. Vince was my carnal but also he was a straight knucklehead who thrived on chaos. Be it the destruction of his own life or mine.

I decided that being a man wasn't about all that macho, prison bullshit; it was about making your own choices and standing by them. As long as you were in the right then you were in the right. Getting caught up in the drama was only a path that led to your own destruction. Real recognizes real, and as long as you were a man, dudes in prison would recognize and treat you with respect. All that other stuff was just sucker shit.

I didn't want to get caught up in all the bullshit and destroy any chances I might have had in the future. A lot of dudes in prison were always trying to drag other dudes into their drama because they were too weak or insecure to deal with it themselves. I always thought that it was harder to walk away from a fight then it was to just knock a motherfucker's head off.

It was like the old cons said, "A hard man shatters but a strong man endures."

And I wanted to be strong so I could endure. Death or a life bid just wasn't in my future I decided. It was easy to hang with your boys and to be down with them and do what they did but it was harder to stand by the side and make your own way so that you could succeed against all odds when everything was stacked against you.

Travieso, with all his wisdom, fell into the trap. If anyone could have succeeded I thought it would have been him because he was as strong as they came. Like a mountain, you know. But he crumbled, he took the easy way out. He did what everyone expected of him.

I didn't want to be like that. I wanted a future. I wanted a life beyond these walls. I wanted to be my own man and not up under somebody's wing or in their clicka. Not just another vato loco, convict tragedy. That day was the turning point of my life. Or at least I intended it to be.

A couple of weeks later I was chilling with my homeboy Mike on the yard.

"Damn, Guero," he said. "You really fucked me up with all that bullshit a couple of weeks ago."

"Yeah," I said. "Why do you say that?"

"Well, dog," he said. "I always figured that if anybody made it outta here, you know, outta prison, outta this life, that it would be you. And then it seemed you were gonna throw it all away like so many dudes in here."

"Yeah, homeboy," I said. "I know what you mean."

My homeboy lit up a joint and passed it to me. "If you gonna stick somebody, make sure it's for a good reason, you know. Like for some marijuana or something," Mike laughed.

It was cool—I knew he was only making light of a serious situation.

"Mike," I said as I passed the joint back. "Don't they got some college classes or something in education?"

"Yeah, dog," he answered, "I think they do. Why, you gonna sign up?"

"I think I just might, you know. I want to use my time constructively," I told him.

"Yeah, I know what you mean," he said. "Kinda like how I do tattoos, gamble, and do drugs, right?"

I did a double take on him when he said that, but when I looked back he was smiling. I took the joint back and told him, "Yeah, homeboy, kinda like that. I think I'm gonna get back in UNICOR, too."

"Damn, homeboy. Let me find out you turning into a model inmate. You gonna stop smoking weed, too?"

"Naw, dog. Never that," I said as I hit the joint again and flicked the roach that was burning my fingertips at the perimeter fence. "You know I'm a stoner for life, homeboy," I told him and laughed. He laughed too as we continued walking around the track.

About six months later I was back in UNICOR working as the grade one expediter and taking four classes in education through the local community college. I had heard from some prisoners that came in that Dave was in Milan, a low security federal joint in Michigan. I never heard anything about Vince again so I guessed he was surviving with his family out in Cali.

Word came through that my carnal, Travieso, got sentenced under the 3-strikes law and was now doing life in Cali.

Dudes on the pound were still talking about the little run and bust at the other spot. Cops bringing in drugs, heroin everywhere, massive sendouts, thousands of books of stamps, ounces of marijuana, dudes getting stuck, it was all the rage in prison. And dudes were still talking about Dave.

I saw this dude Fish who was Dave's homey from Detroit. He had just transferred in and when he heard I was on the pound he stepped to me.

"What's up, Guero?" he said.

"What's up?" I answered as I gave him a pound.

"I can't believe that shit with Dave," he told me.

"Yeah, I know what you mean," I said.

Fish gave me a look of disgust mixed with disbelief. Then he summed up the whole affair: "That shit was fucked up."

I could only nod my head in agreement.

About The Author

Seth Ferranti, federal prisoner register # 18205-083, is the Gorilla Convict Writer. In 1993, after faking his suicide and spending two years as a top-15 fugitive on the US Marshal's most wanted list, he was captured and sentenced to 304 months under the federal sentencing guidelines and committed to the custody of the Attorney General. A first-time, non-violent offender, he's served 12 years of his 25-year mandatory minimum sentence for an LSD Kingpin conviction. His story has been profiled in the pages of *Rolling Stone* magazine. His current release date is October of 2015.

During his incarceration Ferranti has worked to better himself by making preparations for his eventual release back into society. To that end he has earned an AA degree from Penn State and a BA degree from the University of Iowa through correspondence courses. He plans to continue his education and pursue a Masters degree at California State University Dominguez Hills.

In addition to his studies, Ferranti writes about the prison experience. He's been published in numerous magazines including *Don Diva, Slam, Vice, FHM, King, Feds,* and *The Ave.* He is an internationally known prison basketball journalist who's been featured in Spanish, French, Italian and Mexican magazines. His articles on prison ballers regularly appear on hoopshype.com and prisonerlife.com.

Prison Stories is Seth Ferranti's first book. Check out the author's website at www.gorillaconvict.com to contact him or to comment on this novel.

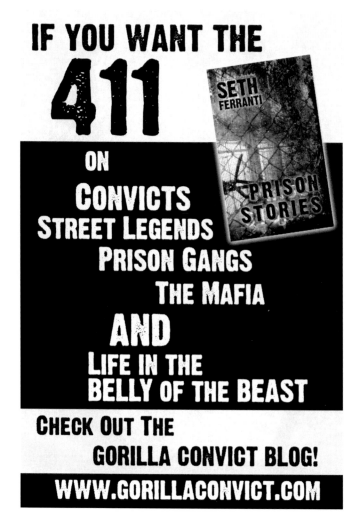

Coming Soon From

GORILLA CONVICT PUBLICATIONS

Prison Ball
By Seth Ferranti

Prison Stories II: The Seven Deadly Sins
By Seth Ferranti

For release information on the above-listed titles:
Visit www.gorillaconvict.com

To comment on this book or contact the author:
Visit www.gorillaconvict.com.

The next book by Seth Ferranti

Prison Ball

Chapter One:
The story of Ron Jordan, a prison basketball legend

From the inner city ghettos to the NBA, when you're talking hoop dreams, it's all about the championships. You can have mad skill, killer hops and handle, or the monster slam dunk. But if you don't win, it doesn't matter. What happens when you juxtapose thuglife with hoop dreams? I'm talking about basketball gangstas in prison. They still hoop, still ball, even if they're prisoners of the War on Drugs. But is it still all about winning? Even on the inside? When you have a ten-year mandatory-minimum sentence are championship dreams still important?

FCI Fort Dix is a cluster-fuck of convicts, snitches, INS detainees, mobsters, studio gangstas, white collar criminals, punks, playa haters, crackheads, whalers, and thugs. Over 4,000 prisoners of all nationalities crowd within the low-security prisons' double-razor-wired fences. The inmates are housed in twelve-man rooms, dormitory-style in the

crumbling dilapidated buildings that once housed army cadets completing basic training on the converted military base.

The prison world is one of negativity. One of tensions and anger. Ignorance and hate. But as prisons go, Fort Dix is pretty tame. Most inmates have short sentences, are awaiting deportation or are long-term prisoners at the end of their bids. Stabbings and violence are relatively infrequent. The prisoners at Fort Dix have one eye on the street as they prepare to re-enter society or journey back to their country of origin.

Still, while locked up, the inmates look for something to relieve the boredom and monotony of prison life. Entertainment is at a premium on the inside. There's not a whole hell of a lot to do. Prisoners can watch TV, read a book, or go to a prison-rec-league basketball game.

The first thing you notice when you enter the gym is the amplified, rambling trash-talk. The man on the mike is Noodles and he calls it like he sees it. Noodles is the organizer, commissioner, and de facto personality of the league. Between his rapid-fire dialogue, Dr. Dre's "Ain't Nuthin' but a G-thing" blasts from the PA as the players warm-up, shooting lay-ups.

Noodles told me he would always know who came to play that night by watching the layup lines. "Dudes that came in bullshitting, you could tell," he says. "When they came in serious, it was showtime." And in the gym at FCI Fort Dix during the 2000-01 Winter A-League intramural season, there would be mad showtime.

During the games the gym would be crazy packed. Dudes would be getting there early. Trying to get courtside seats. Pounding on the stands. Jumping up and down, stomping their feet, and going nuts.

On the floor it was standing room only as prisoners crowded around the court cussing, hating, gambling, and giving props to players or dissing them. With the music, the microphone, the excitement, the adrenaline, and the play-by-play, the tournament was bananas.

The games represented an interlude, a break form the pressures of prison life. A time for the crowd and the players to forget their sentences and problems. A time to relax. To be taken away and escape the reality of being locked up. The electricity brought the diverse prisoners together as they transcended the prison complex through the spectacle of the game.

Picture a high school gym packed with prisoners: drug dealers, bank robbers, parole violators, felony gun possessors, and deportable Dominicans, Colombians, Chinese, Jamaicans. The crowd would live and die with each crossover, spinmove, three-point shot, slam dunk, or behind-the-back pass. The screaming prisoners would release their tensions and feed off the atmosphere created by the games – and in particular, one player, Ron Jordan.

THE LEAGUE

New Jersey O.G.'s Smooth and Mustafa decided to assemble and coach an A-League team for the winter season. Nothing special, just something to represent them and their unit, 5703, on the compound. They wanted to keep it real, though. These two convicts did ten years together at Rahway – a brutal New Jersey State Penitentiary in the 80's experiencing vicious blacktop battles and much drama – before meeting up again in the feds.

Smooth was the passionate, vocal, crazy-type. He would rather have played than coached, but he wasn't the youngster he once was. Mustafa was a calm-devout Muslim who didn't lose control. Staying focused as Smooth stormed the sideline at games yelling and screaming at his team, the crowd, the refs, and opposing players. They made a good coaching tandem – Smooth's fire and Mustafa's ice.

The coaches recruited the uptown players – Pup, the veteran, and Ron Jordan, the gunner – as the centerpieces of their team. They knew Ron would be firing shots, but they figured he would buy into their team concept. "He ain't never seen a shot he didn't like," Noodles says of Ron. "It's like smoking weed; he would put it in the air." Rounding out the team were Baby Shaq, a complimentary inside presence, Solo, the human jumping jack, and Capone – also known as Conan the Destroyer – a physical, monstrous presence in the paint.

As the season started, Smooth described his coaching philosophy: "Taking a group of guys is like putting together pieces of a puzzle. You have to critique them, make changes, and find out what chemistry is needed."

After an 0-5 start it seemed chemistry was lacking.

Ron Jordan was out of control. He was forcing his game, shooting crazy threes, and trying to please the crowd. He would shake his man, step back, shake him again and instead of going to the basket he would step back and shake his man again. Ron would hit him with the crossover, bring it back between his legs, and cross his man over again. He wasn't satisfied with one move and the bucket. He wanted to juke the whole team. His Rucker park antics and unconscious constant shooting proved detrimental to the team and alienated his teammates as the losses piled up. "Ron didn't pass the ball," Mustafa said later. "He had to learn to pass the ball. He had to learn to trust his teammates."

Smooth agrees. "Ron Jordan had an Allen Iverson heart," he says. "He tried to do it all himself. The guys didn't want to play with him." Even the crowd hated on him, shouting 'You don't play no D, you jacking rec. You shoot too much.'" The word on the pound was that no one wanted to play with him. Ron even told me how some Chinese and Spanish cats would come up to him after games and criticize him in their native tongues. When Ron inquired what the fuck they were saying, a bilingual inmate would translate: "He say, 'you shoot too much.'" It got so bad that even the police, when counting, would stop and tell Ron he shot too much.

Mustafa and Smooth considered folding the team as Noodles ridiculed them on the mike. He dissed them saying they were coaching a B-League team. They even considered trading Ron Jordan, but Pup, Ron's homeboy from Harlem, wouldn't hear of it. Pup was known as Hard2guard due to his offensive prowess and scoring ability. He'd been around the system – almost ten years – for a crack conspiracy charge. Pup is a smooth character, a veteran of penitentiary ballcourt battles. The cerebral type. "It gonna be rough," Pup tells the coaches, "This what we started with. This is how we gonna finish it. Understand what I'm saying! Don't worry. We got Jordan. We gonna ride him to the championship."

Later Ron confides: "If it weren't for Pup I would quit or go to another team." This statement shows the loyalty these two uptown cats shared, but Ron still needed discipline in his game. "It's all about me, " he'd say. But his game was wild, chaotic, out of control. It mirrored his life on the street.

THUGLIFE

Young black male – synonym for criminal, thug, or predator – Ron Jordan was born Ronald Paul on August 20th 1972 in Harlem Hospital. He says his dad was "a stickup kid, straight gangsta" who was slain in 1980, shot seven times in the chest when Ron was eight. "When I was a kid, " Ron says, "he hit me with like $30, $40 and I would go to school and buy a wad of candy."

Ron was raised by his maternal grandmother with two sisters and two cousins in Harlem. He saw his moms periodically and got involved in the drug game "pitching and running" at age 16. His moms used to say 'it's history repeating itself' as she witnessed Ron submerging into the street culture that took his father's life. Ron's days consisted of smoking weed, selling crack, roughing people off, and getting money, but his one true passion was playing basketball.

"When I'm on the-court, nothing else matters," Ron says. He mentions the tournaments and courts he frequented: AL-Murf, PAL, Riverside, Gauchos, Milbank, 145th Street, Harbor, Kingdom, Yonkers, and West 4th. He smiles as he explains how he "was hitting crazy threes, dropping 77 in Harlem, and not passing the ball to nobody."

He tells me, "Nigga's still got tapes of that shit," as he names the street legends he balled against. Names like Mike Boogie, Terminator, Master Rob, The Dancing Dugi, and Marc Jackson roll off his lips as he says, "I was going around playing in tournaments and making a name for myself." But it didn't last.

His moms died in 1991 and this tragedy set in motion a slew of arrests and convictions that culminated in his incarceration today. "When my mom died I didn't care about what happened to me," he says. "I decided to go all out in the game." And he's not talking about basketball.

At 18, shortly after his mother's death, he was arrested with 21 vials of crack cocaine. Later that year he was robbed and shot in the stomach with a .380 for $1,500. "I woke up with a tube going into my nostrils and down my throat," he says. His stay at St. Lukes Roosevelt Hospital lasted six days and Ron claims, "the bullet is still in me." After he was shot, he says, "that's when I really started carrying guns. It was either gonna be me or them."

At 19, he caught his first gun-possession charge and did a year at Greene Correctional Institution in upstate New York. He hit the streets again in '93, had a two-year run, and caught another crack charge. As he served a 3-6 year bid at Rykers Island and El Mira, he was indicted on an Attempted Murder charge, which he eventually beat. He was paroled in '98. A couple of months later his grandmother passed and he caught the fed charge. He went to trial still mourning her death. Ron was convicted of Felon in Possession of a Weapon and sentenced to 92 months in the feds. Thinking back on his life Ron reflects, "I believe God's been merciful, because I should've been dead or in jail for the rest of my life."

Ron Jordan kind of rocks back and forth as he talks. He describes himself as "fearless, determined, and at the same-time tugged-out." His hands move, conveying his thoughts as he points his finger in agreement, or stands up to emphasize a point. Every move is deliberate. No motion is wasted.

He looks at you from under his eyelids with a kind of half-smile that hints at some secret knowledge. Then he looks at you directly almost daring you to say something or to question him. It's like when he's balling – daring you to beat him, to guard him, to stop him. He likes to keep people off balance in life as well as basketball.

He walks like a gangsta – not an animated ghetto walk though – but with a gait that belies natural and lethal grace. Almost like a panther. Sleek, powerful, quick, athletic. The kids a b-baller, but he's built like a football player standing 5-foot-11 and weighing a solid 210 pounds. He can be quiet and respectful, but playful like a child. He has a wicked sense of chaoticness that conflicts with his maturity. He can be combative, argumentative, and confrontational – but also is easy to get along with.

He presents himself as confident, self-assured, focused, and smart. He laughs, but doesn't really smile, as he mocks and "gets rec" on other prisoners. He confides to "a lot of anger built inside, a lot of hurt and pain," which formulated his character. Prison put halt to his wilding and misadventures in the game, but thuglife still manifested itself, seeping out of him when he plays ball.

For more information on **Prison Ball** visit
www.gorillaconvict.com